ROBERT OLMS

RIVER DO

Three nights ago I had to bury a dog. I've buried five dogs in
my lifetime. Three of them I had to shoot. After you shoot your
first dog, you become known as someone who will shoot a dog
if the dog needs to be shot. There was another dog, my own, that
got into a porcupine. Everyone expected me to shoot it, but
I didn't. I took the quills out with pliers. As I was doing
it, she gashed my arm with her teeth, but I knew she didn't
mean to.

Burying a dog isn't like burying a cow or horse or skunk or
woodchuck or even a cat. Once, when I was a kid growing up
on the farm, I was supposed to bury a cow, but instead me and
two of the hired men pushed it into the Connecticut River and
then spent the rest of the day drinking beer and fishing for carp.

from **"HOW TO BURY A DOG"** in Robert Olmstead's
collection, **RIVER DOGS**

River Dogs

River Dogs

STORIES

ROBERT OLMSTEAD

Vintage Contemporaries

VINTAGE BOOKS • A DIVISION OF RANDOM HOUSE • NEW YORK

A Vintage Contemporaries Original, March 1987

FIRST EDITION

Portions of this book originally appeared in *Black Warrior Review* and *Granta*.

Library of Congress Cataloging in Publication Data
Olmstead, Robert.
River dogs.
(Vintage contemporaries)
I. Title.
PS3565.L67R5   1987   813'.54   86-46182
ISBN 0-394-74684-8

MANUFACTURED IN THE UNITED STATES OF AMERICA

10 9 8 7 6 5 4 3 2 1

Author photo copyright David Tobin

For Cindy

Contents

River Dogs

River Dogs

THAT SUMMER WAS HOT, hotter than the hobs of hell. Most mornings I'd spend in the cellar, sitting in the corner with my back against the wall. It was cool down there. The oil tank in one corner looked like an elephant, gray and sweaty, that had run its head through the foundation, a seam running along its side.

While I was down there, I'd listen to the radio, read books, shoot darts, and make stuff up. I wrote letters, too. We learned to write letters in school that year.

At noon I'd come out into the light. The sun would be high overhead. I'd drink from the outside faucet and then hike down the hill to the mailbox to send out my correspondence and see what I'd hauled in from my previous mailings. Things like bumper stickers and posters I usually kept. Letters from congressmen I canned, except for one from Boston. He was starting to write me personally. He told me about his family and later on, in July, he began to describe the interworkings of the committees he was on.

He wrote that I should burn the letters because the information was highly confidential. Better yet, he wrote that if I had access to a paper shredder, I should use it. Of course I kept these letters.

The road to the mailbox was long and unpaved. After a good rain, it mudded up, and by the end of winter it was like a washboard. Stone walls ran down both sides. That morning, though, it was dry and hot. I imagined falling off a bicycle or horse and shook all over at the thought of scraping my arms and banging my head. I cut into the sumac and jumped onto the wall to my right. I walked along it until I reached the main road, which was paved.

There were four letters in the mailbox, but only one was for me. The rest were bills for my mother. The letter for me was from Washington, from the congressman. He had written the letter himself, and wanted to know if I thought he should run again. He told me there was talk of a war, a real war, one that nobody could survive.

I slapped the door shut and turned back up the road, but before I got more than a few steps, somebody called to me. When I looked to the other side of the road where the voice had come from, I saw Duck sitting in the weeds behind the other stone wall. I could only see him from the neck up. He was sucking on a cigarette that was unrolling as he smoked it. He wore a greasy John Deere cap, pulled down tight against his skull. When Duck smoked, he puckered out his lips. That's how he got his name.

"Hey, Duck," I said, but he didn't answer. He just looked at me from under the bill of his cap, so I walked over. Duck was sitting on a grain bag he'd spread out in a patch of poison ivy. He never got it. He claimed he ate a little stem of it every day, so as to counteract the poison from inside his body.

"You and me got a little job to do," he said.

"What is it?" I asked.

"You'll see. Come with me."

Duck was a real fool, not your average run-of-the-mill fool. I learned a lot from him, though. I probably learned more from him than from anybody else. Most of the important stuff in the world was skimming around in Duck's mind. He told me stories about Korea. He told me that the women over there were different. Their thing went in a different direction, crossways instead of up and down.

Duck said he used to be a rear gunner in a B-52. After a mission they'd just hose out the turret under the plane. Nothing left to speak of. He also told me what the Nazis used to do to women.

My father said it was all a bunch of bull. Duck was born in a trailer in Claremont, he said, and had never been out of the state except for once when he got washed over to the Vermont side of the river after his brother pushed him in. I guess Duck almost drowned. Duck himself told me about the time he was ice fishing and fell through the ice. What saved him, he said, was that he always made it a habit to tie himself off to a tree whenever he ice fished. I was beginning to have some doubts about the stories Duck told, but I didn't appreciate my father casting his own doubts the way he did.

In spite of this, I followed Duck around like a puppy. He had convictions. He always lied. If given the choice between the truth and a lie, he always lied and I usually believed him.

"Hey, Duck, there's talk of another war," I said.

"Your congressman."

"Yes, today's letter."

"Not yet," Duck said. "We got to hitch a ride."

Duck picked up his grain bag and headed for the middle of the road. I sat by the mailbox and watched him pace from side to side. When he heard a truck coming, he parked himself right on the double yellow line with his hands in his pockets. This is how Duck always got his ride.

"Duck, where you going off to today?" the driver said.

"Walpole," Duck said, hiking a leg over the side of the truck. "We got a little job to do."

I jumped in after him and sat with my back to the tailgate. Duck stood up with his elbows on the roof. He tucked his cap inside his shirt and braced his feet against the hubs of the wheel wells. When the truck hit fifty, his loose clothes snapped out behind him and his hair plastered back against the sides of his head. Chaff swirled around him, but he stood his ground. I got something in my eye. Tears ran down my cheeks for two miles before it washed out. Duck never did look back. I slid closer to the front where the air was a little better. Duck had his chin raised. He drew in the hot wind that whipped toward us through his flared nostrils.

When we got to Walpole, Duck rapped on the roof of the truck with his knuckles and the driver stopped. We both hopped over the side. Duck slapped the side of the truck, and the driver took off. We walked down the street past white clapboard houses with black shutters. Duck finally stopped at one, checked the number, and then proceeded up the driveway. He rang the doorbell and flicked pieces of chaff and sawdust from his clothes while we waited.

Finally a woman dressed in shorts and a man's dress shirt came around the corner of the garage. Her shirt was tied at the waist and had paint stains on it. In her hands she held a pair of electric hedge clippers, the orange cord trailing out behind her, disappearing around the corner of the garage. She raised them a little higher when she saw Duck.

"I came for the puppies," Duck said.

"We've decided to keep them," she said, raising the clippers a little higher. She tried to look at us with hate, but the best she could do was more pitiful than anything else.

"He said you'd say that," Duck told her.

"It's true," she said. "So you can just leave."

Then she spotted me. We knew each other from church.

She sang in the choir. Whenever she sat down, she always spread her robes so her knees showed.

"Does your mother know what you're up to? I'm going to call her and tell her what you're doing."

"When does your husband get home?" Duck said before she could rip into me any more.

"He'll be right home and he'll tell you the same thing I've told you."

"You got any soda?" Duck asked, but she only stared. "How 'bout a cigarette? Can we leave our bag here?"

I could see she was about to cry, so I jabbed Duck in the side and told him we'd come back later. I knew I was in enough trouble as it was. I knew she'd call my mother.

Duck didn't say anything. He and I walked down the street into the village. We went to the church and stood out front. Duck looked around and then hurried out back. In a few seconds he returned with a case of empty soda bottles. He walked across the street and cashed them in at the Esso station and bought soda and a package of bologna with the money.

We wandered over to the bandstand on the common. We crawled through the lattice that skirted the bottom and stretched out on the cool bare ground. Duck ripped open the cellophane wrapper with his teeth or at least with what was left of them. He held the whole wad of meat in his hand as if it were a trout. He let it flop up and down and then bit into the side of it. He offered me some, but I didn't want any.

"Duck," I said. "Let's forget the pups and you and me go fishing."

"No fishing today. We got work to do."

"What exactly is it we're doing?" I asked.

"Today's dog day. We got dog work to do."

Dog day meant there was some work to be done with dogs. This could mean breeding them, doctoring them, fixing them, peddling them, or killing them. I never knew what the day's business was likely to be until right up to the end. Today I had a pretty good idea.

"Let's go fishing," I said again, but he just kept chewing on his bologna.

After a while a boy and a girl climbed into the bandstand. Duck had fallen asleep. The boy and girl began kissing. I sat looking up at them. My nose was only a few inches away from the girl's bare feet. The boy wore sneakers. I could read the label on the sole.

"Open your lips a little more," the boy said.

"Like this?" she said, and then there were more kissing noises.

From where I sat I could see her feet move slightly whenever they kissed. They rose off the deck board for a moment and then settled back down. The boy's sneakers shuffled to the side each time, her side, and hooked between her bare feet a bit more with each kiss.

"That's enough," she finally said.

"But I love you," he told her.

"If you love me, then why do we have to take chances?"

"Guys have needs, you know."

"But I'm afraid," she said.

"Don't be. When two people love each other like we do, there isn't anything to be afraid of."

"But what if I get . . . you know."

"You won't."

"How can *you* be so sure?" she said.

"There are ways of preventing that."

"Sometimes they don't work. You know what happened

to someone we both know. What do we do if that happens to me?"

"You call ol' Duck."

Duck said this in such a reasonable tone I found myself nodding in agreement. I looked over and saw him sitting there nodding his head, too. The girl gave out a scream and then she and the boy took off on a dead run. Duck pulled at his skinny chin and looked around.

"About time we got going," he said. "We got a lot of work to do."

Duck rolled a cigarette, lit it, and sucked hard, hard enough to draw it down by a third. He rolled his eyes round and round in their sockets. He began humming to himself. I watched a centipede crawl across the back of his hand. Unsure of myself I started to giggle, still wondering about the conversation I'd just heard.

Once Duck finished his smoke, we crawled out into the late afternoon sun. From where we were, we could see a car in the drive, so we walked over. The husband met us at the door. He looked tired.

"Hard day at the office there, Chief?" Duck said.

The husband took us to the garage without saying a word. Inside was a bitch and her litter of pups. She looked to be purebred, but her pups didn't.

"Some mongrel watered down the gene pool," the husband said. Inside I could hear the kids bawling. There was no sign of the woman. I could understand why the kids were upset, and any other time I would've been, too, but at the moment I just wanted to head down the road.

In no time we were back on the highway with the pups in the sack. Duck had a carton of Camels tucked inside his shirt and five bucks in his pocket. That would buy him a lot of bologna. He gave me a pack of cigarettes and he insisted on giving the man a receipt for the money. "For tax purposes," he said.

By now it was starting to get late. The sun was halfway down to the mountains that humped up beyond the river. The air had begun to cool and the sweat that had soaked my shirt earlier in the day was now cold against my body. In an hour or so, I knew my mother would start looking for me, if the lady hadn't already called her. I knew she hadn't, though; my mother would have called her sister or her aunt and they would've tracked me down by now.

The pups squirmed and squeaked and yowled. Duck plodded along a few steps ahead of me, the sack slung over his shoulder. I heard that Duck tried to kill a man once. In fact, it was my mother's cousin. Duck threw a corn fork down the silo chute at him when he was climbing up. At first people were mad about this, but the more they talked about it the more they agreed that my mother's cousin deserved it. It was probably something he said to Duck, they figured. Nobody liked my mother's cousin. His mouth had a way of getting him in trouble. Anyway, if that fork hadn't wedged itself in one of the doors halfway down, my mother's cousin would have an air-conditioned chest right now. That's my father's talk.

It was nearly dusk and we still hadn't caught a ride. I was going to catch hell sure as anything, but I didn't really care. It wasn't hot anymore and that made me feel better. The dew was falling and all about the mist was rising. We hadn't seen another person for at least half an hour; no trucks, no cars, no tractors, no cattle in the pastures. I began to wonder if a war had started and we didn't know about it. Maybe the only ones left were me and Duck and a bagful of pups.

"Did you ever see a baby born?" Duck asked without

looking at me. "I saw a baby born once. Ain't like a calf or a pig or a dog, you know. Ain't even like a kitten. Human baby don't just pop right out. Strangest thing I ever saw. Blood all over the place. We lost him, though. The damn fool didn't even know she was pregnant. She was so fat I'm not surprised she didn't know. Told me she'd shit them right out in the toilet before."

I didn't say anything. I didn't think Duck was talking to me. I had other things on my mind or at least I was trying to have other things on my mind. Now it was dark and we'd hiked just about all the way back to my house. The pups had stopped scrambling around in the bag. We came to the corner where I'd met up with Duck earlier that day. Above me at the top of the hill I could see the lights of my house. They looked small against the dark, as if they were deep inside a shell. To our right the dirt road continued on down to the river. Duck didn't hesitate; he turned right and would've disappeared from my sight if I hadn't followed close behind.

At one time this road had been an access road to the ferry that crossed the river before they built the steel bridges into Brattleboro and farther up into Bellows Falls. A long time ago a circus came to town. When they tried to get the elephant across on the ferry it sank. They needed six yoke of oxen to haul that elephant out of the water; then they buried it along the banks of the river somewhere. Me and Duck used to look for it before we got into this other line of work. I always wanted to find that elephant my great-great-grandfather buried along with his neighbors and a bunch of clowns and midgets and maybe one or two bearded ladies. I can see him standing beside a bald-headed strong-man with a handlebar moustache and leather straps on his arm.

11

Off the main road the brambles tore at my clothes. They came at eyelevel and were hard to see in the shadows. I held my right arm up beside my head to ward them off. Ahead of me, Duck plowed along, weaving in and out of the darkness.

After a quarter mile, the road opened up into a meadow planted with corn. The corn was high and tasseled off. I couldn't see Duck, but I heard him thrashing through a few yards ahead of me. The pups started up with their noises again. They were yipping and crying. I followed the sounds.

We used to play war games in that corn. We'd take three-foot steel rods, wrap a handle on one end, and then pop a crab apple on the other end. With a flick of the wrist you could send that crab apple soaring through the sky. I've been plunked on the head by many a green crab apple.

I looked up into the face of the moon. The ring of soft, milky light meant it was going to turn off cold. I pushed on, even though I couldn't hear the sounds anymore. I rushed ahead until the corn gave way and I smacked into the bag slung over Duck's shoulder. I fell back on my rear end, my face wet with piss and puke that had soaked through the bag from the puppies.

Looking out between Duck's legs, I could see the river. It was huge and silent, moving in the same way clouds move across the sky, and the path of the moonlight across its breadth seemed firm enough to walk on. The river was moving southeast to the ocean. Its weight seemed heavy, so heavy that at any moment it would plunge through the earth.

I looked up at Duck. He was leaning back on his heels as if he were fighting the draft of a trailer truck. His heels were dug deep in the silt and sand as if he might go flying through space into the black water.

Duck took out one of his new Camels and lit it up. His

shirt was stained from his shoulders down to his belt. I drew my knees up to my chest and wrapped my arms around them. I could feel the river pulling at me, too. I leaned back to keep my balance and was certain that if I'd tried that anywhere else I would've fallen flat on my back.

Off on the side the pups yipped and cried in their bag. The burlap rippled and bulged as they squirmed and twisted. Duck finished his smoke and flicked the butt into the water. He watched as if this was some kind of test. He bent down and hefted the bag. He bounced it in the air two or three times. He reared back, swung it in a full circle, over and over, and then halfway on the upswing, he let it fly. The bag hurtled through the air and disappeared. It seemed like forever before we heard the splash and saw a sheet of water flare up and catch itself in the moonlight. Then we saw the bag riding on the current. It was open and the puppies were crawling out. They boiled up to the surface and fought to stand on top of the bag.

I sat and watched. I watched them pass through the path of the moon, treading and paddling on top of the swamped bag. The ground seemed to drop out from under me and spin off to another place. I sat and watched long after the sounds of bullfrogs in the eddies and the leaping fish came back to me. I sat and watched the spot long after Duck had wandered back up the road, leaving me alone, sitting next to the black water of the river on its way to the ocean.

A Good Cow

BY THE TIME WE GOT DONE with the Rudman cow, she was shot full of so much cortisone it was coming back out the needle holes. Even though she was about fourteen, with hide like tree bark and pins you could hang your overcoat on, she was still a decent milker. She had bad legs though, a definite drawback.

The rest of the herd shuffled around in the loading pen, the Rudman cow amongst them. They would be sold and shipped down country by noon. We waited in the alleyway for Scribner to call.

My grandfather sat on a milkstool, his cane between his legs and his hands wrapped over the crook. Every once in a while he spit a ribbon of Beech-nut onto the concrete. We sat without saying anything for forty-five minutes. In that time, no less than fifty flies landed on his forehead and took off again. He paid them no mind.

"When does Scribner get here, anyway?" My question didn't startle him as I figured it would.

"By noon. He is supposed to call from Brattleboro first." The heat made me dizzy. Surrounded by flies and humidity, my mind jumped around. It had a method, too. I could feel it jump up as opposed to over or down. I could hear my blood pumping. I had to move before I threw up. The old man hadn't let me stop so we could get breakfast.

The old man didn't budge, though. He was still as a tree stump. In weather like this he wasted no effort, not even to swat a fly.

15

Just as I was about to move, not being able to sit there any longer, a white billy goat walked into the alleyway. Neither of us moved as the goat approached, ducking his head and sidestepping to keep us both in view. He was probably wondering what in hell was going on. His chin whiskers were yellow from where he'd pissed on himself. He was a rancid old thing, but we didn't move.

First the goat walked over to the old man and sniffed him in two or three places. The goat made his way down to the puddle of tobacco juice and licked it up as if he had to prove how dirty old goats could be.

"Shit," I said, standing up. The goat jumped and braced himself, about to make a move. The old man's cane swiped him aside the head and sent him scuttling off into the barn. He still didn't know what was going on.

Scribner was a good customer. The cows we bought in the Northeast and Canada were in turn bought from us by Scribner and trucked to Maryland and Florida. Scribner wasn't as particular as some brokers, but he did like a cow that had good legs and could step right along because most of his cows went into free-stall barns. Cows had to be able to walk to the feed bunks and then into the milking parlors.

He'd been supplying dairies that milked seven to eight hundred cows around the clock. These dairies had sprung up over the last few years since milk prices shot up so high. Housing and feeding cows in the South is cheap because of the weather. They feed cows everything from swamp grass to orange rinds, I've heard.

What makes things rough is that they've been dumping their milk back in our markets, upsetting the balance of production and consumption. Some people refused to sell cows south. The old man's brother gave him some grief over it, even though we know the old man's brother sells

Scribner cows, something Scribner told us one day as if it were a big joke on the family.

Anyway, a good cow, in Scribner's mind, had long pasterns and a smooth rump. "You'd think he was buying trotters," the old man remarked one day. Regardless, the Rudman cow was not his idea of a good cow. A cow like her would lose her legs in no time. Oftentimes an old cow like that will slip on the concrete, go spread-eagle, and split her pelvis. We've had to shoot a few like that. Usually we call the track, though, and they become food for the greyhounds, or we call a mink farmer. That's a pretty damn ugly sight, too.

"If you think Scribner'll take that Rudman cow, you're nuts," I said.

The old man looked up. "She's a good cow," he said quietly. For a minute I almost believed him, but then I realized what he was up to.

"She's a good cow all right. Good for hot dogs or bologna."

I knew this time he wasn't going to slip one past me. There wasn't any way in hell Scribner would buy that cow. In fact, when he was up in the spring he'd complained. He told the old man he was losing his touch and didn't know the difference between a good cow and a bad cow anymore. Everybody laughed and so did I.

It was still early. Scribner wouldn't be calling for another half hour; then it would take him nearly another half hour to drive up the interstate to Westminster. I figured I had time to wander through the barns. I held my cane for driving cows by its crook and rolled the top over and over in my hand. The old man insisted we use canes instead of electric prods. The same day he told me prods were inhumane, I saw him break his cane over the nose of a bull that wouldn't get on the truck. The family used to own these barns when

17

I was a boy. Its official name was Westminster Commission Sales, but everyone always referred to it as Westminster or the Auction.

A reporter from *Harper's* came here one Thursday night about thirty years ago and bathed himself in the warmth of the taciturn yet bucolic life of a New England auction. He filed a story two days later on the experience. He noted how thousands of dollars exchanged hands with the nod of a head or the wink of an eye. He thrilled in the fact that these people didn't need contracts, clauses, or negotiations.

He probably arrived at the Port Authority sometime on Friday. No doubt he'd already pounded out his story, so he proceeded to regale his friends with stories of a different kind of stock exchange while they sat around the coffeepot.

In February of the next year, the IRS paid a call. They were in agreement that much had been done without benefit of contracts, clauses, or negotiations. This upset them a bit because they had no record of the volume of business the reporter from *Harper's* wrote about in his piece. We sold the barns to another concern and negotiated a settlement. To this day the old man refuses to talk to reporters about anything.

Reporters are like that, though. Once they took a picture of an old tenant house we were about to tear down and ran it under an article on poverty. Another time, during the oil embargo, CBS wanted to do a story on all the cordwood we were selling. We sent them up the road to Griswalds. Sure as hell, Griswald got himself on the six-o'clock news and then got audited that same year.

We still used the barns to hold cows we bought in Vermont. We trucked them in from around the state and then sold them to a number of buyers, Scribner being one. They usually didn't spend more than two days here before they were on their way south.

The barns seemed a lot smaller to me now. The bleachers surrounding the sales ring held only twenty or thirty men, and before they had held hundreds. I wandered through the maze of pens and chutes the goat had disappeared into.

"Bobby!" my grandfather's voice bellowed from the main alleyway. "Go up to Ernie Williams' store and buy some Moxie. Get plenty of ice. Be quick about it. Scribner'll be here shortly."

Scribner liked his Moxie and he liked it cold. Ernie Williams' store was the only place that still carried Moxie. I crossed the river into Walpole, bought the Moxie and a bag of ice, then headed back to the sales barn.

"Bring that cooler in here. What did your mother pack for lunch?"

"Tuna fish and egg salad," I replied.

"Give me an egg salad and a cup of that iced coffee."

"Don't you want some Moxie?"

"No. Tastes like diesel fuel."

The old man chewed slowly and sipped at his iced coffee. "Get the noses from behind the seat."

Noses are a fairly ingenious contraption. They look like a pair of oversized pliers. Instead of jaws at the end, the steel loops out and then back in with a steel ball forged on each tip. They clamp within three eighths of an inch from each other. Each ball fits nicely into the nostril of a cow's nose. When the handles are clamped shut by the attached rope, you can control a cow's head and body.

"Draw that Rudman cow into the chute." I chased the Rudman cow into the chute used for doctoring cows, the same chute she was in not more than three hours ago. The

19

old man clamped the noses on in one smooth motion and trussed the rope over a beam. He drew the cow's head up until her front feet were barely touching, a sight which pained me a little.

"Get the cooler." I carried it in from the main alleyway. The old man was eating the other half of his sandwich. "Get one of those gloves you use for breeding cows."

"What for? You aren't going to breed this old bag. She isn't in heat, and we haven't got any semen anyway."

"Just get the glove and don't argue with me. Want to learn this business, you do what I say." I came back with my right shirtsleeve rolled up and a plastic glove on that went clear up to my armpit.

"Clean her out just like you were going to breed her." I reached in and cleaned the cow, wondering what in hell he had in mind. All the time I had my hand up her ass, I stared at my grandfather quietly chewing on his egg salad.

"Now stick that ice up her ass."

"What?"

"Stick the ice up her ass and be quick about it. Scribner'll be here any minute. Don't get any shit on the Moxie, though, b'Jesus." The ice was cold, and the Rudman cow gave out with a low moan from down in her throat as if she were calving. She thrashed a bit, but stopped, preferring the ice to strangulation.

"Let her go," I said, "she's got five pounds in her." With a quick tug on the rope he released the knot. He gave a slight twist to the noses and they unclamped. The Rudman cow backed out. At first she walked tenderly and then high-stepped about the pen like a Tennessee walker. Her back was straight and smooth and her tail head was rounded off nicely as she sucked in her guts. Scribner arrived shortly thereafter.

He and my grandfather dickered over every cow but the Rudman cow. He liked her a lot. When they had struck a deal they both drank Moxie while I helped his driver load the trailer truck. As we drove out behind them, the old billy goat stood in the alleyway and watched us go.

On our way back down the highway, the old man told me to fuel up the truck because we had to be in Rutland by seven the next morning to buy a dairy.

That night at supper, I told my mother everything her father and I had done that day. From my chair I could see her standing at the sink looking into her dishwater.

When I told her about the Rudman cow, she stiffened like a board and drew her neck down into her shoulders. She held still like that for a long while before she turned and looked at me.

"You did no such thing," she said with calm conviction.

A Place to Stay

WE DRAFTED ALL THE WAY into Bellows Falls, behind a semi deadheading back to St. Johnsbury. The trucker knew some people Lewis John knew. We hooked up with him in PA, where he was just waking up at a 76 Stop on Route 81. He told us he had a mint Super Glide in his mother's garage in Claremont, so when he saw Lewis John's cherry red Sportster with a Vermont plate, he didn't feel so far afield.

We'd worked the year in Texas, south of San Antonio. I didn't have a place to stay after we lit up the line, so I came north with Lewis John. We figured we'd stay at his place for a month until the next big line job opened, maybe down in Australia. Lewis John had been leaning toward Australia ever since he heard Tasmania was two hundred miles off the coast. He said he wanted to see the devils.

Early that evening we pulled into the Dery Café on High Street. We took off our helmets and lay back against our packs. I put my feet on the front pegs and Lewis John crossed his legs over the gas tank of his bike like a skinny Buddha.

"So, Lewis John. When's the last time you were home?"

"Not since San Antonio."

"She's all you said she was." I scanned the plywood over the windows and the garbage heaped in the alleys.

"She's something all right," Lewis John said. "See those tracks down there? My cousin broke a guy's arms over those rails. That boy was a wild one."

If I hadn't been so tired, I think I would've turned my bike around and aimed it out of there. Rural Vermont wasn't

23

exactly like the travel posters, but then again, I didn't have anywhere else to go.

"We'll go up to the homestead and see the family, but first I need a beer." Since Lewis John didn't drink, this threw me a bit.

"Lewis John, you don't drink."

"No, no," he said, cocking his head to see through the plate-glass windows of the bar.

Suddenly the front door, crisscrossed with steel straps and dented high and low, flung open. A young woman stepped onto the sidewalk. She stood with her hands on her hips. Her ash-blonde hair hung down her back in a long braid. Her bare arms and legs were tanned.

"Addie," Lewis John said quietly, as their eyes locked.

With three long steps she crossed the sidewalk, stepped on a foot peg, and swung astride him. She buried her face in his neck for a long time.

Bellows Falls was an old mill town, as best I could figure out in the dying light, and appropriately named. Down below I could hear the river gasping and blowing, slashing through chutes and slides. The whole town was balanced up here on the rocks.

Next to me, I could hear Lewis John whispering the words to nursery rhymes into Addie's ear, first "Rock-a-Bye-Baby" and then "Mary Had a Little Lamb." A young guy, maybe twenty or twenty-one, came from the bar and handed me a beer.

"River's high this time of year," he said, staring off. "See that mountain over there? That's Rattlesnake Mountain. Across that river is New Hampshire. You a friend of Lewis John's?"

I nodded my head and drained the neck of the bottle.

"Me, too," he said, and walked back inside.

24

Addie turned her face and peeked at me from under Lewis John's chin.

"Who's your friend, Lewis John?" she asked.

"Name's George Bright. He's from Idaho. His people are real cowboys. One of his great-uncles shot Billy the Kid."

None of this was true, but I didn't say anything. Being a cowboy from Idaho was sure as hell a step up from being a lineman out of Syracuse, New York.

"Your father's funeral is Monday," she said, turning back into his neck.

"Addie, I didn't even know he died. Must've been just after we left Texas," Lewis John said, addressing the last sentence to me. "Jesus, I didn't want him to die. Addie, we're going up to the house. Want to ride along?"

"I'll be up in a little bit. You go see your mother."

"Come on, George," he said to me.

Addie unknotted herself from Lewis John and stepped up on the walk. He didn't bother with his helmet. He just backed away from the curb and roared up the street. I followed close behind. After ten minutes I was hopelessly lost in the winding maze of back roads. The pace was a little quicker than safe, but no doubt Lewis John knew these roads and knew them well. I kept my eye on the taillight in front of me and on the trees and fields that shot by on the chance I would catch the glint of a deer's eye. Deer and bikes don't mix.

Before long we reached a crossroad. At the bottom of one lane in a hollow, a barnyard was lit up with a halogen light. The light glowed out from a seam of mist that curled through the hollow like a caterpillar. It seemed tiny from where we sat at the top. Lewis John pointed down the hill. By the time he swooped to the bottom, he'd been through four gears and I hadn't even started.

He waited for me by the front door of an old farmhouse I took to be the homestead. Inside the house, lights were on in every room.

"Is that you, Lewis John?" came a vacant, faraway voice from inside when he rapped on the door.

"It's me, Ma."

"Addie called to tell me you and some cowboy were coming."

"He's not a cowboy, Ma. He's a lumberjack from Canada. First name's Pierre and the last name is French. Ma, would you open the door?" Lewis John pointed at his head and made circles with his finger.

"Now you boys wipe your feet," she said opening the door and walking away from us without looking back. We followed behind after going through the motions of wiping our feet. Inside, the kitchen was warm. The woodstove had a small fire in it to take the dampness out of the cool air that had settled in the hollow. A mound of bread dough lay heaped on the butcher block in the center of the kitchen. The old woman folded the dough toward her and then pressed into it with the heels of her hands. There was so much dough that her hands disappeared up to her wrists. She gave the dough a slight turn and pressed into it again. She repeated this until the dough became smooth. She looked up after a few more turns.

"Addie says she's going to marry you this time and you two are going to move into the tenant house. I think that's nice."

"Yes, it would be nice," Lewis John said.

He was making coffee. He moved efficiently about the kitchen. I found an easy chair by the stove and drew it closer. Even though it was summer, I was chilled from the bike trip. That plus a year in Texas serve to thin one's blood considerably.

"How did the old man finally do in the end, Ma?"

She stopped her kneading again and stared at a row of cast-iron skillets hanging over my head. "Well, he died, you know."

"I know, Ma. Addie told me. We left Texas before your note got there."

"That nice man Ballone said you were in transit. For a minute I thought it was a place. I called at the home office in Kittery. They're going to Australia next. Are you leaving for Australia, Lewis?"

"It's a big job, Ma, all expenses paid. Three-year job. Power line's over a thousand miles long."

"Maybe we could visit," she said, pounding her small white hands into the dough. Tiny air pockets were beginning to form under the surface coating.

A black cat rubbed its back against my boot. I reached down and rubbed its head. It jumped into my lap and laid on its belly with its front feet extended, and began to purr. I could feel it flexing its claws into my dungarees and then releasing. It kept that up for quite a while. After three days on a motorcycle, it felt good.

"How's the dairy, Ma? William making a go of it?"

"Your brother could use some help now that your father's dead."

"Ellie and the kids? You didn't know I was an uncle, did you, Pierre?" Lewis John looked at me.

"Are you married, Mr. French?" Lewis John's mother asked.

"He's married, Ma. His wife's in Syracuse. He left her." This part of my history he had right.

27

"I'm sure they'll work it out, Lewis. Are you going to Australia, Mr. French?"

"No, he's not, Ma. I think I have him talked into going back to his wife and kids."

"That's good, Lewis. Where's Addie? She was to bring me some margarine. Lewis, I'm going to nap for a while. When Addie comes, you wake me." With that the old woman left the kitchen and went into the living room. From where I sat I could see her sit in a rocker and put her head back. She fell asleep within a minute.

"William your brother, Lewis?" I said. The sound of my own voice sounded odd after being quiet so long.

"Coffee?"

"Yes."

"He's my older brother," Lewis said, handing me a mug. "He and my father ran the dairy. Now it's just him. There never was room for all of us, so I hit the road. A buddy of mine worked for Seaward years ago. I learned the trade and I've been at it ever since."

"That would be Tommy."

"Yeah, Tommy. He hired you."

"Yeah, Tommy hired me away from Niagara Mohawk. Good man."

Lewis John went to the cupboard and took out a dust-covered bottle of Jameson's. He poured a shot in each coffee mug.

"It's been two years and this bottle was the last bottle I took a sip from. Seems only fitting," he said, lifting his cup and taking a drink. "Damn, you never lose the taste for it."

We sat like that for at least an hour. We didn't talk. Lewis John began to move about the room, opening drawers and cabinets. Before each one he'd say "silverware" or "cups" or "can opener" or "dish rags," and every time he'd be right. He was halfway around the kitchen when I dozed off.

I woke for a few seconds and heard him in the pantry saying, "Fifteen pounds of flour? Yes, fifteen pounds of flour."

I fell asleep again. You get accustomed to sleeping like this when you work a power line. It's like the army. Sometimes you're on the right-of-way thirty, forty hours at a stretch. Sometimes it takes you half a day's drive through the bush just to get where you need to be. Sagging lines, walking spans, skinning bells all took time. I woke up again.

Lewis John had a stool pulled up to the butcher block. He was staring at the mound of dough, shaking his head and saying, "She ran out of margarine. She ran out of god-damn margarine."

"Lewis John," I said.

He looked up at me and smiled. The Jameson bottle was sticking out of the dough, empty.

"Be quiet," he said, "you'll wake up my mother."

"Lewis, what is it?" came her voice from the other room.

"Nothing, Ma. Just a bad dream." He lowered his eyes toward me and asked, "Did I ever show you my room?"

I shook my head. He stood and motioned me to follow. We climbed a flight of stairs to a room at the top. Inside was a bed, a desk, a chair, and a dresser with half a dozen baseball trophies on it. I went over to the trophies. Inscribed at the bases were such things as High School All-American, MVP 1964 American Legion Tourney, and Bellows Falls High MVP 1963.

"These yours, Lewis John?"

He smiled.

"You must've been quite a ballplayer."

"Red Sox scouted me all through high school. I even went to farm league. I made it to Pawtucket, Triple A."

"What happened?"

"Knees, you ask Addie. She was in the seventh grade. She was my first fan."

Lewis John crouched down on the floor.

"I was a catcher. I caught Dick Radatz once."

"Lewis, what's William like?" I asked, seeing William's name on a small trophy for pitching.

"He's my brother. He lives in the trailer back up the lane. He'll run the dairy now that the old man's dead. They both used to love the ball games. The old man would hit pop flies for half a day for me to shag down."

"William's older," I said.

"He's older. He and the old man would take turns pitching. William had a helluva curve."

"Why didn't you come home and work on the farm?"

"These people need me for other things." He left for downstairs.

When I caught up with him, he was rummaging through the pantry. Finally he found what he was looking for, another half-empty bottle.

"Lewis John, what do you mean they need you for other things?"

He turned and looked at me. "They need me to go to Australia because they'll never go. They need me to climb steel towers and tell wild stories." He took a drink from the bottle and made a face.

"Lewis," I began, attempting a half-assed apology, but he held up his hand and smiled.

"We grew up differently. Let's just leave it at that."

We leaned back against the kitchen counter and drank from the bottle, passing it back and forth. Our minds went in different directions. I thought about my wife, and though I'd already faced up to the fact long ago that I had nothing left to prove and never did to begin with, I felt the weight of it all over again. I had walked out.

God knows where Lewis John's mind went. I didn't know him and had to admit I never would. Admitting something like that makes you realize you don't know yourself all that well. Time, distance, sweat, and muscle only teach you what you already know, but don't want to.

"You going to marry Addie?" I said.

"I doubt it. She could do a lot better than me. The girl has a pure heart. Why?"

"I only wondered, Lewis John. A man has got to be allowed to wonder about things."

I poured a tumbler half full from the bottle and sat back down by the stove. As I drank I could feel the heat seeping through my body. My last thought before I fell asleep was that I was grateful I had a place to stay.

I slept there until the sound of an engine coming down the lane woke me. From the glow of the halogen light, I could see Addie step down from the pickup. She walked to the front door. She had a package of margarine in her hand.

"It's Addie, Lewis John."

He was huddled in a corner by the wood box. He had a Red Sox cap pulled down over his eyes and his catcher's mitt in his lap.

"Addie," he said, the same way he did when he first saw her at the Dery.

He bounded to his feet and swept her up in his arms. I'd seen him do that in Nuevo Laredo. There he hoisted the girls high and spun them until they were afraid. This time he moved around in slow tight circles, his cheek against her

31

breastbone. She wrapped her arms around his head and perched her chin on top. She stared into the high corners of the room, almost through the walls.

"It's gonna rain, Lewis," Addie said softly.

"Steve, why don't you bring in the gear?" Lewis John's voice seemed to come from inside Addie's chest. "You can wheel the bikes into the machine shed."

I went outside. The night air was warm. Out of the dark I could hear crickets and the thunking sound of frogs from the stock pond. I didn't know who Steve was, but at the moment that's who I was supposed to be. The machine shed was neat and clean. Cords were rolled like lineman rope. Bolt boxes and socket sets were complete and separate. On the walls, wrenches were hung by size. In the back, bags of fertilizer and seed were squarely stacked on pallets. The compressor hose was coiled and even the vise was screwed shut and wiped clean.

Outside in the feedlot, the cows moved like ghosts, milling between the bunk and their stalls. To my right the house went dark and then, one after another, candles were lit and placed in the windows.

For the first time I felt a long way from home, a home I really had no right to even think of as home. I felt like calling my wife, but instead, I hung a pack from each shoulder and lifted a duffel bag in each hand. The packs were light. Inside we carried only a few changes of clothes. The duffel bags were substantially heavier: belts, ropes, wrenches, jackboots, and spurs. We made a lot of money climbing three hundred feet into the air. I felt a long way from home. I wondered if there was a pay phone in town.

Back inside, Lewis John and Addie were dancing slowly around the kitchen table.

"There he is," Lewis John said. "He can marry us."

"Him? He's a cowboy."

"No darlin', that's just a front. You see, Steve here is a militant Baptist missionary. He works the high lines half the year to earn money to buy Bibles and passage to Hong Kong. Then he spends the other half smuggling the Bibles one by one into Red China. He can marry us."

Addie looked at me. Her eyes welled up and I thought any second she'd start crying.

"Stop it, Lewis. Goddammit, just stop it."

I didn't know what to say.

Lewis John sat down by the stove where I'd sat earlier. Addie went over and kneeled between his legs. She grabbed the cuffs of his jacket sleeves with both hands.

"Lewis," she said softly, "if the Reverend will marry us, I'm willing."

"Okay," he said. "I'm willing, too. He's got a fine voice, clear as a bell."

The two of them stood before me arm in arm. Lewis looked old and tired. He had a five-day growth of whiskers and his face was windburned. He was still dressed in wind shirts and leathers. Addie stood next to him looking like his little sister. She was a little red from too much sun. She stood erect, then reached over and held his arm with her free hand. This steadied him.

I dropped all the bags at once. A spud wrench and spurs banged on the floor. From the other room Lewis John's mother asked who was there.

"Ma, come stand with us," Lewis John said. "Me and Addie are getting married."

The old woman toddled into the room, touching each piece of furniture as she passed it. She went to lean against the butcher block and stuck her hand squarely into the pile of bread dough.

"Goodness," she mumbled. "What an old fool." She wiped her hand on her apron and noticed Addie.

"Dearie, I didn't see you. Did you bring the margarine?"

"Yes, Mrs. John, it's in the fridge."

"Ma, hush. The Reverend's going to marry us."

"Oh, Lewis John, now what are you up to?"

"Go, Robert," Lewis John said, using my real name for the first time all day. Addie and his mother must have sensed it. They looked at me intently, as if they were trying to read something.

We all stood there like that, poised, waiting. Lewis John nodded his head and said it was okay. Quietly he urged me to go ahead. I started slowly, trying to remember how it went.

"Dearly beloved," I said. "We are here to join Lewis John and Addie in marriage. Do you, Lewis John, take this woman to be your lawfully wedded wife and to honor her in sickness and health and to love her and be honest to her?"

"I do."

"Addie, do you promise to do the same?"

"I do."

"Lewis John, we need a ring." Up to that point I thought I'd done okay, but I honestly felt we needed a ring to top things off. Neither Lewis John nor I wore one because it could get you electrocuted.

"Lewis," his mother said, raising her hand.

We watched her take her gold wedding band off her finger. Her eyes were filling up and she kept dabbing at them with the back of her hand. Addie's lips were tight against her teeth, and tears were starting down her cheeks. Lewis John took the ring and put it on her finger.

"I now pronounce you man and wife," I said. "You may kiss the bride."

When they kissed I walked out onto the front porch. I drew the cool air deep into my lungs with long breaths. Far to the east the sky was shot with red, but in the hollow the yard lights were still on. I walked to the center of the drive to Addie's pickup and folded my arms on the hood. I stared back up the lane and felt the dew seep through my sleeves.

Running west along the ridge was a high line. The top of one tower caught the sun at odd angles before letting it pass through. I felt good imagining those lines spanning out three hundred miles to a house due west of here.

I knew if I pushed it, I could be there by noon.

for Tommy White

What to Do First

WHEN BIG GEORGE GILBUS'S WIFE REFUSED to sleep with him after he came home drunk one too many times, he decided to hit the road. That very night, he weaved his way about the house gathering those things still important to him. He emptied the pantry shelves into a rucksack with a few sweeps of his arm. He put his guns in the rack behind the seat of his truck, along with his fishing tackle. His best dog on the seat next to him, he started driving north. He would go to Cutler's place.

Cutler lived in a trailer on the edge of the Adirondack Park. He'd lived there before the Park Commission came into being. When the surveyors came through they told him the tongue of his trailer rested on state-owned land. He had to move his trailer two feet south. Cutler did so, but one dark night he dug up his septic system and replanted it thirty feet north. Every time Cutler went to the toilet, he said, "Take that, Rockefeller."

Cutler had decided to build a house and Big George figured he could help him build it. He was a carpenter by trade and knew that Cutler wasn't good at doing much unless he was jacking deer or getting revenge.

It was 6:00 in the morning when Big George came to the top of Cutler's hill. Cutler was standing in a big square hole. He was drinking coffee, silently measuring the four invisible walls of his new house.

"Big George! Now what do I do?" Cutler shouted.

"You never did know the difference between your ass and a hole in the ground," George bellowed.

Cutler pointed first at his skinny rear end and then at the ground. "The former and the latter," he asked, breaking into a toothy grin. "What brings you north, George?"

"I heard you were going to build a house, and work's slow down country," Big George said, his mouth feeling like cotton.

"The old lady shut you down again, I see." Both men laughed, but this time George knew it was different. This time his wife hadn't cried. She'd only started tucking blankets into the couch.

George's dog jumped through the open truck window and took up a position on the mound of earth that had been excavated from the foundation. She bayed at the harvest moon that was now a white shadow on the southwestern horizon.

"Cutler, you have to lay a footer to build your walls on."

"How do you do that?" Big George realized this was Cutler's game, but he didn't mind. He always knew the answer Cutler wanted regardless of the question. He wished his own life was so cut and dried.

"First you get a beer and drink it slow," George said.

"Well, that I can do, but drinking it slow takes willpower. Something I've always been short on." Big George and Cutler went into the trailer and sat down at the kitchen table. During the first two beers they spoke quietly of the subtle changes that were taking place as winter approached. They didn't mention such things as the leaves turning, the vast fly-over of geese, or the declination of the sun. Instead they spoke of the smell of white ash burning because it dried the quickest, the snap of trees in the morning as they locked in the cold October air, and acorn shells cached neatly in the leeward roots of oak trees.

"So how much money do you have for this project?" Big George finally asked, his thoughts coming back from last night and the look on his wife's face. An ash log had burned in the fireplace.

"About three thousand," Cutler replied proudly.

"Three thousand dollars! You don't even have enough money to get out of that hole in the ground." As soon as he'd said this, Big George knew he'd hurt Cutler's feelings. "We need a plan of action." Cutler could be a little thin-skinned at times, George thought, somewhat like his wife. George decided he'd better go easy.

"Well then, Big George, you make up a plan of action while I take a leak."

Big George sat back and pulled at his chin. He had cast doubt on one of Cutler's schemes and now felt obliged to patch it up.

Cutler came back hiking up his trousers by the belt loops. Big George heard him mumble, "Take that, Rockefeller."

The two men walked quietly through the woods. Cutler wanted to show Big George a huckleberry patch that was rife with signs of black bear. Though dry leaves covered the forest floor, neither man made a sound. Cutler bounced along from bare spot to bare spot while Big George took painful strides, watching every step.

Cutler motioned toward a fallen tree they could use for a blind. The men sat for an hour before a she-bear and a big cub came to feed on leaves and berries. Their coats had begun to grow out, long and shaggy. The black bears swept the bushes clean with their paws. Then they sat back and preened like cats in the low-angled sunlight. They licked their paws, sucking the berry stains off their pads. After a while they wandered off in the direction they'd come in from.

"I brought you up here for a reason, George. They make this stop every other day or so. I'm building that house so's I can hang one of those bearskins on the wall."

"We can do it. With three grand I know we can come up with something." This project was something George could reach out and touch, and could rely on his knowledge of spans, loads, and flex. There were some things he understood.

"Well, what do we do first?" Cutler's eyes danced in his face.

"First, we have to rethink the plan of action," George said. He paused a second. "And have another beer." George really didn't want the beer, but he knew it would be easier than changing the procedure.

Back at the house the only paper was brown paper bags. George ripped one open and began redesigning Cutler's house. Cutler sat back and gazed at the ceiling tiles as he told George what he wanted.

"I've got to have an expansive porch, George. That's important. A house without a porch ain't friendly. And I want a loft with windows open to the south. Don't worry about closets. I don't have many clothes." George jotted notes to his right as Cutler rambled on about antlers, gun racks, and the granite he wanted in the hearth.

Big George thought about his own house. He saw the pantry, the living room, the kitchen, and the bedroom. It was a small ranch house on the outskirts, never too far from whatever house he was building. He stopped listening to

Cutler and started sketching a diagram replete with dimensions, materials estimates, procedures, and details of small parts. He worked methodically, counting out figures on his fingers. "More bags," he said to Cutler, who promptly yet carefully opened them at the seams. After a few hours he sat back exhausted. Cutler had been cleaning his guns, no doubt trying to decide how he'd shoot his bear, George thought. Cutler stepped around gingerly to view the work.

"Aw, Georgie, she's a beauty. You even put in a place for my bearskin."

"It's all there, friend."

"What does she ring in at George?"

"With some wheeling and dealing, you could probably do it for, say, eighty-five hundred. Now remember, it's not really a house, it's more of a camp or a lodge. That's right—a hunting lodge."

Cutler beamed at the prospect of having his dream house built. "A lodge," he said. "A lodge. I like that, George, but it's a little rich, don't you think?"

George started to explain how they could get financing, find a barn for salvage, make their own shingles. He looked up from the sketches to make another point.

Cutler was staring intently at a fly on the table. George stopped talking and Cutler looked up.

"George, that sounds good," Cutler said slowly as if waking from a long dream. "Can we start today? What comes first?" George reached back into the refrigerator for two more beers.

Outside it was dark. George stared at the window for a while, trying to see something. When he couldn't, he still didn't look away. Cutler started a fire in the stove. He rummaged through George's sack. He emptied a can of tomato soup into a pot on the stove. Into that he added a can of corn, one of beans, one of carrots, and one of onions. "A feast, George, a veritable feast," he said.

The men ate without talking, sopping up the stew with hunks of bread. George watched as Cutler spooned the stew into his mouth with the reverence of one who appreciates good food. When Cutler finished, he sat back and belched. "Fit for a king, George," Cutler said, "but I've got an even bigger treat for you." Cutler took a dish from the refrigerator.

"Nutmeats," Cutler said. "I took 'em from the bellies of three gray squirrels I shot this week."

As the men ate, George thought about the last time he and Cutler had eaten nutmeats from a gray. Both men had taken deer that autumn and were rip-roaring drunk. They'd run through the woods smashing into trees in their long underwear. George had rocked huge rotten trees back and forth until they crashed to the ground. The smaller ones he embraced and ripped out at the roots.

"Let's run the dogs, Cutler," George said. "Must be plenty of coon still left in those woods." George suddenly wanted to move. It made him uneasy to think about the past now that it seemed so near at hand.

"That's an idea, George. Get your rifle and I'll get a spotlight." They met where Cutler had his red-bone hound chained. George's dog, also a red-bone, was lying nose to nose with her. Cutler had a .22 pistol holstered at his waist and a miner's helmet on his head.

"Where in hell did you get that thing?" George said.

"A couple of fellers from Pennsylvania came by one night. I told them I'd guarantee them five coon if they'd trade me the helmet," Cutler said proudly as he reached to the battery pack on his hip and flipped the switch. A brilliant beam of light shot from the top of his head.

"Shut that damn thing off and unleash the dogs. You look like a lighthouse."

Once loose, the dogs chased each other around in circles. "Go, you bitch," Cutler yelled. The two dogs ran into the big hole and tried to go up the back side, a vertical wall of dirt. Cutler yelled again. The dogs honed in on his voice and bounded back out, into the woods. "Fool dogs," Cutler muttered. George and Cutler followed them in about three hundred yards, then waited. They smoked cigarettes, cupping their hands over the ends. The trees loomed about them, starkly lit by the fullness of the moon. The forest floor was a tight pattern of darkness and shadow.

"Georgie," Cutler said, "what was it this time? You been into the rum a bit much?"

"Ah hell, you know how it goes."

Cutler took off his helmet. "Man's greatest delusion is that one woman is different from another."

This bolstered Big George even though he didn't believe it.

"I *am* a good man, Cutler," George said. "I work hard and I have a good reputation. I have a lot of friends. Sure I stop after work, but you have to when you're in the business I'm in."

"Just one thing, George," Cutler broke in. "Never sign your name to nothin', especially after eight at night in a gin mill. That's my motto."

Before George could reply, the high-pitched whine of Cutler's hound came from the direction of the huckleberry patch. That was soon joined by the deep baying of the other dog. The men set off at a dead run. The dogs had treed the coon high in the crotch of an oak tree. The limbs looked like a tangle of cobwebs against the moon.

Cutler shined a path of light into the tree, moving it back

43

and forth with his neck until he spotted the coon's tail. The men worked their way around the base of the tree, the dogs never once letting up. Cutler's hound kept running six or seven feet up the tree and then twisting out at the last second so as not to fall on her ass.

Cutler directed his headlamp into the coon's eyes. The animal was paralyzed in the light. George picked it off cleanly with a single shot just under its chin. The animal somersaulted to the ground. The dogs tussled with it briefly and set off again, only to be called back by George.

"Too easy, eh, George?"

"Yeah, I kind of thought there'd be more to it. Never used to be like that."

Cutler shut off his light and stuffed the coon inside his coat. He moved close to George. "You want to run some more tonight or not?"

George smiled at his friend and shook his head.

"Surviving's easy, George, if you have to do it. Carpentering ain't hard, is it, if you know what to do?"

"No," George said, "no it isn't, not if you know what you should do and do it right."

They leashed the dogs and began the walk back to Cutler's trailer. The dogs fell in step behind them. Some nights George and Cutler had hunted in the cold till sunrise, but tonight the air was warm for the time of year and there would be no frost. Both men were sweating under the woolens they'd put on as the evening chill set in. Now it was warmer than it had been during the day.

"Cutler, she says I need professional help," Big George said without breaking stride.

"May be, George. It just may be. What do you think?"

"I don't drink any more than the next man," George said. Nearing the trailer, George could see Cutler's face. Cutler's

44

gaze was directed at his trailer and the small island of light that surrounded it.

"Well, George, I know what we gotta do first."

"I don't think I'm thirsty." George felt burdened by his extra clothes as he walked to his truck.

"I don't mean that. We gotta skin this coon. This pelt's worth fifty bucks toward my lodge. If I can get fifty coon this fall, that's twenty-five hundred toward my hunting lodge. I'm getting closer, ain't I, George?"

"You sure are, Cutler." George opened the door of his pickup, and his dog jumped in. George climbed in after her and turned. "You sure are. You can do anything if you have to." George gunned the engine and reached for the door. "I have to go home, Cutler," he said. Cutler nodded his head as George turned his truck around and aimed it down the hill.

Cody's Story

CODY AND HIS PARTNER, G.R. Trimble, were loggers. G.R. had a splendid piebald Percheron twitch horse named Buck that stood eighteen hands, and Cody had a one hundred-horsepower fully articulated John Deere skidder equipped with grapple, winch, and arch, that could skid five hundred board-feet equivalent of hardwood logs.

The men lived in the horse trailer with Buck. They had bunks and shelves that folded up during transport and down when they set up camp. They had a TV, electric baseboard heat, and a microwave oven. All of these ran off a little Homelite generator they took in swap for some cordwood.

It was a good life for the two gypsy loggers, even in the winter, when on certain nights the dark silence heaved open with the sound of hardwoods cracking and snapping from the cold within their very heartwood. Such nights Cody would sit up bolt straight in bed and curse silently to himself. G.R. was merely thankful it didn't get as cold as it used to in the old days.

G.R. was older than Cody and had a reputation. They say that when he was up in Saskatchewan he got shorted on an overrun of logs once, so he went down to the mill. When reason failed, he threw the sawyer's bird dog down a well, packed up, and left.

People treated G.R. with respect, just in case the story was true. G.R. always responded with great courtesy, cementing in the minds of everyone he met that the story was indeed true. The more kindly he acted, the more convinced they were that he threw the dog down the well. G.R. was a politic man.

Cody was married to a woman in Winchester, New Hampshire. She had a boy from a previous marriage. When the boy was young Cody loved him, but as he grew older and took on the looks of another man, Cody could see in him his wife's first husband, and as the boy grew, it was as if the other man had moved back in. Finally Cody left for the woods with G.R. He seldom got home, but always sent money to their joint account. Being away helped him start to love her again, and by now he'd been in the woods with G.R. so long he'd forgotten why he'd come in the first place.

Their last year together, Cody and G.R. wintered on the leeward side of Monadnock. G.R. opened his money belt and bought a used D-7 to clear the right-of-way. They hewed out a suitable landing on the main haul road. Arterials ran in at up to 20 percent grades, too steep for most men, but not for Cody and G.R.

Sunday was the only day Cody and G.R. didn't work. They'd hole up in the trailer, where they serviced their saws and sharpened chain while they watched *The Three Stooges* on TV. G.R. would cringe and say "Oh God" whenever Moe raked a crosscut across Curly's noggin, splaying the teeth in opposite directions and making him screech like a cat in heat. Because he was a real stickler on safety, G.R.'s fascination with the Stooges brought him much pain.

"My way or the highway, boy," he'd yell at Cody, when they were in the woods.

"Don't call me boy," Cody would yell back over the roar of the skidder.

"Okay, boy," G.R. would reply, dragging out the last word

48

before disappearing into the trees with the winch line over his shoulder, hooks and choker assemblies bouncing against his chest.

On this Sunday, the first snow of the year had come down country and gripped everything. The generator ran out of gas at about 4:00 in the morning. The trailer was freezing, the walls coated with sharp white needles of hoarfrost. Buck was blowing billows of hot breath that were crystallizing in the air and coasting to the floor. "Cody boy, get me a beer, would you?" G.R. said from deep inside his blankets.

Cody and G.R. drank beer on Sunday mornings. They bought the beer on Saturday night when they went grocery shopping because it was against the law to buy it before noon on Sundays. Cody and G.R. liked their beer on Sundays.

Cody reached into the case under his bunk for a beer. He passed it up to G.R. with a can of tomato juice. G.R. took a swallow and refilled it with the juice.

"This one's for you, Buck ol' boy," he said nodding to the horse. "If it weren't for you, we might've froze to death."

Cody tried to go back to sleep, but it was just too damn cold. He burrowed down in his bed covers for his shoes and trousers. Once he was dressed, he started the generator. It was almost 7:30. Cody squeezed his way around some boxes and dished up oats for the horse. Buck swished his tail and snuffed into his feedbag. He was a good horse.

"Boy, that tastes good," G.R. said, staring at the empty beer bottle. "You know, I can't eat breakfast on an empty stomach."

"Sure, G.R. That's a good one," Cody said.

G.R. dressed while Cody cooked eggs, potatoes, and a rasher of bacon in the microwave. The men washed down their breakfast with beer and tomato juice. By eight o'clock they had their benches, jigs, and files set up. Each had fifteen chains to sharpen. On each chain they had to sharpen the cutters and file the rakers. They turned on the TV and went to work. It was almost time for *The Three Stooges*.

The men worked carefully, side by side, inspecting each link for wear and stress. A snapped chain at high speed could raise hell with a man's will to live.

The only time G.R. ever used another man's saw, he was bucking up frozen hard maple. When he set the saw to the wood, it skated along the tree, cutters clipping off into the air. The chain broke, whipping around his top hand. They saved his hand, but it took two hours to separate the glove, steel, meat, and bone. It was understood they'd each use their own saw and chain. G.R. tied blue ribbon around his chain and Cody used red.

This Sunday the Stooges were going west in a covered wagon with three fat sisters, Faith, Hope, and Charity. The girls made the boys fetch wood and break holes in the ice for water. Their horses ran off and they were attacked by Indians. The girls made the boys sleep outdoors under a tarp. By morning they were buried in snow.

The high point for G.R. was when Moe got slapped in the face with a limb Curly let go. Moe poked him in the eyes a good one with his fingers.

"Boy, that had to hurt some," G.R. said, rubbing his eyes.

"It's all phony," Cody said. "If he really did that, it'd blind him."

"I'd like to get those boys in the woods for a day," G.R. said. "I bet I could teach them a few things. Snap them in line."

"For Chrissakes, G.R., it's all bullshit. That stuff doesn't really happen."

"It does more than you think, Cody, my boy. More than you think."

Cody finished his chain while G.R. switched the channel to *Meet the Press*. Cody worried about G.R. lately. G.R. didn't seem to have any diversions except the Three Stooges. He talked about them like they were his boys. Cody watched G.R. cringe whenever the boys got hurt and heard him declare revenge whenever they got screwed by someone. Cody knew G.R. was serious when he said he'd like to take the boys out into the woods and teach them how to be loggers.

Cody and G.R. continued to work all morning, sitting in front of the TV. Cody made sandwiches, thick slabs of beef between bread. The men drank and ate and worked while they watched TV.

"We'd best start the engines tonight," Cody said.

"Why?" G.R. asked, cocking his head sideways toward Cody.

"Winter, G.R. Those engines will never start in the morning. Till this weather breaks, we'd best leave them go around the clock."

"Ether, Cody boy, ether."

"Not in this weather, G.R. You'll blow the heads."

The men sat quietly. Buck ate hay and sucked water from his bucket.

"G.R.," Cody said quietly, "you feeling all right?"

G.R. nodded his head without looking at Cody.

"G.R.," Cody said, "we always leave the engines run in this weather. We never use ether."

G.R. nodded his head again.

"I know, Cody. I know. I know."

"G.R., that ain't like you."

"I know, Cody. I been doing that more and more of late. I miss stuff. It's like when I was stationed overseas, Spain. I got up in the middle of the night to take a leak. All the boys were on guard duty. So I'm standing there in the can draining Big Willy, and the whole room starts to go up and down and here I am pissin' all over the walls. I thought I was sick as a dog, so I go back to my bunk figuring I'd better see the doctor. Well, I get back in the barracks and the concrete floor is going in waves just like the ocean. Now I know I'm sick. Two days later I find out it's a goddamn earthquake."

Cody stared at G.R., trying to fit this into what had prompted the conversation. G.R. began to rummage for his mackinaw.

"Where you going?" Cody asked.

"Let's go take a leak, Cody. The sun's high and fine."

G.R. had no way of knowing, Cody thought, because there were no windows in the trailer. Cody shut off the TV anyway and followed G.R. out the side door. The sun was low on the southern horizon and wouldn't start to climb until after the solstice. Cody dusted off the machines and unlatched the hoods so what sun there was could warm the batteries. G.R. backed Buck out of the trailer and walked him around the landing half a dozen times to limber him up. The horse stepped high, not too pleased with the whole affair.

Cody watched G.R. amble alongside Buck, whose nose was at the same level as the top of G.R.'s head. Snow collected on Buck's fetlocks in hard, round balls. His shoulders alternately bulged and receded and his haunches swayed rhythmically. G.R. picked up the pace. The two of them pranced around the perimeter of the clearing.

Cody had to admit that Buck earned his keep. They used him for gleaning the swamps, holes, and isolated stands for the best tree. Buck was smart. He had the sense to set over whenever he hit a snag. G.R. would set the choker and Cody would be on the haul road yarding the logs. Buck would twitch the logs a long ways up to Cody on his own without a jam.

That horse is the most important thing in G.R.'s life, Cody thought. They'd logged both coasts and as far north as Hudson Bay together. Buck was old, though, and wouldn't last much longer. G.R. knew it, too, and it had to be on his mind.

G.R. brought Buck up to the Cat where Cody was tinkering with the terminals.

"We're a little stiff today, Cody. Gonna be a long winter this year, I'm afraid."

"No longer than any other."

"I meant more by that, Cody. I meant winter would be longer."

"I know, G.R., winter will be longer this year." G.R. backed Buck off and began around the landing again.

"G.R.," Cody yelled, "picket that horse and let's hike up the haul road. There's deer sign up there."

"You go, Cody, I'm going in and watch TV. There's a cowboy movie on."

Cody started up the haul road with his Deerslayer and field glasses. When he reached the first level he climbed the bank and bushwhacked up the mountain. Halfway to the summit he was forced to skirt a thirty-foot rock face. When he reached the top, he walked out on the lip where the snow had melted off and the rocks were warm in the sunlight. He sat down, cradling the shotgun in his lap.

Water was trickling from under the snow behind him, fanning out to his right and left in wide arcs coursing across the rock and then dripping off the edge. Night would come, turning the fans into an icy veneer and the drips into icicles.

Far below he could see the blue hull of the trailer and the yellow skidder and crawler on the edge of the landing. They were encircled by G.R.'s and Buck's track. Cody tapped a cigarette on his thumbnail and lit it. He tried to relax, but kept thinking that G.R. was a little different this morning in a vacant sort of way. Men changed, he knew that. He'd seen it before. He himself had felt it, the feeling of something creeping up on you. The woods were full of men who'd sat down and died, men with a full larder and an income. The more willful hadn't waited for death. They took it to her.

Cody sat and smoked. He just had to get away. He turned around and looked at the mountain that rose up behind him. He imagined Larry, Moe, and Curly tumbling down the mountain toward him with a black bear in hot pursuit. He imagined G.R. riding up to save them on Old Buck, waving a double-bit axe over his head. "You did good, boys," he'd tell them. "You always run downhill from a bear because its front legs are short and it can't go so fast."

Cody looked down the mountain again and saw G.R. running in circles. Cody raised his binoculars. G.R. was spelling Cody's name in the snow. He was standing on the loop of the Y, waving his right arm back and forth. Cody waved his arm and then saluted.

Through the binoculars, Cody could see the smile on G.R.'s red face. He could see a tuft of white hair where G.R.'s shirt was open at the neck. Cody felt better sitting on the rock with the sun on his face and G.R. waving at him. He stretched his legs and opened the collar of his own shirt. He lay back on the rocks, sore and tired from the long week's work. He could smell the pine and hemlock in the air. He fell asleep feeling a little relieved.

When Cody woke up, the sun was fading behind a snow-capped mountain to the southwest. Its light played out in deep reds and purples. Cody stood and stretched, aching with cold. He crossed his arms on his chest and shivered. Turning to make his way home, he stepped on an ice patch to his right. He slipped, his body slapping full length against the rock, and began sliding toward the edge. The only sound was the echo of his gun clattering from rock to rock on its way to the ground.

As Cody slid, everything seemed to pause just for him, all mechanisms stopping so as not to divert him from this moment. His body warmed and his thoughts came like pictures, some he'd never seen before. Then he was floating, unable to figure his orientation to the ground below and not all that concerned with whether his head was up or down. There was no rush of air and his breathing seemed easy to him. Just as he began to worry, he was in the top of a blue spruce, dropping through its branches, limbing them with his legs and arms.

Cody locked his arms around a branch, annoyed that this would be more difficult than he thought. He hugged the branch against himself.

For a second it bent under him and held. At that moment the world about him lurched back into gear as if someone had popped a giant clutch. The branch sheared off and he rode it the rest of the way to the ground.

Cody lay there in the dark a long time, then began taking inventory of his body. It was all there and it worked. He began to wonder if what had happened had happened at all. He found his gun and set out for the trailer.

By the time he got there it was dark. He ran a lead cord and trouble light out to the skidder. He worked quickly, fearing the batteries had cooled and the oil had thickened.

He remembered the time G.R. started a fire under one

machine to warm it. Those were the days when everything G.R. did was safe, or at least he'd explain that everything he did was safe.

Cody shifted the skidder into neutral range, switched on the ignition, and pressed the starter. The engine chugged and huffed and then fired up in the sharp night air.

Cody backed her up and then drove forward, breaking the tires free of the ice that was forming. He idled her down, checked the fuel, and went in for the night, walking lightly on the balls of his feet.

The trailer was warm and bright. Saw chains were hung on the wall, blue ribbons for G.R., red for Cody. On the same wall were silver hard hats and duckcloth overalls. Cody's supper was in the microwave waiting for the button to be pushed.

G.R. sat on a bale of hay watching *60 Minutes*. He was eating chili dogs and chicken noodle soup. While he chewed his food, his mouth was half open and his jaw popped.

"Where you been, Cody?" G.R. asked.

"Starting up the skidder." Cody didn't recognize his own voice.

"What for?"

"G.R., we leave it run. I already talked to you about it."

Cody ate his supper, lighting up his last cigarette to go along with his meal. He felt confused and lost, as if G.R. were a total stranger who for no reason had robbed him.

"G.R., remember the time you started a fire under that Massey loader to warm it up?"

"Tried and true method, Cody my boy."

"Good, G.R. That's real good," Cody said, shoving a chili dog into his mouth.

"Watch this, Cody. Dan's going to nab this poor bastard for shutting off an old lady's electricity last winter."

"Goddammit, G.R., something's happening and I want to know what the hell it is."

G.R. stood up and turned toward Cody. He craned his neck and puffed out his chest. "I'm losing my edge a little, Cody. That's all. It's damn hard to maintain when you go the way I do."

"That's a crock, G.R."

"No, Cody. I'm feeling it a little. I'm feeling it right now, and if I can't feel it, then I can't do nothing." G.R. sat down.

"Cody, if I ever get too daft to be out in them woods, I want you to shoot me."

"Sure, G.R., right between your goddamn eyes, and then I'll shoot old Buck and carve a niche inside that mountain. I'll set you up on him with your hands wired to the hames. I'll bury you there for some asshole to dig up in the year three thousand."

Cody felt his stomach churn. He eyed G.R., sitting only a few feet away, intent on the TV. For a moment he considered packing it in and going home—something had a hold on him. Cody squeezed through to Buck and fed him a couple cubes of sugar. The horse tossed his head and shifted his weight. The whole trailer bounced. Cody put his face and chest against Buck's body. It was warm and moved slowly as Buck breathed.

Cody took out the curry and brush and began to groom him. He combed out the mane, tail, and fetlocks. He curried his coat until it was sleek and shiny. Then he wrapped his arms around the animal's huge legs, hugging and squeezing them.

When he was done, he leaned back against Buck's chest. The horse rested his chin on Cody's head, breathing deeply, the weight of his head growing heavy as he relaxed.

Cody eased out from under the horse and moved to the

front of the trailer. G.R. was already in his bunk, asleep. Cody shut off the TV and lights and climbed into his own bunk.

He lay there for a long time. Tomorrow they would be on the far boundary of the cutting unit, into maple and beech. On a concave slope with a wash down the center. It would be an interesting challenge. G.R. would build it up as insurmountable only so that his method of logging would seem that much more amazing. Things would be all right then, Cody thought. Things would be better in the morning.

Buck stamped once and then there was only silence in the trailer. The horse was asleep, his four legs locked into position. Cody relaxed a little more and then he heard G.R. whisper.

"Cody. What's that noise?"

"It's the skidder," Cody said.

"Of course, of course. Better set that idle or you'll foul the jets."

"It'll do for tonight," Cody said, feeling his stomach clench up again and start to swim. He fought back the feeling. He fought back his fears for G.R. and his fears for himself.

"Colder than hell," G.R. said, still whispering. "Might not make it through this one. They'll find us with icicles hanging out our noses."

"G.R., I'm pretty damn cold myself," Cody lied.

"We better do something," G.R. said.

There was a long time when neither spoke. Cody didn't want to but he tried to remember the images he saw while he was falling. Just as he would begin to get a lock on one, it would slip from his mind's grasp and he was left only with an empty feeling. He gave up on the ones he hadn't recognized, but by then he couldn't remember even the ones that had seemed familiar.

Finally G.R. crawled out of his bunk and got in bed with Cody. Cody rolled onto his side and G.R. lined his body behind him. They lay there feeling the warmth of each other's body. Cody felt better having his friend so close, haunted as he was by his tumble off the cliff.

"Just one thing, Cody boy," G.R. said.

Cody felt G.R.'s chin whiskers scratching against the back of his neck.

G.R. moved closer. "There'll be no kissing on the mouth," he said.

Cody threw back his head, hitting G.R. in the nose, and laughed. G.R. grabbed his hurt nose and began to laugh, too. They laughed and sighed and Cody began to cry, softly so G.R. wouldn't know. He lay on his side, his face inches from the wall. G.R. was behind him, his arms folded and his face was in the corner made by Cody's shoulder and the mattress.

"G.R., I needed you tonight," Cody said.

"Now, Cody, you've got to take charge more."

"Stop it, G.R. Stop it. I almost died tonight," Cody said, his tears too full to hold back. "I almost died on that goddamn mountain." Then he told the whole story, feeling for the first time the pain in his arms and chest.

G.R. didn't say anything for so long that Cody thought he'd fallen asleep. Then he felt G.R.'s hand on his shoulder and heard him speak, as if he were talking to himself. "Is it true, Cody, that your whole life passes before your eyes?"

Cody didn't answer. He only lay there and listened. He heard the John Deere's diesel knocking outside in the night. He imagined a thousand small explosions going off inside its block, like all the scenes he couldn't remember and never would.

59

Onions

"I WANT TO KNOW what in hell you're going to do with your damn onions now, Raymond Knowlton." Raymond's father didn't wait for an answer. He stamped his foot like a little boy, splashing mud up his pant leg. He slogged across the driveway, hitting every puddle he could, splattering anybody who was too close.

Raymond sat on a packing crate and picked his teeth for something to do. He watched two men wrap chains around the axles of his John Deere 4020 and draw them tight to a flatbed with come-alongs. He watched them climb into the cab, turn over the diesel, and drive to the highway. The last thing he noted was the deep blue Pennsylvania license plate as the rig left Savannah, New York, disappearing down the highway.

People milled about him, collecting the items that had been auctioned. Everything that wasn't nailed down had been bought by somebody. Some things brought more than expected, others less.

Raymond saw his father moving from crowd to crowd. He'd glower at the purchase, huff and stamp, and then move on. The old bastard is putting a curse on everything, Raymond thought. People shifted uneasily as the old man moved toward them.

Four Amish fellows came from the barn walking two by two, a length of harness stretched out between them over their shoulders. Several people snickered, but Raymond saw

61

their eyes that flashed out over their long beards from under their black hats.

Down at the warehouse his cousin Earl was loading pick-ups and flatbeds with compressors, refrigeration units, roll-away tool boxes, spare parts, and empty onion crates. Earl, you're a fool, he thought.

"Raymond," a quiet voice said.

He turned his head slowly and looked up to see Boyd Resin, the auctioneer, and Hans Madden, the man from the bank who handled his account. He squinted, trying to see their faces. They stood side by side and the sun broke over where their shoulders met. He stepped to the side. He could see them now.

"How'd we do, boys? Debtors' prison?"

"Actually we did okay, son," Madden said.

"We who, Mr. Madden?" Raymond said.

"I mean all of us, Raymond. You still have half the land and all your buildings."

"And just a few tons of onions, I'd say, Mr. Madden."

"Now Raymond," Resin said, "if you can move those onions—and I mean within the month—you can come back. Madden here will float you a loan. You won't be as big as before, but you'll make out."

Before he could reply, they walked away. A few tons of onions, as Raymond put it, was more like two hundred tons. Every onion broker in the country had been contacted, but not a one had shown up for the sale. There was an onion glut. Raymond, being new to the onion business, couldn't unload his goods. The old-timers were having a tough enough time calling in every last favor they were owed.

He sat back down on the crate. He watched the last of the people leave, the scavengers, the ones who'd drive two hours just to buy an old bolt box or a pulley or an old milk can they could decoupage and put in the den. No one had spoken to Raymond. At least at funerals people say they're sorry, he thought. At an auction, though, they come in a big parade to see who the screw-up was and why he went under.

Raymond sat and watched. His cousin Earl walked over. "Well, all loaded. Every last stick of it is gone. Now what do you want me to do?"

"What do I want you to do? What do you mean what do I want you to do? Sweep the floor? No broom. Shut off the lights? Electric company will do that. You don't realize, you damn fool? You just loaded your life and sent it down the highway."

"Raymond, don't yell at me."

"Don't yell? You're running around here breaking your neck to ship out everything we own, and you say don't yell? Don't you understand there's nothing to do? We are *done*. The whole family's down the tubes."

Earl didn't move. He stood with his long arms clamped against his sides.

"Go to supper, Earl. I'll finish up here," Raymond said quietly.

After Earl plodded up to his house, Raymond walked down the lane to the warehouses. To the west it looked like the sun was setting into Montezuma Swamp.

"Someday I want to live long enough to hear a big hiss and see steam billow out of you like a locomotive the size of a planet," he said aloud to the swamp. "Then I want to see this black muck turn to dust, and the ditches sucked dry."

"Who the hell are you talking to?" His father's voice came

from the shadows of the warehouse. "Now you're rantin' and ravin' like a goddamn crazy man. If you still have half a mind, come here."

Raymond walked to the side of the warehouse. On the black wall his father had a series of calculations and equations written in chalk.

"I've been doing some figuring, boy. If we can move them onions for these few pennies here, we can jump right back into potatoes. Now even given the worst of markets, in five years we can be right in the thick of it."

"What in hell do you know? Last year we grew two hundred acres of potatoes and a couple acres of onions and we made a bundle off the onions and lost our shirts on the potatoes. This year we go onions and lose it all. It's Chicago. They dictate the price. Supply and demand—bullshit!"

"Now son, I gave you some rein and you hung yourself good, but you ain't dead yet. I ain't gonna say I told you to stick with potatoes, but I did and that's what we're getting back into. Now look here."

The old man went over the figures, but Raymond wasn't listening. From the warehouse he could smell the onions. Without the refrigeration units, they'd rot in a month.

He should never have let them talk him into selling the units. The onions will sell, they said. Madden had a buyer. My ass, he had a buyer. It was one big put-up. He knew them refrigeration units would sell good.

The old man was gone. Raymond turned and saw him halfway up the lane on the way to his trailer. Raymond walked through the side door and looked at his onions in the dim light coming through the doorway. He threw the breaker switch and the fluorescent tubes high in the trusses flickered, then lit. As each light came on, the mountain of onions grew. Millions of yellow globes the size of your fist nestled in together. They smelled rich and pungent, but if they weren't gone soon, they'd freeze, and then, when spring came, they'd rot. He hit the breaker switch and left for the house to wait for something else to happen.

The month dragged by. He made a few phone calls. At last he offered to give the onions away.

The broker was quiet for a moment. "Raymond," he finally said, "maybe we can work something out."

"Go to hell," Raymond said, slamming the receiver down.

His last hope died at the end of the month when he woke up to a frost. He put on his overshoes and went to the warehouse. His onions looked like a pile of hairy snowballs, millions of them.

Raymond's wife went back to substitute teaching, Earl went on unemployment, the old man collected Social Security, and Raymond checked his onions and sat. He sat through most of the days that winter.

He would split a little wood and sit by the stove, his stocking feet on the hearth. He tried his hand at carving decoys, but gave up after the first few looked like onions with a few knobs.

Earl and his father would stop in to talk and plan and figure. For Christmas, Raymond's wife had bought her father-in-law a pocket-sized solar-powered calculator. The old man loved to figure. Only now he'd say, "Let me compute that for you."

Early in March the old man called Earl and Raymond together in his trailer. He sat them down at the table and poured them each a cup of coffee.

"Boys, in another month we're going back into business. I'm cashing in my life insurance and I've got a few War

Bonds. Madden says he'll do better than match it. But one thing, there'll be no onions. We're going back into potatoes come hell or high water, and this time around we'll all be partners. Three votes to everything. I put up the money, you put up your backs."

Earl was happy, but Raymond saw through it all. Whenever there was a vote, Earl would throw in with his uncle. Raymond's father was now taking it all back. He hated him for doing it, and hated himself even more for feeling that way.

"Sounds good to me. Sounds great," Earl said, but neither Raymond nor his father responded. Raymond looked into his coffee and his father looked at him.

"You in, Ray?" his father asked.

"I suppose," Raymond finally said.

"Good," the old man yelled, slamming his fist down. "Now, boys, we are going to go back to the regional market. We are going to sell by the road and we are going to these supermarkets and sell under contract. We'll haul our own potatoes."

Raymond muttered, "Shit," and the old man looked at him.

"What's the matter with you?"

"Nothin'! Must just be something I ate." Raymond was thinking back to when he was a boy and the old man still ran the farm. Gangs of men would come in and follow the potato digger, handling every spud that broke out of the ground. Then they'd bag at night and truckers would haul all day. Even as a boy he was expected to do a man's work, to make a man's decisions.

". . . and Raymond, change those overalls. They smell like onions."

"I like the smell," he said.

"You'll come around sooner or late," the old man said, wagging a finger at him.

"Let's go, Earl, we have a lot to do. You're a partner now, how do you like that?"

"Pretty good, I guess, but I think Raymond's got more say."

"Piss on it, boy. Comes a time when you have to do what you have to do."

Raymond walked the lane to the warehouse. He threw the breaker, but no lights. At the loading dock, he pulled up the overhead doors by hand. They clattered up their tracks and let the sun come in on his onions.

At the bottom of the heap the floor was wet and slick from the juices. He breathed deeply and stepped on an onion. It squished flat and gray under his shoe. He smiled and stepped on a few more. He kept this up until a car pulled in. A county seal was on the driver's door. A man stepped out, grimaced, and quickly put a handkerchief over his mouth and nose.

"By God, I knew it was bad, but I never realized," came his muffled voice. "You're Raymond Knowlton."

"What the hell's wrong, you got the flu?" Raymond said.

"No. I'm from the county board of health and these damn onions have got to go."

"Go? Why?"

"You can't smell it? The whole town smells it when the wind changes. By summer people will be stunk out of their houses."

Raymond turned to the mountain of rotting onions. He'd looked at them every day for months. He had a chair in the warehouse where he'd sit and look at the onions for long spells at a time, trying to figure things out.

"Smell's all it is. Smell doesn't hurt anybody."

Tears were coming to the other man's eyes.

"Where's your father?"

"My father doesn't own these onions, I do."

"Raymond, these onions are rotting. They stink and make everybody uncomfortable for miles around."

"Let me think about it."

"Raymond, I can make you bury them, but it takes time to get the orders and I don't have time."

"I'll get back to you on it."

The man drove up the lane to the trailer. Raymond watched him go inside. He knew the old man would use this as a lever to make him get rid of his onions. He'd outsmart them, though. He didn't know just how, but he knew he would.

The week passed. The weather grew warm, almost hot. Raymond drove the two miles to town for groceries. All the way he was wondering how the old man would play it. He could hear him saying, "Now let me compute that for you . . ." The old man hadn't said a word about burying the onions, though. In fact he'd told Raymond he actually admired him, the way he stuck to his guns, even if he was foolhardy.

As Raymond entered the village, he saw a number of people wearing surgical masks. The grocery store's air conditioning was going wide-open. As he made his rounds with a shopping cart, people who saw him coming turned down another aisle.

He rounded the produce aisle and saw the onions, big purple Spanish ones, two to a package. They cost just a few cents. Poor bastards, he thought, holding a package in both hands.

After the produce he came to the household items. Whole shelves for cleaners and air fresheners were empty. Half-empty boxes of lemon and pine scent spray cans were on the floor.

At the checkout, the grocer nodded his head and said, "Raymond."

Raymond nodded back, but didn't say anything. He left through automatic doors that hissed and swished. For the first time he smelled something funny in the air. His onions. He looked around. Everyone seemed to be staring at him.

He emptied the cart into the back of his truck and left town, feeling all the way that people were looking out windows and pointing at him as he passed by.

When he went by the warehouse, he looked up the lane at his father's trailer next to the empty barns and machine sheds. In the front yard was a payloader and a backhoe. Both belonged to the town.

"So that's it," Raymond shouted over the noise of the truck engine. He looked at the machines and knew what he would do. He'd get his shotgun and hide out in the onions. They were his onions, and he'd keep them. I pity the poor man who opens that big door, Raymond thought.

After he put the groceries away he called his old man over at the trailer.

"I see you're going to do some digging."

"That's right, son."

"I called to tell you I was going away for a few days to do some fishing."

"Did you tell the wife?"

"No, might you let her know for me? I think you understand, don't you?"

"I do, son. I understand better than you think."

Sure you do, Raymond thought after he hung up, sure you do.

Raymond loaded his gear in the truck and left before his wife got home. He drove his truck down by the river and parked. He waited until dark and then hiked across the fields to the warehouse.

The muck was so black it looked white in the moonlight. He slogged through wet spots where he sank up to his knees. The mud and water in the deep irrigation ditches almost swallowed him more than once. By the time he slipped in the side door, the muck lay on him in a thick, greasy coating. The last thing he noted was a light in his father's trailer.

Inside, the warehouse was hot and black. For the first time the odor of the rotting onions brought tears to his eyes. He stepped forward and felt the onions squish under his feet. He rested his gun on the floor and from his pack he took a spotlight and rope. The spotlight he propped on mashed onions, aiming its beam toward the peak. He flung the knotted rope high into the trusses and drew back. It caught between a gusset and the bottom cord.

He looped the sling of his shotgun over his shoulder and began pulling himself up the onions. He sank to his knees and then his waist. Toward the top the smell was stronger. Raymond grabbed the sling off his chest and put it into his mouth. He bit down hard on the leather. Through his trousers he could feel the heat. Some of the mash started up his legs. He lost a shoe, but he kept pulling himself, hand over hand, higher onto the heap.

Once at the top, he lay flat on his back, his arms and legs outstretched, floating on top of the rotting mass, the shotgun balanced on his stomach. He was tired. His body was covered with muck and rotted onions. They were in his pockets, his shirt, and his pants. He knew that in a few hours the old man would come for them.

At five, the timer on the coffee machine kicked in. Raymond's father sat up in bed. At his age, sleep came and went quickly. He was at this moment as lucid as he would be in the middle of the day. He reached for his trousers by the bed and pulled them on over the thermal underwear which he'd worn to bed. He then poured his coffee and sat down at the kitchen table in his stocking feet, his calculator at his right hand. When he got up for his second cup, he moved a lamp directly over the solar cells. The zero came to light, but was faint. He would wait for the sun.

At six he heard the discharge of a shotgun from down the lane. He paused, the coffee mug halfway to his lips. As the sound began to die, he held it, amplified it, and made it echo again and again. When he could hold it no longer, he made it up out of the silence in his trailer. It echoed and again disappeared. The percolator bubbled and hissed as it began to cool. The old man went to the phone, feeling slow and burdened.

"Earl," he said into the receiver, "this your Uncle Knowlton. Be a good boy and help run that loader this morning. I'm feeling my age just now."

"Sure enough, Uncle Knowlton. Be right down."

In the warehouse, Raymond's eyes, glowing like hot coals, focused on the shaft of light that beamed through the hole in the roof. His jaws tightened and his lips curled into a thin smile as he slid another shell into the chamber.

The Mason

Used to be when he was a younger man, Moss Whitehouse could lay block faster than a Frenchman. Now he mostly keeps to himself, on the mountain that heads up the Daggert Hills. And every so often that mountain rumbles and once in a while his woman can be seen clipping along in the pickup truck, her long blonde hair tossing in the wind.

When Moss got out of the service in 1954, he went into his brother Clancy's construction business and soon became a partner. As all partnerships go, especially those between brothers, they argued. Moss would get irritated because Clancy ended every argument grinning, as if they'd just finished playing a game, whether he'd won or not.

But the business did well. Moss, a good ten years younger than Clancy, loved construction. They owned a hoe, two Cats, two ten-wheelers, a twelve-ton lowboy, mortar mixer, mud sucker, compressor, trowel machine, mortar tubs, zip saw, tanks, torches, and eighty-eight pieces of tubular scaffolding, along with a lot of other stuff.

Moss was born to be a mason. People swore he could see inside stone, brick, block, and tile. When he blasted a rock, nothing would happen until Clancy nudged it ever so slightly with the D-8. Then the rock would fissure and fall open in a hundred pieces. It was Moss who blasted through Cobb's ledges when they straightened Route 9 east of Wilmington. Whether he was blowing out a thousand tons of granite or

73

laying a soapstone hearth, he spoke to the stone in a way no other man could hear.

But one night in the office Moss couldn't take Clancy's grin any longer. "Why in God's name do you always grin like some damn Hindi nabob?"

Clancy's grin widened. "Because I know a lot of stuff you don't, my boy."

"So tell me, Mr. Smart-ass."

"I planned for this conversation, Moss. I planned for this conversation since you was six years old and slapping mud pies together in the front yard buck-naked."

"Planned what?"

"Me and the old man would come home from work and see you there. The old man said you were born to be a mason. Alls I saw was a bare-assed kid covered with muck, but I had faith in the old man."

Moss listened. On a limited basis, he knew something of fate. The extent of it was, once your number was up you were dead meat. He'd seen that in the war. One night a guy would wash up and straighten out his affairs. The next day he'd be stuck in a bag and shipped out, still warm but dead. When he realized his brother and father had recognized some proclivity of his and then groomed him for twenty years without saying anything, he was scared. "As of right now, the partnership is dissolved," Clancy said. "We're done."

"Bullshit," Moss said.

"No BS, the partnership is officially dissolved," Clancy said, walking up and down the room. "Yes, my boy—you and I are done. But," he whispered, "we aren't burning any bridges."

Clancy knew that the stone possessed Moss, and by knowing this he had a hold on him. Clancy went to the broom closet and returned with a dusty cardboard box. From the box he took stacks of business cards, billing forms, proposals, contracts, stationery, and a ledger book. On every piece *Moss Whitehouse Masonry* was printed in gold letters.

"Clancy, what is all this?" Moss said. He stared at the raised letters of his name.

"Now you're in business for yourself, and you got to learn to be a businessman. From now on, every block you lay is yours. I dig holes, you fill them. It's that simple. Get your ass in gear. You have four foundations and two patios waiting to be done by Moss Whitehouse Masonry."

That night the Whitehouses gathered for dinner. Mother Whitehouse, a stout woman with white hair, sat at the head of the table. She was robust and moved her arms much like a man would. Clancy sat on her right and Moss to her left. This, she had declared after her husband, Harold, died, was how it would be when they gathered as a family.

Beside Moss sat his wife. Louise was an intelligent woman who loved him for his strength and the long periods of silence which she mistook for contemplation. Though in Korea he had seen waves of Manchurians—high on opium—dance through the foggy night, their swords swirling and dipping in the firelight, the only thing he usually thought about was stone, and, on occasion, the difference between using nitroglycerin and ammonium nitrate in dynamite. While you gained stability with ammonium nitrate, he contended that you lost a certain amount of resonance.

Tonight she was proud of him. She moved her leg flush against his and placed her hand on his knee and drew it slowly up the inside of his thigh.

"Clancy," Moss said, "do you have the key to the dynamite shack?"

Louise laughed. Moss used to take her there before they

were married. He'd kiss the hollow of her neck and slide his hands over her bare shoulders amidst the wooden boxes of explosives.

"What's so funny?" Moss asked.

"Nothing," she said, covering her mouth with her hand.

"We have a blast in the morning," Moss said, ending the conversation.

Across from Louise, Ruth sat next to her husband. The two women looked at each other and smiled, sharing knowledge as two sisters would. Lee Ann, Clancy and Ruth's little girl, sat beside her mother. Moss and Louise had no children.

"Moss," Ruth said, "doesn't Clancy always have the key whenever you need it?"

The women laughed while Clancy and Moss didn't even attempt to understand.

"He'll have his own key now," Clancy said.

"That's good," Louise said, causing Ruth to laugh so hard that she started to cough.

"Ruthie," Clancy said, grabbing her shoulders.

"Oh, I'm all right," she said abruptly.

Ruth was a thin woman and often sick. Some winters knocked her down for weeks at a time. Clancy would carry her about the house when she was too ill to get around on her own. She had a special place among the Whitehouses because, sickly or not, the woman was spirited and independent.

When she and Clancy first dated, she always made him help with the dishes after dinner at the Whitehouses. They would hold hands under the dishwater, or Ruth would invent an itch on her nose and make Clancy rub it because her hands were wet. As the courtship went on, the itch became more daring.

Some mornings she took off from work and invited Mother Whitehouse for tea. When she was ill, though, she locked her apartment door and wouldn't let anybody in till the day old Harold threatened to smash her door down. They moved her in and Clancy out. He had to get an apartment.

"She's a good girl," Harold told his son. "If I were thirty years younger, I'd take a run at her myself. Don't let her slip away. By the way, I don't mind you taking her out, but have her home by midnight."

"I am going to ask her to marry me," Clancy said.

"That just might be easier all the way around, m' boy."

She was Harold's favorite to the day he died.

Lee Ann was more like her grandmother. Grandmother Whitehouse had never had a daughter and thought of Lee Ann as her own. Of course she always deferred to Ruth, but when alone she swept the little girl up into her arms and danced about the house. Harold came home early one Saturday and found them waltzing in the kitchen. He politely asked for the next dance and the three of them moved slowly around the table.

Lee Ann had once ridden her bicycle two miles before dawn to bring the men a thermos of coffee. She was awkward and quiet. Moss thought her a little homely at the time. For a while she watched them work, then Clancy stood her up between his legs while he sat in the backhoe and showed her how to run the swing lever for the boom.

"Now, whenever I say to, you pull that lever," Clancy told her. She nodded her head and pursed her lips. Moss stood on the bank. At first he was impatient, but soon became fascinated. "Go," Clancy said, as soon as the full bucket cleared the trench. Lee Ann pulled back and swung a yard of earth to the right. Clancy dumped it. "Back," Clancy said. She pushed the lever forward and the boom swung past the hole, all the way to the left. "Now what do you do?" Clancy asked, his lips close to her ear.

She pulled the lever a touch and slowly swung the boom over the center of the trench. Clancy roared his approval and began to dig again. He looked up at Moss, whose mouth was half-open, a cigarette dangling. Over the roar of the backhoe, Moss couldn't hear the instructions Clancy was giving. All he saw was the little girl running the machine.

Then Ruth drove up in her car. She was frantic because Lee Ann hadn't told her she was leaving. Ruth saw the bicycle and Moss on the mound of earth. She walked up to him, and from where they were standing, she saw Lee Ann in the machine.

Moss looked at Ruth. She was smiling. He watched her mouth the words "You goddamn Whitehouses," as she slowly shook her head back and forth. He was surprised only by the fact that Ruth cursed. He'd never heard her do that before.

At the dining room table, all of the Whitehouses were sitting together, six of them spanning three generations. Their conversation rarely went beyond the day's events, the matters at hand. Right now, the conversation was about dinner, beans that had been baked all day in mustard, molasses, and brown sugar. With the beans they had hot bread, and frankfurters ordered from a butcher in Pennsylvania.

Ruth tapped her glass. "We need a toast, Clancy," she said.

"Yes, yes we do," he said looking from face to face.

"It's your place to do it. Go on now."

Clancy sat back and thought a moment. No matter how hard he tried, he couldn't stop thinking of his father. Harold would've been charming—he had a way about him. Finally, Clancy cleared his throat. "I would like to toast the new business of Moss Whitehouse Masonry, owned and operated by the best mason around."

Mother Whitehouse was quiet, but no one noticed until she reached out and took a hand from each of her sons, squeezed them, and then let go. Neither man said anything. She looked at Lee Ann. "Honey, I wish your grandpa could be here tonight."

Everyone looked at the old woman.

"Harold's with us, Mother," Ruth said.

The old woman sat up and then said, half to herself, "No he's not," and began to eat once again. The others sat quietly. Finally Clancy spoke.

"Jesus, Ma," he said, taking his mother's hand in both of his.

She looked up and smiled. Her eyes were wet. "Eat your dinner, don't mind me. Go ahead, eat," she said.

Everyone smiled and began to talk again—except for Mother Whitehouse and Lee Ann, who looked at each other as they had before, their eyes locked on things deep within.

Moss Whitehouse Masonry never lacked for work. Even Clancy was impressed as he watched the business flourish. Moss could be seen at sunrise, a cigarette pinched in the corner of his mouth, horsing blocks into the air, building walls. He took the cigarette out only to light another one. It took two tenders to keep him busy. To be a tender for Moss Whitehouse was something few men could do.

Within five years the two businesses grew in reputation beyond all others from Springfield to the New York State line. Clancy cleared the site, dug the hole, landscaped the grounds, and put in the driveway, while Moss built the foundations, patios, chimneys, and whatever else wasn't wood, steel, or plastic.

By this time, Moss had bought a mountaintop and half

the Daggert Hills that rolled out behind it. He parked a long house trailer on it, and moved Louise out of Deerfield into the trailer. Here they'd live until the house was built. Clancy dug the foundation and paved a driveway that wound back and forth all the way to where the front door would be.

In June they burned the stumps and slash. Clancy ran the D-8 and Moss the D-4. They worked all morning, heaping and pushing the pile into its center, where Moss had laid a bed of twenty tires like a griddle.

As the machines pushed stumps into the burn, the fans off the diesels blew into the fire and caused it to roar higher and burn hotter.

At noon they stopped for lunch. Ruth and Louise had a picnic table set up with casseroles, cold meat, and lemonade.

"Couldn't you two make it any hotter?" Ruth asked Clancy, fanning herself with a paper plate.

"Hotter than hell already, I'd say, Ruthie. Wouldn't you, Moss?"

"We could throw you on, Ruthie," Moss said, "but I think you'd only sizzle a little, maybe sputter some."

"Nobody gets my Ruthie but me," Clancy said, wrapping his arms around her from behind. He whispered into her ear and then pinched the lobe between his teeth.

"Clancy, stop." She turned to face him, put her arms around him and her cheek against his chest.

They ate lunch on the summit in front of the trailer, the radio playing inside. Next to them the hole for the foundation lay deep and wide. Beyond that, the burn roared and crackled, sucking in dust and leaves on the air it consumed, at times panting and heaving because it couldn't get enough. Below them, the valley yawned all the way to Connecticut.

"Let's dance," Ruth said, pulling Clancy to his feet. They

started off to a slow waltz, Clancy's heavy shoes moving lightly over the ground.

Louise reached over and took Moss's hand in her own. She watched him as he watched the burn. After a while he let go of her hand and put his arm around her shoulder. The four of them took the rest of that day off from work.

Moss was dead set against cutting into his business to construct his own house, so he lit up the building site with floodlights. Late at night people drove through the valley along the Deerfield River and saw the entire top of the drumlin ablaze with light.

Louise sat in front of the trailer on those summer nights and listened to the sound of the mortar slapping over and over again in the mixer. She watched each sixteen-inch block being set into place and knew that by midnight he would come to bed and fall asleep. They hadn't made love much since the business had started, and now even less. She tried to imagine that she was the reason he was building the house, that all his time away from home and his long silences were for her, and sometimes she believed it. If nothing else, she made herself believe they shared a history that would sustain them.

Moss's house grew. It became his habit, if he liked the materials, to order a little extra for each job he did and then use the surplus on his own house. To pay for the extra materials, the cost of which he fully assumed, he and his men worked hard to bring in each job faster. To do this, he invented several techniques about which he swore his men to secrecy. Only he knew how to build a three-story block chimney in one day without the mortar squeezing out of the joints, compressing beyond its ability to bond. He did let out a few secrets, though.

The key to his rubblework, he later let on, was in not

making it perfect. The irregular fieldstones had to be left uncoursed like a stone wall or it didn't look right. Each stone had to be cocked independently, depending on its own characteristics. If they were coursed, they looked stacked and top-heavy. He revealed this only because knowledge of this fact had nothing to do with having the talent to master the stone.

Ordering materials in odd lots made for a curious yet graceful structure. The solid stone and brick climbed without becoming undignified and bulky. Old friends had taken to stopping by on Sundays, when Moss worked only at home. They came up the long sweeping drive and brought picnic lunches. Louise was happy to see them, because she missed these people from when they lived in Deerfield. She dandled the babies and discussed the advantages of breast-feeding with the women, while the men watched Moss lay blocks. As the months went by, the numbers grew. Everyone he worked for wanted to stop by, and felt honored when Moss didn't refuse them.

Late that summer it started raining and didn't stop for five days. The first two days, Moss tried to work. But when a load of block rolled over in a washout, there was little he could do. Once he and Clancy righted the truck off the winch on Clancy's D-8, they shared a quart of beer in the pickup. Then they each left for home and dry clothes. The third day Moss spent running about the shell of his house checking for leaks. He found none. That night he went back to the trailer.

Louise was happy to have him home. Moss paced the length of the trailer and then sat down at the window and watched the rain streak the pane. He got up and started a kerosene heater at his feet. Louise watched him from the kitchen. She was leaning on the sideboard, watching him fiddle with the pilot on the heater. He stood abruptly and looked around him.

"Moss, what is it?" Louise said.

"Nothing, Lou, just antsy."

"Moss," she said, "I want to go to bed with you now, while we're both awake."

"I'll be right back," Moss said, heading for the door.

The door slapped shut, moths gripping the screen and batting against the outside light. She watched him jump puddles and then disappear through the lancet arch that led down into the basement. A second later, the top of the drumlin was flooded with light. Through the noise of the rain pounding on the roof, she heard the sound of a hammer and chisel against stone. She turned out the trailer lights and sat in a rocking chair by the window. She put a magazine on her lap and began to rock. The floodlights from the shell of the house cast bays of blue light through the trailer windows and across her body. She rocked and listened most of the night.

When Moss came in for breakfast the next morning, Louise had an urn of coffee made and potatoes frying. A cup for Moss was cooling on the kitchen table. He liked to gulp down his first cup and then take his time with the second.

"Good morning, Moss," Louise said.

"Seven-thirty and you're not even dressed." He kissed her neck and reached inside her robe.

"Get away," she whispered as she moved into his body. "Your hands are freezing cold. Wash the dust off you. You taste like chalk."

She watched him go to the kitchen sink and wash the fine white dust from his hands and face and forearms. He looked out the kitchen window. Through the rain he could see his house. It looked stark and cold.

"You seem pretty cheerful for not being able to work," Louise said, coming toward him.

"I'm about to polish off my best piece of work, Lou," Moss said. He wrapped his arms around her and began inching her robe up until his hand cupped the bare flesh of her thigh.

"Let's eat first," she whispered.

Louise was asleep when Moss slipped out from beside her and dressed. He pulled a blanket over her shoulder and then slogged through the mud back to the house.

Once in the shell, he sat and smoked quietly on a pile of soapstone intended for the hearth. He looked at what he had accomplished. He looked three stories up at his roof of six-inch precast Portland resting on twelve-inch I-beam purlins. He and Clancy had placed them with a crane they brought in for a weekend from Greenfield. Moss had set the cables and then rode the concrete slab into the air. Descending, he stood on the hook with one foot in the curve and the other on the point. Moss had felt relaxed as he rode at the end of the two-inch cable. Remembering how he and Clancy had shown off, he laughed to himself.

At the foot of the driveway he heard Clancy's International gearing down as it climbed the hill. He listened to the engine and in his head shifted the gears with Clancy. The truck carried a load of bluestone flagging left over from a job they'd done early that summer in the Quincy Market area of Boston. They'd restored a number of terraces, garden walls, and private walks. This entailed being away from home for several days, but they needed the job since work was becoming scarce near home.

Boston had been trouble. An auditor for the city noticed

the extra stone on an invoice and wanted to know what it was for. Moss explained that it merely came in on the same flatbed and that his company had paid for it. "Jesus, boys," the auditor had said, "I think I understand, but I don't know how I explain this to my superior. He might call a hearing. Could take time."

"How much time?" Clancy had asked before Moss could say anything, knowing full well they were being played for a couple of country boys.

"A helluva lot longer than it would take you to do my driveway in Saugus. Here's the address. I'll be gone the weekend of your completion date."

"Good as done," Moss had said, moving one eyelid as if in a wink.

That Friday, Moss moved his stone across the state line into New Hampshire, where he rented a barn to store it. He also bought a ton of hay from the farmer. He and Clancy did the driveway themselves early on Saturday. First they shook out the hay and then blacktopped it over with a few inches of tar. Only when the frost set in would the driveway turn into a jigsaw puzzle. By then Moss Whitehouse would be snowshoeing in the Berkshires.

Because of the rain, Clancy had gone to New Hampshire early that morning to pick up Moss's stone. He was just getting back.

Clancy swung from the cab onto the bed of the truck. Within minutes he set the cables and hoisted each pallet onto the ground. He then jumped to the ground from the bed and walked toward the house, leaning into the wind, his slicker snapping at his legs.

Moss waited at the arch with a cigarette already lit for him. "Clancy, I got a little surprise for you."

Clancy looked up. His face was drawn and tired. His

cheeks were pale and his eyes were red. "I have to talk to you, Moss."

"Wait till you see what I have," Moss said. Clancy looked hard at his brother. The only time he'd seen him this excited was the day they'd dredged a steel box full of silver coins out of the Ashuelot River.

"Well, what in hell is it?" Clancy said. "More silver coins?"

Moss rubbed his chin. "This is different, Clancy. Come see for yourself."

Clancy took off his hat and slapped it against his leg, then followed his brother back into the house through a maze of Roman and Gothic arches. None of the ceilings or floors had been completed, so Clancy had to look up at the concrete roof to keep his bearing.

"What do you think?" Moss pointed at the far wall. As Clancy's eyes became accustomed to the brightly lit room, he saw a huge marble stone in the center with two smaller ones on the right and one on the left. Chiseled into the center stone were the names of their mother and father. To the right was a double stone bearing the names of Clancy and Ruth and to the right of that one, a single stone with Lee Ann's name on it. The stone on the left, another double stone, had the names Moss and Louise Whitehouse chiseled into it.

Moss stood smiling. He didn't see Clancy reach for the workbench.

"What do you think, Clancy?"

"Moss," Clancy said, "it's Ruthie. She's dying."

Ruth Whitehouse was dead by Halloween. Moss and Louise went to Fletcher's during calling hours on the thirty-first, dodging bands of trick-or-treaters who roamed up and down the sidewalks. Clancy and Lee Ann were already greeting townspeople and business associates who came to pay their respects. A number of people commented on what a nice job Fletcher had done, but not, of course, to any of the Whitehouses.

She was buried to the right of Harold Whitehouse in the North Cemetery, leaving enough room for her mother-in-law to squeeze in when her time came. Moss had taken off several days from his work to complete the stone. He spent time at DeRossiers, where he learned to do delicate work on monuments with acids and paraffin. He decided against these techniques, using instead his finest point and teeth chisels. He polished the surface with wet sand and pumice.

At the cemetery people called the stone his most magnificent work. At the top of the stone, a profusion of flowers flowed from an urn at the base of a willow tree. The branches of the willow seemed to wrap around fluted columns that rose up each side. The dates of Ruth's birth and death were chiseled in. Clancy said nothing except thank you, not knowing what else to say.

Thanksgiving was approaching and the women decided Moss should take Clancy hunting while they prepared dinner.

Since Ruth's death, Clancy had plunged into his work, stopping only to check on Lee Ann, now a high school senior.

She stayed at her grandmother's house. Some nights Clancy slept in his pickup. He seldom went to his own house.

Thanksgiving morning, before light, Clancy took a twelve-gauge pump from the cabinet and Moss took a thirty-thirty Winchester. This way, they reasoned, they'd be ready for either deer or birds. From Moss's house they struck out across open pasture until they hit the old Post Road, which had been abandoned before automobiles came into use. This led them into the Daggert Hills, where they stopped to rest at a stone wall. They sat quietly, letting everything settle about them before they began to hunt.

"Moss," Clancy whispered, "two things've been on my mind of late." Moss didn't say anything. Clancy sat awhile longer. He lit a cigarette, making sure that his match was cool before he dropped it and that he had a bare spot of ground for his ash to fall.

"Two things, Moss," Clancy began, his words a little louder now. "The first thing is something the old man told me when he was dying."

"Goddammit, you here to hunt or talk?" Moss said.

"It was after he got the cancer and mother wouldn't let him smoke in the house anymore. He told me that years ago he shot a pheasant and two partridge and gave them to mother's mother. He said she seemed happy with the birds and made it a point of telling him so. A week later he took a load of rubbish to the dump along with his twenty-two so he could pick off a few rats. When he emptied the barrels over the bank, the pheasant and partridges came flying out, plucked and frozen. I asked him if he shot any grouse, as I'd been reading about them in a magazine at the time. He said grouse and partridges were the same. I asked him why they had different names and he said he didn't know."

"Why are you telling me this?" Moss asked.

"Because it bothered him, and now it bothers me."

"A lot of things have two names." Moss tried to think of something with two distinct names but couldn't.

"Not the damn stuff about names, but his story. Why'd she throw out the birds, especially after making such a big fuss over them?"

"I don't know, Clancy. How the hell should I know? Alls I know is you're screwing up the hunt."

"There's one more thing, Moss. Something Ruthie told me when we were going to the doctor's, the day he told her she was dying. Louise told her she wasn't happy. She couldn't get out of her just why, but she said she was miserable."

"What're you talking about? She has plenty of money. In fact she has it all. She keeps the books and writes the checks." Moss knew she wanted children. It was something that bothered the whole family, but they knew it couldn't be helped. The best he could do was just set the thought aside.

Moss didn't say a word.

Finally they began to hunt. Clancy shot a partridge.

When they got back to their mother's house, Lee Ann took their mackinaws and then gave each man a hug. "Dinner's ready," she said.

Clancy handed the partridge over to his mother.

"Clancy, how wonderful." She called Louise from the dining room to see the bird. All the excitement made Clancy a little uneasy.

"A partridge," Louise said. She turned to Moss. "And what did you catch?"

Moss didn't look up but continued unhooking the leather laces of his hunting shoes. When he finished he stood erect and methodically picked burrs out of his wool pants.

"Moss had a shot at a buck, but then . . ." Clancy paused and cocked his head to one side. "I forgot what I was going to say."

"Uncle Moss, let me read your fortune."

Moss turned and looked at the girl as if he was unsure

89

who was talking to him. She returned his look, standing squarely before him. Such a look from him unsettled most people, because it seemed to come from a remote place, and now, with the news of Louise's unhappiness on his mind, the distance he was traveling within was even further away.

The girl didn't back down. Her uncle intrigued her. Riding between Clancy and Moss in the truck, she had witnessed the effect he had on other men. Although it sometimes frightened her, she was always compelled and mystified by it.

"Moss, let me read your fortune in the cards."

Without speaking he sat down. Lee Ann unwrapped her cards from a silk scarf. She then tied the scarf over her head in a tight cap. Moss watched, but he didn't see.

"Dinner's ready," Mother Whitehouse called from the kitchen. Lee Ann collected her cards and wrapped them in her scarf.

"So what's my future?" Moss mumbled to himself.

"I can't tell you," she said walking away, leaving him surprised that she'd heard his question.

Lee Ann came back to the living room after she'd set out the steaming dishes of potatoes, squash, and onions on the table.

"I don't know about you, but the rest of us are ready to eat," she said.

Lee Ann sat next to her father, in Ruth's old chair, and throughout the meal she kept her father's plate heaped with food. Louise asked Moss several more questions about the hunt, but he kept his answers short and stared at his plate or at his brother. Grandmother Whitehouse started to tell a story, then stopped when she came to a part where Ruth was involved. Even the sound of forks and knives was hushed.

Lee Ann propped her elbow on the table and leaned forward. She told a story about one of her teachers named

Adler, who was said to keep a fifth of vodka in his file cabinet. Some other seniors were conspiring to get his key and unlock the drawer. In a few minutes she had Louise and Grandmother Whitehouse laughing.

Louise then began a story about when she was going to high school in Springfield. Moss held a forkful of potatoes halfway up to his mouth, just gazing at her. In the middle of the story, she stopped for no apparent reason and looked down at the napkin in her lap, but Lee Ann carried on with questions about Louise's school and friends.

Moss and Clancy finished their eating in a silence the women took pains not to notice.

In that part of the country, it was a long, cold winter. Work came to a standstill. Clancy hired Moss to haul gravel on a road job that lasted only a few weeks. By February, there had been the usual number of suicides in the back country and bouts with alcohol in the towns.

Moss took it upon himself to defy the winter. He would snowshoe alone back into the Daggert Hills and blow up trees and rock formations.

He used a variety of explosives. For some stones he used black powder so they wouldn't burst, but rather lift in the air and go to the right or left a few feet. His most spectacular blast involved one hundred yards of hedgerow and stone wall. Trunk lines inserted with delays at twenty-five milliseconds connected five C-4s wrapped in cordite.

He trailed primacord a safe distance away to a clearing. When he could hear only his own blood pounding in his ears, he pushed down on the rack bar, developing a detonation pressure of over a million pounds per square inch. Shattered rock and pine shot skyward and seemed to hover in a violent blossom. Smoke hung over the site as everything else settled. The explosion echoed off the hills and cannon-balled down the valley. Moss lowered himself onto one knee and lit a cigarette. He surveyed his work and concluded he could maybe lighten up on the plastics next time. No need to waste good explosives.

One day Clancy went with him, not knowing Moss was packing five charges in his knapsack. By the time Moss set off the fifth, Clancy was in his truck winding his way over the roads back to Deerfield.

Finally a letter came for Moss from Newport, Rhode Island. The Newport Historical Society was in the process of restoring Old Newport. They'd heard of his work in Boston and, though he'd only been a subcontractor, they were impressed by what he'd done. He was asked to review the prints and come to Newport as soon as possible to sign contracts. They would even buy him out of any contracts he might already have signed.

Early in March, Moss drove down and negotiated a deal. All expenses would be covered. Clancy Whitehouse Excavation would receive the contract for all site work, excavation, and hauling. When Moss told Clancy what he'd accomplished, Clancy grinned for the first time in weeks.

"You should see this lady who runs the show," Moss said. "Those people have so much money they don't know what to do with it. My whole goddamn double-wide trailer would fit into the gate house of some of those mansions. At one place, they had a doll house for the kids big as Fletcher's."

Clancy listened as Moss went on and on talking about fireplaces you could park a car in and black marble from northern Italy, but the mention of Fletcher's dogged his thoughts.

"She said I was quaint," Moss said.

"What'd you say when she said that?" Clancy asked.

"I didn't say anything. I didn't say a damn word, and the more I sat trying to think of something, the more they kept offering. If they'd have shut up for a second, they could've saved a lot of money."

"What do you mean?"

"King River water-struck bricks," Moss said with gravity.

"Those damn things cost forty-three cents apiece," Clancy shouted.

"I know, but that's what they want. The Rich Blend. I've always wanted to work with them. I'm going up to Gray, Maine, in a month and put in the order. Half a million bricks."

"Moss, I don't know. This isn't any two-man operation. It ain't like the old days."

"Damn. Are you losing your nerve? I've never heard you talk like that. Old Harold must be rolling over in the grave."

"I don't know. Things are different now. They're just different."

"We've got to get a move on," Moss said, and walked away.

Late in March, Moss drove northeast into Maine with Lee Ann. She was on spring break and Clancy had urged her to get away for a few days.

Louise had been looking forward to the trip, but had to stay in Deerfield and take care of Mrs. Whitehouse, who'd slipped on ice and broken a bone in her foot.

The old woman fought off help as long as she could, until one afternoon, two days before the trip, Clancy and Moss picked her up and sat her on the kitchen counter.

"Louise would benefit by spending time with you," Moss told her. "She needs something to occupy her."

Given the gentle persuasion of her boys, who towered over her even as she sat on the kitchen counter, she agreed.

*

Lee Ann sat quietly as the truck bounced along the highway, catching every so often in the line of slush left down the center by the plows. She hardly knew her uncle, and he knew her even less. Family life, as the Whitehouses knew it, revolved around work. A good distance after that came funerals, Christmas, Easter, and Thanksgiving.

She offered him some coffee from the thermos. He took it and thanked her. He steered with one hand, the other on the stick shift. The steam from his coffee cup, perched on the dash in front of him, condensed in a small circle inside the windshield. Moss stared at the highway ahead. The snow was still winged high along the roads and glazed over from the constant wind blowing in off the ocean. The sky was gun-barrel gray, and often the only sign of life was wood-smoke coming out of chimneys.

"What's the big deal about these bricks?" Lee Ann said.

Moss turned and looked at her. The faint smell of perfume came to him through the smells of coffee, wool, and cigarettes. She held his look until she became nervous and told him to watch where he was going.

"King River bricks are made in a wooden form greased with water. They bake the bricks for four or five days in a kiln built by stacking the bricks themselves. They come out black and purple and orange and raspberry and every color imaginable. They're bricks made the old way."

"That's it?"

"What else is there?"

"I don't know. I thought there was more to it."

"Well, you've got a lot to learn."

"I know," she said, plainly irritated.

"More coffee?" he asked.

"Sorry, that was the last," she replied.

Late that afternoon they hit Old Orchard Beach, where they planned to push on to Portland, where they finally found a new hotel.

"That's ugly enough," Moss said out loud.

"It does look strange," Lee Ann said.

"We may as well stay here. This trip's on the History Society of Newport."

"That's not their name," Lee Ann said, laughing.

He felt his cheeks flush red. "Then what is their name?"

"The Newport Historical Society."

Moss looked at her as if she'd sprung full-blown out of the earth. He slowly turned his head away and looked out his side window. She was suddenly a young woman and no longer waltzed about in her grandmother's arms.

The hotel was fairly unimaginative in its use of stone, Moss thought. It disgusted him to see steel lintels used to break up the facade. They rented two rooms side by side and then met for supper in the dining room. Moss was already seated when Lee Ann came in. She had dressed for dinner, and Moss had never seen her dressed up.

She was beautiful. She carried herself with her shoulders back and her head slightly tilted as if anticipating a question. Her eyes opened wide and she smiled when she saw him. "Moss?" she said. "What is it?"

"You have Ruthie's eyes," he said. "I never noticed that before."

"While you've been working, a lot has happened you probably haven't noticed."

Moss didn't reply. He took a roll and broke it. When the waitress came, he ordered a beer and Lee Ann ordered wine.

Moss didn't say anything in front of the waitress, but once she left he asked Lee Ann what in hell she thought she was doing.

"I drink in bars," she said.

"You're not even eighteen yet," he shot back.

"I will be in a month."

"That's not the point."

"Jesus, Moss, what's the big deal?"

"Don't talk like that." They looked at each other for a second until Lee Ann raised her brows, opening her eyes even wider. Moss felt a wall inside him collapse, like the time the Ashuelot jumped its banks and went its own way.

"Forget it," he told her, "it's on the ladies of Newport. How'd you know their name, anyways?"

"I'm learning to keep Dad's books."

"He doesn't keep his own books?"

"Not since Mother died."

The waitress brought their drinks and asked for their orders. Moss told the waitress he hadn't driven for six hours into Maine for nothing. He wanted clams and a lot of them. She continued to look at him, expecting him to order for Lee Ann. Lee Ann watched him fidget for a moment and then she ordered clams as well.

"What the hell was she looking at me for?" Moss said when the waitress was gone.

"In a restaurant, the man is expected to order for the woman."

Moss nodded his head. He watched the way she held the stem of her glass and how after each sip she would lightly trace her lips with her tongue. He looked at the pale silvery hair that lay close to her face.

"Do you remember when the Ashuelot flooded?" Moss asked.

"I was only a little girl then."

"It was something to see," he said, imagining himself riding the crest.

"Tell me, Moss."

He paused. "You see, the Ashuelot is a low-gradient river. There were heavy snows that winter and a wet spring. The headwaters filled too fast. Keene is sited on a swamp, a floodplain. The river jumped its banks and poured through, loaded with silt and flotsam. It left its mark on everything."

He looked up and saw her smiling at him. He stopped talking and looked away. He isolated each part of her face in his mind, and considered the parts: her nose, her forehead, her chin, her cheeks, and, finally, her eyes. She sat quietly as he did this.

The waitress brought their food and they ate.

What started out as a two-day trip turned into three weeks. Moss had heard of King River bricks and had seen them on the Quincy Market job and also once on a trip to Strawbery Banke. King River was the only brickyard left in the country that still fired its bricks in a scove kiln, and Moss wanted to watch the whole process. After three days he called Clancy and told him they were staying to see the burn, but that he would send Lee Ann on a bus out of Yarmouth so she wouldn't miss too much school. Clancy said the girl needed to get away.

The King River crew accepted them immediately, due to the size of the order and Moss's interest and respect for the craft. He worked alongside them and was treated as an equal. It took them a week to stack the three hundred thousand bricks that would form their own kiln. The stack was forty-five feet long, thirty feet wide, and twelve feet high. Arches were struck every forty inches, supported only by shared stress.

Once the kiln was completed and scoved with a mask of clay, Moss lit the torches. It sounded like six D-8s under load at full throttle as the torches sucked up two thousand gallons of fuel oil a day for five days.

The heat reached twenty-two hundred degrees on the afternoon of the fifth day. It was time to shut down the torches and switch to slabwood before the bricks melted into a lump. Moss helped fill the arches with wood for the final burn. In the early morning hours, though, something went wrong with the kiln. A section of wall was cool.

Moss started to follow two of the men up a ladder to the top. Lee Ann grabbed his shirt.

"What are you doing?" she asked.

He turned quickly, too quickly, surprising her.

"Moss."

"Up the ladder."

"Moss, you can't go up there."

"It's okay," he said, and then climbed the ladder.

Immediately he felt the searing heat through the soles of his shoes. He stepped quickly to keep his soles from melting. Several times he lost sight of the other men, whose forms wavered in the billowing steam and smoke rising from below. He was forced to wrap his arms around his head and peek out from beneath his elbows.

Finally he joined the men kneeling over the cool spot. They gave him a thumbs up. As they turned to run back across the top, Moss saw the sun rising through the immense cloud he was in. This was the first time he'd seen the sun rise, because the rest of the time it had been hidden in fog and overcast.

When he burst out laughing, the other two men thought

the heat had gotten to him. They each took an arm and hurried him off. At the bottom Lee Ann grabbed and held him.

"Are you okay?"

He looked at her face. He wiped the sweat from her forehead with his fingers. "It's okay." He hugged her.

After the burn, Lee Ann didn't want to leave. Moss knew he'd miss her company. He looked forward to his dinners with her.

"Go home, Lee Ann," he told her at the bus station. "You have no say in the matter."

"I don't *want* to leave."

"You'll miss too much school. You don't want to end up an old dunce like me."

"You're neither old nor a dunce."

"Go on. Clancy has enough on his mind without worrying over you."

"I don't want to ride any damn bus. I'd rather hitchhike."

"I catch you hitchhiking, I'll slap your butt, even if you are almost eighteen. Now go home."

She turned hard on her heel and boarded the bus. He watched her climb each step.

At one time, Newport had a life. Captain Kidd got drunk at the Black Pearl after sailing in from Nova Scotia, where he had watched his crew dig a hole to bury treasure and then blew out the backs of two heads with a brace of pistols and lifted the third off its shoulders with his cutlass. Smugglers met in the back alleys, their shoes echoing on the cobblestones, and slapped one another on the back after they burned the British cutters *Liberty* and *Gaspee* to the water line. Years later the air was black and stinking from the cauldrons where whales were melted down for their oil.

Some women walked in attic rooms and tore at their hair and clothes, while others just stared and stared when they thought about their losses in the North Atlantic for the sake of whale, cod, and seal. Even now, at night the fog barrels in off the ocean so heavy you can't see your feet. And on Thames Street there are still bars with harpoons over the till, and occasionally drunks roll off the wharf and have to be fished out.

Moss, Clancy, and Lee Ann arrived on such a night. They took rooms at the Sheraton Islander across the causeway on Goat Island, within walking distance of the restoration site. It *was* a different kind of job. Money was no object.

Lee Ann had come to serve as timekeeper and secretary. Mother Whitehouse's foot had not yet mended, and Louise had offered to stay and continue nursing her. She had yearned for Moss to say no, hoping Lee Ann would stay, or that Clancy would bring them all along, but by now she had decided that when Moss returned, she would be gone.

"Moss, you sure have a thing for the best hotels," Lee Ann said.

"Lee Ann, this is hardly a vacation," Clancy said. "The sooner we get done and shed of this damn tourist town, the better for all of us."

Moss and Lee Ann looked at each other and shrugged, but Moss could see the pained expression on her face. They knew it was Clancy's habit to visit the North Cemetery every few days and leave flowers, and that now he wouldn't be able to. Moss was worried Clancy wouldn't last the job. He'd never been so far from home before.

"He'll be all right," Moss said while Clancy was signing the register. "He just needs something to occupy him."

"I hope you're right. He scares me sometimes. I wish Louise could've come, and Grandma, too."

"They'll be down in a few weeks, once we get on top of things."

"All set," Clancy said, hoisting his bag like a sailor. "Let's get up on it." He stopped and looked at them. "What in hell's wrong with you two? Seasick already?"

Lee Ann hugged her father, and Moss slapped him on the back. They walked to the elevator, laughing, Clancy in the middle.

The Newport job was a new venture for both men. As general contractors, they would spend more time as overseers than as workers. Moss let out the brickwork to a company run by a Portuguese family. Everyone who worked for the company was related and fought like hell to outdo the rest. Clancy let his share of the work out to a firm that owned twice the iron he did but did about half the work.

The ladies from the Historical Society stood by the fences most days and watched Moss standing bare-chested in the midst of a swarm of stubby, olive-skinned masons. He would yell, "Salazars are ahead. Salazars are real masons." This would make the Goncalves angry, and make them work harder.

At night he disappeared into their world and drank their homebrews and ate shellfish. Occasionally he brought with him a bottle of Rosa Lusa, and the Salazars and Goncalves would cheer. The old men would unfold their marlinspikes and show him the secrets of knotting, splicing, and marling. The young men would look on, fascinated for the first time by the ancient art of their fathers. The children found reason to touch Moss, and the young women would follow him with their eyes.

101

Often the old men sat and chided the boys for doing the work of Italians. They had been seafaring men and expected the same of their sons. One night there were generations of masons arguing with generations of sailors. One of the fathers wrestled his son to the ground and threatened to send him off to the Outer Banks to fish for cod.

Everyone was awed by the deep purple and black bricks. The Salazars and Goncalves handled them like precious stones. Moss hired a half-dozen college students as laborers. They built scaffolds, stripped forms, backfilled, and hauled brick. One day the straw boss, a kid named Rudy, came to Moss with a complaint. The masons, he said, were the laziest goddamn bunch in the world. He and his crew were sick and tired of their attitude and unwillingness to help themselves.

Both Lee Ann and Clancy were also in the office when Rudy told this to Moss. Clancy was about to lay into the kid, but Moss held up his hand and smiled.

"So you think masons are lazy?" he said.

"I sure do. Yesterday, for example, we hadn't completed the last section of staging, so they went home, instead of building it themselves."

"Now listen, Rudy," Moss said, "there isn't a bigger fool on the face of the earth than a mason. Alls they know is how to pick it up, slap mud on it, and set it down. You keep brick and mortar stacked so high they can't see the sun and those masons will make you a lot of money. Don't give them anything to confuse them. Pick it up, put it down. Why should I pay them scale to build staging when I can get you to do it at less than half the price?" Rudy loved hearing that masons were stupid, and went away satisfied.

Moss and Clancy began to laugh. Lee Ann was mad that they'd toyed with him, so when Rudy asked her out the next night she accepted.

Clancy and Moss ate alone. They spread prints out on the restaurant table and tried to work out a few details over dinner, but were constantly interrupted by people who'd watched them work or were in the Society. Everyone insisted on buying them a drink, and before long Clancy was drunk and homesick. By one o'clock Lee Ann still hadn't returned.

"Moss, promise me something on our father's grave."

"Anything."

"I have to go north for a few days. You don't need me here anyways. You're running the whole damn project."

"That's bullshit."

"No, Moss. That don't bother me. Never did. Me and the old man knew it from the first. He said by forty you'd run it and I said by thirty-eight. Well, you surprised us both. You're only thirty-five. Anyways, if I have to sit through another goddamn tea or listen to those Portuguese jabber one more day, I'm gonna go birdshit."

"What about Lee Ann?"

"That's the promise. Promise me you'll look out for her. Just tell her I had business to look after. I'll be back in a week or so. She's a woman. I know that now."

"You leaving?"

"You're goddamn right, but I'll be back. Mark my words."

"Clancy, wait," Moss said. "Louise, tell her—I love her. The best I know." He paused and looked at his hands resting flat on the table. Before he continued, he wrapped his thumbs under the edge and clenched the wood till his knuckles turned white. "Tell her to do what she thinks is right."

"I know, Moss. I've known it all along."

With that Clancy packed up and left. Moss thought about

Ruthie. He knew that by morning Clancy would be laying flowers on her grave, and that he wouldn't come back to Newport. The last thing Moss thought of before he fell asleep that night was that he wished he'd hugged his brother before he left.

At three in the morning there was a knock at Moss's door. He got out of bed and opened it. Lee Ann was standing in the hall.

"Where have you been?" Moss said quietly.

"Did father go home?" Lee Ann asked.

"Yes. Where have you been?"

"Rudy took me to dinner and then to the Black Pearl." Moss looked at her. "He ordered dinner and wine for both of us, then we went to the beach."

Moss knew what she meant and couldn't help but feel hurt. "I suppose you told him what a bastard I am."

"No. I told him you were a mason. I told him you were my boyfriend but we'd had a fight. I feel bad. We all made a fool out of him."

"Go to bed, Lee Ann."

Just before dawn, Moss dreamt he was on top of the kiln at King River and the mass of bricks was puffing out under his feet and the sun was starting to rise. He woke up and saw Lee Ann standing at the end of his bed.

"Moss," she said, "I'm cold. I'm afraid to be away from home."

"Come here, then." Moss moved to one side of the bed. She lay down next to him. He reached out and touched her almost white hair and then eased his arm behind her head until her cheek lay against his bare chest. Moss lay beside her and listened to her steady breathing; he felt his heart pound inside his chest. He knew she must've felt it, too. She brought her hand up and placed it between her cheek and his chest. After a while she fell asleep. Moss eased out of bed and sat by the window. He watched the harbor lights until they went out at dawn.

The nights that followed, his wanderings took him through the backstreets and alleys where cobblestones still paved the way. Each night he would visit a different family and sit on their porch till he was the only one awake. Then he would walk back to the hotel alone through the heavy night. Sometimes Lee Ann would go to a movie or to a party on one of the beaches or at one of the estates. She usually went with Rudy and his friends. But no matter how late it was when he returned, she would come to him. He would move to his side of the bed and she would lay next to him with her cheek against his chest.

Clancy resumed business around western Massachusetts. He drank late most nights and fell asleep with his clothes on. One of his last sober acts was to help Louise load her belongings into the Buick. At his mother's request he sold Moss's stake body and one of his bulldozers and turned the money over to Louise.

As the three of them parted, Mother Whitehouse squeezed Louise tight to her chest and told her she would always be her daughter. When Clancy hugged her, he lifted her off her feet. He told her to come back when she had worked things out, and not to forget he was an eligible bachelor.

"The man is possessed, Clancy," she said, but Clancy didn't reply.

He kissed her on the mouth and then headed for the basement of Moss's house with a quart of Jim Beam.

Mother Whitehouse stood alone, looking at the unfinished house, the trailer, and the sky beyond. She felt as though she'd lived too long and was now a stranger to the world. She felt no pain, but she was tired and weary. She would go home and rest.

The last night in Newport, Moss threw a huge party for the crew. He and Tony Salazar got tattooed and had their ears pierced. Moss had a pawing bull put on his right shoulder blade. Tony got a cross and anchor exactly like the one his father had. While Tony and Moss and their entourage were at the tattoo parlor, the women dressed Lee Ann in a full skirt and short white blouse. They put gold hoop earrings on her and high-heeled shoes.

By the time the two groups met at the Black Pearl, Moss's case of Rosa Lusa was gone. The men and women seemed to collide in a swirl of color and noise. Moss and Tony took off their shirts to display their new tattoos and didn't put them back on. The room filled with the sound of glasses, laughter, and dance. The air grew heavy with the scents of perfume set in motion by the sway of bodies.

From several feet away, Lee Ann stared at the bull on Moss's shoulder blade. Every time he flexed his back, tiny flecks of blood rose out of the new tattoo like beads of sweat. She stared until she heard one of the Goncalves shout Rudy's name. He was walking toward her, smiling. "I wanted to see you before you go," he said.

Moss and Tony Salazar were across the room throwing darts. A few women stood behind them, touching Moss's back and Tony's arm. The old men were elbowing one another, laughing at how brazen their women had become. Tony stood shoulder to shoulder with Moss, puffing out his chest.

"Lee Ann, I'd like to talk to you. Alone," Rudy said.

They stepped outside into the orange and yellow lights that mottled the darkness.

"The best part of the summer has been you," he said.

"Rudy, please don't."

"I'm going back to school in a week or so. Springfield. I'll be nearby. If old Moss crosses you again . . ." He let it drift off, not knowing how to finish. Then he added, "I like you a lot, more than I should, I guess."

"Rudy, he's not my boyfriend, he's my uncle," she said.

Rudy entered the bar, knocking into people as he went. He was inches from Moss's face when he hissed, "You're her uncle, you bastard."

Moss dropped his arms, defenseless. The strength seeped out of him, leaving him weak and empty. He was a bystander unable to stop what was shaping before him. He smiled at the truth, nodding his head back and forth, wanting to thank Rudy and at the same time kill him for what he'd said.

Tony Salazar was the only other one who heard. He showed no emotion when he lifted Rudy off the floor and slammed him against the wall. He spoke to him quietly, so quietly no one else could hear, and then set him back on his feet. They all watched Rudy leave.

The party regained its momentum. Even Lee Ann laughed and allowed herself to be spun around the room in wide circles by all of the old sailors and young masons. As they parted in the morning hours, the women whispered secrets in Lee Ann's ear and each man gravely shook Moss's hand.

Tony Salazar was the last. He kissed Moss on the cheek and whispered, "I told him you were just a mason," and he backed away without smiling. A week later Tony would follow them northwest to Deerfield with ten thousand of King River's Rich Blend in a reefer. The bricks had been stored in a Cranston warehouse for two months.

*

It was late afternoon when Moss and Lee Ann drove up the drumlin. In the workroom, Moss found the stone with his name and Louise's name broken in half. Lee Ann's stone was gone.

Moss told Lee Ann to go inside the trailer and take a nap. He had to make a few visits and let everyone know they were home.

Clancy's International was parked outside the wrought-iron gates of the North Cemetery when Moss arrived. The engine was cool. At the family plot Moss found Clancy lying back against his and Ruth's stone. Lee Ann's stone was to the right of theirs.

"Clancy, let's go home," he said. He stooped low and lifted his brother to his feet.

"Did we make a good buck down there?" Clancy whispered.

"A good buck, Clancy. A good buck."

"I knew it," Clancy said.

Moss half-carried his brother, who was cold and wet, back to the gates. Before he walked through, Clancy swung around and grabbed Moss by the front of his shirt, but he didn't say anything. Moss smiled and Clancy smiled back.

Moss took Clancy to their mother's house and then went home to the trailer. He wanted to sleep for a long time and he did, but at some time before dawn all the things in the room took on long angular shapes in the moonlight. Off in the hardwoods winds were unsettling them and gently shaping them down. Lights and shadows played on her almost-white hair and across his broad shoulders. One of her legs lay across his thighs and the other she stretched out slowly, tightening and releasing the muscles from her hip to her toes.

In her mind she whirled about the dance floor of the Black Pearl, beads of sweat on her forehead and chest. She felt again the sash at her waist and the cotton blouse against her skin. She reached over and stroked the hair, still damp, that lay against his forehead. He turned and kissed her and started to turn back, but she held him and pulled him even closer and he knew he wasn't strong enough to stop. Bays of shadow lengthened across the room and the night silently moved about the house.

A Pair of Bulls

IT WAS NEW YEAR'S EVE. Benware leaned into the body of
the steer. With his right hand, he applied a warm compress
to the animal's open scrotum. Infection had set in. The
animal smelled like a giant rat that has crawled off into a
cellar corner or fallen into the walls through a hole in the
attic floor and died. The smell hung in the air, close as a
wet hunting jacket.

Benware had castrated this animal and one other three
days before. Until then, they had been his bulls. Now they
were his steers. A matched pair of Blue Roans, the offspring
of a Charlois and a Holstein. They were fifteen months and
went seven hundred pounds apiece. Full grown, they'd each
go a ton or better, a four-thousand-pound team capable of
drawing out three times their weight without breaking stride.
They'd be able to handle a scoot full of cordwood or five
hundred gallons of sap in snow up to their bellies. If this
one didn't make it, though, it'd be fed to Frankie Bergevin's
mink. The other steer would end up on the business side
of a meat hook in the cooler.

He rinsed the compress and refolded it into a neat square.
It was a kitchen towel from the drawer by the sink. Angie
didn't like it when he did that. She'd bitch him out for
using a good towel. Benware enjoyed agitating her, liked to
play cat-and-mouse. This time, though, he was tired of his
game even before it had started. His mind was on the steer.
He knew he was to blame for its condition. He'd taken out

his money clip, peeled off a five-dollar bill, and flipped it to Angie.

"Buy another goddamn towel on me," he said, walking out the door.

"They're a new set, Benware Smith, a set my mother gave us for Christmas," Angie shouted at the back of his head.

Benware wanted to tell her to call her mother and let her know that one of her precious towels was wrapped around the infected scrotum of a steer, but he didn't. Angie was a literal-type person and he knew she'd do it, and that would really set things off. Besides the steer, he'd have to contend with Angie's mother and the prophesies of dead Artie, her husband. Benware always referred to her as a "good shit," and everyone seemed to take this as a compliment.

He liked dead Artie even less. When Benware married Angie, it was against the wishes of her old man, who wanted more for her than to marry a farmer. He had lined up a foreman at the shop for his daughter, a young fellow who played on the shop softball team. That Artie refused to give her away at the wedding really hurt Angie, but didn't bother Benware one bit. Finally Artie died. He keeled over at work, falling head first into a machine that threaded screws and bolts. For Benware, though, there was no relief. Artie's legacy was carried on by Angie's mother, who happily took up the cause.

Benware stepped up beside the animal, and rested his weight against its body, his knee up under its belly just in from its hind leg. He reached down, palming the compress in his hand, cradling the scrotum in its warmth. He didn't understand women, he thought, but then he smiled because he knew that deep down he really did. He knew how to size them up. He'd had his share of them, and had to admit he'd won out on most accounts, unlike other men who'd lost out altogether. Frankie Bergevin was one who'd been taken to the cleaners. His wife left him for a truck driver. Benware told him not to let her waitress, but Frankie let her do it anyways and now she was gone. Frankie made the kids start tending the mink so he could drive truck in an attempt to track her down. Frankie knew she was pushing red flannel hash in some truck stop in New York State, but he never could catch up with her. The whole process brought him and the kids quite a bit more income, though, and Frankie seemed to enjoy driving truck.

The steer raised a leg and then put it back down. Benware stepped away as the animal began rocking its ass end, trying to work its bowels.

Benware thought Angie to be a good woman. She kept her weight down and still had nice legs. She liked to dance, though with the farm Benware couldn't take her out very often. That night, they were supposed to go to a party, the Jamboree. Tickets cost ten dollars each. Normally Benware wouldn't have gone the cost, but there was a band, a buffet, and free beer. Ernie Ladd and the Green Mountain Boys were playing. Ernie had a young boy on accordion who played the fastest polkas anyone ever heard.

The boy was playing the night Benware first saw Angie. When he played the "Beer Barrel Polka," Benware walked right up to her and asked her to dance. Angie had to move fast to keep from getting stepped on by Benware's shoes. The faster she moved to keep out of his way, the faster he moved to master her. By the time the polka was over, the dance floor was empty and the other dancers were standing off to the sides clapping. Benware had never felt that way in his entire life. He swept his arm across his chest and bowed to the crowd. Angie looked at him and laughed. She plucked at the hem of her skirt and curtsied. The people hooted and slapped each other on the back.

The place was packed that night. Angie's mother and father were there. Frankie Bergevin and his wife, Toots, were there, too. After things cooled down, Benware took Angie out to the parking lot. They sat on a picnic bench that was chained to a pine tree. The seats were covered with black pitch, so before Angie sat down, Benware took his shirt off and spread it out for her. Then he got his beer cooler from the truck. There were a few bottles bobbing in the water left from the melted ice. Benware had been baling hay all afternoon. He liked to drink beer while he wound his way along the windrows. He liked to look back over his shoulder at the gang of boys who picked up the bales and stacked them in the lofts.

The warm beer hissed and frothed when he spun off the caps. From where they sat, they could hear music and the people stamping their feet. After working in the sun most of the day, the air felt cool and slack to Benware.

"I plan to marry you," he told her.

Angie stood up and walked behind the tree. Benware waited, afraid that he'd scared her off. Finally, she came back. She moved the tee shirt to the tabletop, then sat on it. She kicked off her shoes. She put her feet down on the bench, only inches from his thigh, her bare knees next to his shoulder. Benware thought about swinging his elbow enough to touch her calf, but he didn't. He stared at her knees.

Then it started to rain, slow, heavy drops. They came infrequently as if the air had just now begun to outweigh itself in certain places.

"Don't be stupid," she said.

"Ain't nothing stupid about it."

"Well, maybe I will and maybe I won't. One thing's for sure, I'm not interested in talking about it now."

Benware started to speak, but she jumped off the table and ran inside. Benware sat for a while, finished off the beer, and got up to leave. He saw her shoes on the ground so he picked them up and put them on the bench. Then he went behind the tree and took a leak. He always liked going on the trunk of a tree. Even when he was a little boy, he'd rather go outdoors on a tree than in the toilet.

The steer hunched its back, spread its legs, and hiked its tail into the air. Benware moved back another step. Angie would be upset about the Jamboree. She'd bought herself a dress and a pair of high-heeled shoes, and they'd planned to go with Frankie Bergevin in his new four-wheel-drive Blazer. Frankie had a woman friend who was driving in that day from Buffalo, some babe he'd met on the highway.

Benware began to feel tired, standing there waiting for the steer to take a shit. He sat down on a bale of straw, hating himself for letting the animal get in this condition. The pair of them were fine last night when he made his rounds, sweeping in their hay. This morning, though, he was in a hurry to get chores done, and hadn't checked them. He wanted to be in the forest cutting firewood, maybe take a deer. It's funny, he thought, how a deer will hear a chain saw and walk up to investigate, but if they so much as hear a twig snap they're off to the races. Anyway, he bucked up cordwood all day and when he got back to the barn in the afternoon, the scrotum was swolled, shot with infection.

Benware rinsed the towel and applied it again. He knew the steer didn't mind the infection. It didn't seem to care when Benware had sliced it open with a razor, pulled out its testicles, and crushed the cords off. The steer flinched

115

just once, then settled down and stood patiently, the blood draining onto the floor, forming a puddle between its legs. The testicles lay steaming in the gutter, as big as oranges. Christ in heaven, Benware had thought at the time, he'd seen people with a toothache moan and whine for days on end.

An hour earlier, Benware had given the big steer 50 cc of penicillin and began the compresses. Angie boiled the first kettle of water and now she was in the bathroom taking a shower. Benware arched his palm so that the compress would enter the gaping hole.

The animal hadn't touched its feed. Its neck was stretched and taut. If left alone, the jaw would eventually lock up. In its face, Benware could see half its life gone. It didn't mind, or at least it didn't give any sign of minding. Animals were like that. It was the one quality, in Benware's thinking, that pushed them above people, not that it would take all that much.

The best method for nutting a bull is pinching off the cords with a pair of Burdizzo clamps. When you close them off, the fingers come together nice and tight. Most other brands leave a little bit of light showing. What you do with the Burdizzos is locate the cord leading to the nut. You get it between the jaws, high enough so as not to crush the nut, and then you press the handles together like a giant pair of pliers. A good pair of Burdizzos were costly, though, and Benware had lost track of who'd borrowed his. There was only one pair around and all the oxmen shared them.

Benware remembered asking his father, the first time he watched, if pinching off a bull's nuts like that hurt. Only hurt if you got your thumbs in the way, his old man told him. Angie would get a kick out of that one, Benware thought. He'd have to remember to tell her.

The steer's name was Paul. His mate was named John. Every pair of oxen his father ever owned were named Tom and Jerry, and every pair his grandfather ever owned were named Buck and Bright. They were all dead now, all the Bucks and Brights and Toms and Jerrys and the fathers, too. Benware likened dying to being eaten, like being eaten by a cancer from within. His fathers had been eaten by different cancers. Then, they were eaten up by the earth and whatever tunnels around down there looking for a square meal. Eventually they were eaten by men again. Benware thought that he might have tasted his own father once or twice. When he thought about it, it didn't seem so bad.

Paul shifted his weight, raised his right hind leg, and curled his neck around as if to look at his foot. Benware stepped away and watched him dance back and forth again. The hot compress against the infection had only perked up the smell, now stronger than ever. The scrotum was tender from the heat. Benware would have to wait an hour or so before he tried it again. When he heard Angie yelling across the drive, he cracked open the barn door and poked his head out. He could see her standing on the porch in her robe and slippers. Her hair was wrapped up in a towel that rested on her head.

"Benware," she yelled.

"I can hear you."

"You gonna take a shower? We have to be going in an hour."

"Can't go."

"What in hell you mean you can't go? Where the hell are you anyways?"

Benware opened the door a little wider. She could see him standing in a vertical slot of light formed by the door

117

and the barn wall. His·shadow lay there in the snow at his feet.

"Bull's sick."

Angie didn't say anything for a moment, then said, "Bullshit to you, too." She slammed the door.

Benware laughed. That Angie, she had one of the filthiest mouths he'd ever heard on a woman. Sometimes she talked that way when they were in bed, but he didn't like it much. He fluffed up the bedding under Paul and checked on John, whose scrotum was already starting to shrivel up into his body. Then he went to the house.

Angie had her clothes spread out next to the woodstove. She liked to dress next to the stove, the warmest place in the house this time of year. Benware seldom watched her dress because he was usually up and out to the barn by the time she got out of bed. It was a sight he took great pleasure in, especially when she was getting all dolled up.

"I told you I can't go," he said.

Angie turned to face him. She held her slip in front of her.

"Benware, I thought you were only fooling."

"No, I'm serious. Do you think I want to lose that bull?"

Benware was proud of himself for how he posed the question. He knew she'd have to say no, and no was somehow what the whole conversation was about. Benware was beginning to get lost in this particular thought when Angie brushed past him on her way to the kitchen, making for the phone that hung on the wall next to the refrigerator.

"What are you doing?"

"What in hell do you think I'm doing? I'm going to use the phone."

The kitchen was cold. Standing there in her pantyhose,

Angie dialed the number and waited, drumming her fingers on her hip.

"I know you're using the phone. What's your thinking?"

"I'm calling Frankie and I'm going to tell him that you're not going, but that I still want to go if he doesn't mind me coming along. Benware, I've been looking forward to this party all year."

"I know you have. You call Frankie. You go ahead."

Angie put down the phone and looked at him. He knew he had her talked into not going, although he didn't care one way or the other. It was a matter of who'd win out, and he'd won. Besides, Benware didn't like Frankie. He didn't trust him since Toots had left him. Frankie didn't know how to be out in public. He considered himself someone who'd weathered a great storm and now had the right to lay claims, give advice, pass judgment, and make an ass out of himself.

The worst part of it was after Frankie got a few drinks in him. He'd start cursing his wife, calling her a slut and a whore. Then he'd concoct schemes by which he could cash in on a lawsuit—neck injuries, back problems, and all-round pain. The trick, though, was not to actually get hurt, he'd say, as if this was some kind of secret. During his final stage of drunkenness, Frankie'd get right up in your face and tell you he had a certain truck driver's affliction, but that it didn't slow him down one single iota between the sheets.

"It was busy the first time," Angie said. "I'll try again."

Benware watched her pick up the phone and dial the number. She still hadn't put any clothes on. Benware was struck by how young she looked. He thought about their first night, outside the Jamboree. It seemed like so long ago, though it had only been a few years. Her skin was still

119

smooth and white. When Benware folded his arms, he could feel where the skin had grown slack over his muscles. His body was still strong and when he needed them his arms and legs knotted up and did their job, but they weren't the same as they'd been that night, when they were only a few inches from her bare leg. He could see them sitting there. Angie was the same, but the person sitting next to her was someone different, someone whose chest and arms seemed to glisten in the rain.

Angie talked a little, then hung up and went back to where her clothes were. Benware sat down in a chair and looked up at the ceiling, studying it as if he had never seen it before.

"Frankie said he was about to call. His lady friend called from Buffalo. She's snowed in and won't be able to make it. He was going to tell us that he wouldn't be going himself."

"That's too bad."

"He's coming by to pick me up and the two of us'll go together. Are you sure you can't come? We'll be home before you know it, and when we get back I'll help you with the bull."

"It ain't a bull anymore."

"You know what I mean. Come on, what do you say?"

"No. You go ahead and have a good time. I wouldn't enjoy myself."

Benware refused to back down. He didn't know why she was being so obliging, unless she really didn't want him to go, but that was foolish. He'd stay and not think any more about it.

"You have a good time," he said, looking at her standing naked in front of him. Inside he felt as if she'd triumphed over him. Her talking to Frankie on the phone without any clothes on was her way of taunting him. But if he backed down this time, it would be the beginning of the end. He'd have to tough this one out and play it different the next time. He'd have to play it so that there wouldn't be a next time. He liked the way that sounded in his head, and told it to himself two or three times.

Angie was back by the stove getting dressed. Benware watched her drop her slip down over her hips, step into her dress, and fasten the buttons that drew in the bodice. He went to her and gave her a quick hug and a kiss.

"I have to get back to the barn. You have a good time. Tell Frankie I said to be a good boy."

Angie looked up at him. He tried to see something in her face, but he couldn't. He turned away and left.

Benware kicked snow in front of him all the way back to the barn. He felt like a fool for saying anything about Frankie, and thought again of the look on her face when he left.

Inside the barn, he checked on Paul. The animal was standing calmly in his stall. He stretched his neck and tossed his head as if he'd just come out of a deep sleep.

Benware stood at the window, scratched away the frost on the inside, and looked out onto the drive. He didn't know what he would do when Frankie showed up. For a moment he thought about shooting him. The thought served its purpose, making him feel better. Maybe he'd just run out and rap him on the head a few times. Frankie was like one of those little dogs that hide under the furniture or behind a door and then spring on you, nipping at your ankles, getting a tooth caught in your sock. Benware knew he had to do something when Frankie showed up. Exactly what, he didn't know.

He went over to Paul. He talked to him in a soothing voice, telling him that they'd make it. He'd been through worse, he said, and seen his way clear. The animal looked past him at the wall. His breathing came more steady now, a good sign. Benware moved down to John. The animal's head was as big as Benware's chest. His horns spanned out eight inches beyond Benware's elbows. Benware moved in close and stroked the animal's chin. John stretched his neck and sniffed Benware's face. Benware lengthened his strokes, drawing what pleasure he could from scratching the animal's neck and chin. He could feel his body relax as he thought about Angie going to the dance.

As he turned to look out the window, John snorted and tossed his head. The sweeping horn caught Benware in the ribs. The blow lifted him off his feet and knocked him high into the wall. Benware slid down to the concrete and looked up at the animal. John stood quietly chewing on his cud as if nothing had happened. Benware crawled down the feed-walk on all fours until he was well clear of the animal. His whole side throbbed with pain as the air came back to his body.

Benware stood and looked out the window. He could see the taillights of Frankie's rig pulling out. The only light on in the house was the one over the kitchen sink. He went over to Paul and reached in to feel his scrotum. It was still hot, but it was a little softer than before. Benware stood back and held his side. The pain moved across his chest and into his throat. He stood there until finally he took out his jackknife and cut the strings on a bale of straw. He kicked some in under Paul and then he lay down in the rest.

He reached inside his coat and felt the tender spot. His ribs ached. He could feel his heart beating under his hand, wild at first but then a little slower. He couldn't remember ever feeling it in that spot before. He wondered if it were swelling up, or if maybe it had been knocked out of place. He lay there and held onto his heart like that for a long time.

Bruno and Rachel

WHEN BRUNO BAVASI, JR., RETURNED HOME that spring with the Jewess, there was not much rejoicing on the farm. Seven months earlier, his mother had died, right around Christmastime. Earlier that month, the temperature had dropped fifty degrees in twenty-four hours. The goose began to lay eggs. She laid thirty-five eggs in thirty days. Bruno's mother went to check every day for more eggs, but one day she slipped on the ice and cracked her head open. She didn't make it into the new year. The goose didn't, either. Bruno's father lopped its head off the day his wife died and the housekeeper cooked it on the first of January.

When the Jewess showed up as the new female in the house, there was still the emptiness left by the death of Bruno's mother. She was seen as someone intended to be a replacement, but of course there was no such intent. Bruno never would have considered such a thing.

His mother had been the center of all life on the farm. She had endured through the years when money was tight. She had endured her husband's drinking and whoring when he'd been a younger man. She'd had her boys at home in the same bed they'd been conceived in. Rachel was from the city, a place where Bruno's family had never gone because they were convinced they'd be robbed and murdered in their sleep.

Rachel had black hair and black eyes. She had a long, delicate nose and a space between her front teeth. Bruno's first image of her still braces him against the late night. He

123

sees her playing the piano in the dormitory, wearing her bathrobe and sandals. She was twenty-five years old at the time and told him she was determined to become a person and not a thing. To accomplish this, she'd gone back to school. In fact she'd gone back to many different schools at different times. Bruno listened to her and was certain that she was like no other being on this earth or any other.

Rachel told Bruno that she was a prisoner of Jewishness, and seeking to break out. Her parents were hurt by this, but that, of course, was the name of the game. Carrying around so much baggage, she said, was tiresome.

Bruno told her that *he* always felt better after a drive in his truck, and she said that was a good idea. She sat beside him, one knee draped by her robe and the other next to the gearshift. Bruno told her he didn't really know what in hell she was talking about, but that it sounded very interesting. To make her feel more comfortable, he told her he had a little bit of the same problem. This appealed to her, so she made herself available to him. From that night on, Bruno, through no conscious effort, groomed her for the farm. She mistook for poetry his homesick comments about calves, butternut trees, and frozen ponds. She imagined a place where maybe she could be happy. What she didn't know was that the family had sent Bruno to school because his older brother, Alf, had the rights of the eldest son and they didn't know what to do with Bruno. They hoped he'd find something to occupy him, but they had no idea it would be someone who'd spent three years on a kibbutz.

Rachel was with him that Christmas when he got the news of his mother's death. She was mystified because he didn't cry and tear at his clothes. That he suffered no temporary stint of reclusion or impotence mystified her.

They were married without ceremony or rings by a justice

of the peace a few weeks before graduation. Then they left for Bellows Falls, where they moved into the tenant house behind the barn. A tight little cottage with a slate roof and a woodstove for heat. It had a kitchen, a sitting room, and two bedrooms upstairs. Bruno told Rachel about the times he'd come to the house when families of five, six, or seven people lived there. He'd sneak over to the house late at night, and whoever the hired man was at the time would slip him beer. They'd sit on the slab of stone that was the front step and shoot the shit. He admitted he felt a little strange living there, but Rachel excited him with her plans for decorating the place.

Within time, Rachel became tolerable to Bruno Sr., Alf, and Evelyn the housekeeper. Evelyn was fifty, though her age was of little significance. It happened once that she was called up for jury duty. After that experience, she claimed that there was no justice in the world. She delighted in telling that to everybody at every possible opportunity. The good ones get it, she'd say, and the bad ones go scot-free.

Jury duty and the Red Sox were her life. Late at night she sat in the kitchen and listened to the ball game. Above her head the ceiling was stained yellow from the Pall Malls she chain-smoked. There was a foam rubber pad she rested her fat elbows on as she sat out those hot nights in a house dress or a slip, no matter who was in the room. Sometimes Bruno Sr. sat with her and listened until he fell asleep in the chair.

On those nights she'd talk to him about his wife and Rachel, but mostly about Rachel.

"Rachel's all right, she's a good girl," Evie would say, as the Red Sox went down in order. "I remember when you brought Carolyn home. *Your* father welcomed her right in. Made her one of the family."

125

"Who's ahead, Evie?"

"Boston. Yaz is batting. He's a good boy."

Evelyn worked on Bruno Sr. that whole week while the Sox were home at Fenway. Curt Gowdy did the play-by-play. Most nights Bruno Sr. fell asleep during the seventh-inning stretch. Evie kept on in her low, monotonous voice, sucking on her cigarettes, staring off into the night, talking to the man who by then slept in the chair beside her.

Every morning, Rachel was in the habit of going to the barn with Bruno Jr. She assembled the milkers and then fed the calves. She was more meticulous than the men were about mixing the formula. She watched the calves more closely for scours and pneumonia. Bruno showed her how to let them suck her fingers to keep them occupied. She stroked their chins and made sure they had clean bedding. Within a few weeks the number of dead calves dropped to zero.

Alf and Bruno Sr. didn't like her in the barn, even though their spite for her wasn't as apparent anymore. She usually wore shorts and a halter top and they never knew when she'd come around a corner, so they couldn't piss in the gutters. But the man who drove the milk truck and the man who delivered the grain were a lot more sociable. They found reason to dally whenever she was around. Neither one of them had ever seen a Jew before and they were curious.

"Your people don't like those A-rabs at all, do they?"

"Mr. Ives," Rachel would say, calf milk dripping off her hand, "don't get started on that again. We spoke about that last time you were here and the time before that. Aren't you going to be late on your deliveries?"

Rachel gave Ives her slightest smile, and watched him blush. She shifted her weight and Ives had to fight a bit to keep his balance. He walked away shaking his head. He hadn't come to like her either, though he couldn't figure out why. He was convinced there was something bad about her.

Mornings in the tenant house were Rachel's favorite time of the day. She padded barefoot around the cool rooms. She liked to touch the walls and run her fingers across the woodwork. The disappointment she felt over Bruno's family not liking her couldn't spoil these moments. The pattern on the linoleum was scuffed at the door, in front of the sink, and by the stove. She liked to stand in those spots and think about the kinds of people who'd stood there before her, the kinds of people Bruno told her about. She wondered especially about the women and all the children they'd given birth to.

The families had moved in and out. They lasted only a year or two, moved on, and then, more than likely, came back again.

She remembered Bruno telling about one family, a father and mother and seven kids. Bruno was just a boy the year that family lived in the house and worked on the farm. It was Bruno's job to make sure that every dead calf went out immediately on the manure spreader and was thrown into a deep gully along the river for the coy dogs. In other years this hadn't been necessary. Dead calves were thrown out behind the barn with the rest of the trash, where they'd freeze and be buried by snow and boxes and twine. When spring came, they would be disposed of. But that year dead calves started to turn up missing. The meat of these was usually shot with blood and medication, but the hired man was taking them back to the house and butchering them. Bruno Sr. finally had to take action when one day he spotted the man's kids across the frozen stock pond slapping calf heads with homemade hockey sticks. The little boys ran

127

across the pond while the older ones knocked them down like pigeons. The little boys were crying and squalling but their brothers wouldn't stop. They had plenty of groceries, Bruno Jr. told her, but the man couldn't bear to see those calves go to waste. Bruno Sr. didn't want to confront his hired man, so when the man asked why he was wasting all the meat, Bruno Sr. told him it was Bruno Jr.'s doing and he'd have to take it up with him. The hired man never said a thing, but Bruno could feel him watching every time he drove down the road with a calf or two heaped on the spreader. After this ordeal, Bruno told her, he never could stomach the thought of eating veal.

On most mornings that first summer, the sun coming in the windows formed rectangles divided into quarters on the kitchen floor, rectangles she could stand in and feel the warmth come up through the bottoms of her feet. By the time the rectangle had crossed the small kitchen, Bruno was dressed and sitting at the table. She had him to herself.

"Coffee," she'd say.

"Yes, I'll have a cup."

"People don't like me around here, Bruno. I try hard, but these people never ask me anything or tell me anything. I don't know what they want. I do a good job, but they never really talk to me."

"They like you, Rachel. It's just their way."

"Their way is, I hate to say, bullshit. Ives undresses me with his eyes every time he sees me and the guilt is written all over his pinched little face."

Bruno laughed. He'd never thought of Ives that way before.

"He does look like a chicken, you know," she said, at which point they both laughed.

Bruno looked at his wife and felt a heaviness come over

his body. He looked away. He knew she was right, and he knew there wasn't anything he could do about it. He knew that his father considered most people outsiders and everybody fools. Bruno couldn't tell her that his father had never really loved anybody. He had trouble telling himself that.

"Bruno Junior," Rachel said, "how come you're Bruno Junior and Alf isn't? He's older than you."

"Alf is named for my grandfather, Alfred, and I'm named for my father. My father always said he couldn't give me much except his name. That's why he sent me to school. If I hadn't gone, though, I never would've met you."

Rachel asked him that question often because she liked to hear the answer.

Now Bruno turned his body toward hers. Her chin was perched on the palms of her hands. Her fingers reached up along her cheeks, her fingertips disappearing into her hair.

Bruno reached his arm around her bare shoulders. He reached inside her top and held her breast. She sighed, half from the frustration she felt and half from the feel of his touch. For a moment Bruno imagined her banging away at the piano and then dancing her fingers lightly across the white ivory keys. The world seemed to still itself for him until she reached out and held the back of his neck. At that moment they were both content.

After several of these conversations, Rachel became pregnant. The news of this rekindled the bad feelings. Bruno Sr. went back to church on a regular basis and dragged Alf along with him. Evie would normally have found all this amusing as every Saturday night she drew their baths and starched their shirts, but the All-Star Break had come and gone and the Red Sox were in a slump.

"There's no justice," she muttered to herself. "Bruno Senior," she yelled from her ironing board.

Bruno was in the tub.

"This is the third goddamn shirt you ruined with your tobacco juice."

"So I'll wear a vest," Bruno said, grabbing a towel as if he feared her voice could see his naked body.

"All the way up to your collar? How in hell can you dribble tobacco on your collar?"

"It's not easy," Bruno Sr. yelled back, splashing water on the floor with every movement. "Leave me alone."

Evie made things even worse for Alf. By the time it was his turn to bathe, it was late in the game and not only were the Red Sox losing, they were also being shut out. Rice, Boggs, and Yaz were all hitless.

"Alf," she said, cranking on the words as if her mouth were a torque wrench that knew just how tight to snug them, "you wash that neck of yours and wash it good. This collar is filthy. It's disgusting."

Luckily for Alf, the Red Sox rallied in the bottom of the eighth and hung on to win. Evie had pie and coffee waiting for him when he got out of the tub.

Being hauled into church by his father brought unexpected good fortune to Alf. He joined a fellowship group and took up with a Sunday school teacher named Michele. She was actually the daughter of the Bavasis' next-door neighbors, the Newells, but her old man had kept a tight rein on her. She was six years younger than Alf. When her father saw him in church, though, he gave in and even went so far as to promote the courtship. Bruno Sr. didn't much give a damn one way or the other. He'd known Newell for many years. He liked him, but deep down thought him a fool.

Alf and Michele dated on Friday nights and ate dinner together on Sundays at her parents' house. They discussed going away on retreats in the autumn with other members in the group. Alf was proud of her. Michele had been runner-up to the state dairy princess only two years earlier.

Alf's new love softened his feelings for his brother and Rachel. He now was cordial in the mornings, offering to help Rachel carry pails of warm milk. If you'd quizzed him about it, though, you'd have found no change in fundamental beliefs, just a general lovesick, cow-eyed approach to life. At night he worked harder so they could all get out of the barn earlier. Bruno Sr. hung back, always finding one or two small jobs to do, a cow to be bred or a machine that needed a little maintenance. Alf whined at the delays and Rachel giggled. Bruno teased Alf by being more affectionate with Rachel. He'd bite her ear and she'd coo and poor Alf would go red in the face.

That summer went well on the farm. The corn grew high and the alfalfa was lush. Rachel's slight body showed her pregnancy from early on. Her record with the calves was perfect. She hadn't lost one since the day she started taking care of them. Alf's new love took off some of the pressure, because now the old man ranted about him wandering around like some moon dog. Bruno Sr. was merciless.

"You can't fuck all night and expect to do a day's work," he yelled at Alf every day. "You're throwing it all away because that prick of yours has no mind."

Alf's shoulders would fold in and he'd feel like crying. Alf was confused and hurt to hear his father so angry. The old man knew it, too, so he found ways to turn his invective into concern, which Alf always sucked up. For the old man to ignore Alf's response took an effort, because he thought it the response of a fool, but he ignored it as best as he could.

In late August they had a break. Twelve thousand bales

of timothy and alfalfa were stacked in the lofts, and they'd dried off a number of cows and sent them to pasture. As in years past, they went to Cheshire Fair in Swanzey. They took three vehicles: Bruno Sr. and Evelyn in the station wagon, Bruno Jr. and Rachel in his pickup, Alf and his girlfriend in her car. She had a white Mustang that Alf loved to drive. This was a strange procession to see going down the highway. Bruno Sr. led the way, ignoring the kids behind him as well as the stop signs and red lights, while Evie took up most of the front seat beside him.

Alf and Michele were behind them in her car. She was telling him about how some friends of hers were remodeling a farmhouse. It didn't mean much to Alf, but she wore a new perfume and he could smell it every time she moved. Bruno and Rachel were last in line. He told her stories about novice 4-H kids who sometimes turned up missing at fairs because gypsies snatched them. He worked hard at making her believe him and then, when they were almost at the fairgrounds, he grabbed her knee and shook it. She let out a yell and he laughed at her.

Rachel had never been to a county fair, which she expected to be somewhat like a craft show, with wandering minstrels, jugglers, fire-eaters, and a dancing bear. Once there, they all gathered at the 4-H building, but soon went their separate ways. Bruno Sr. and Evelyn went to the pavilion, where they caught the last of the three-horse hitch and stayed on to watch the Billy "Crash" Craddock concert with the Newells. The men talked about driving up to Canada or to New York State to buy some cows. Mrs. Newell rattled on to Evelyn about the microwave she got for Christmas. Evelyn sat with her head tilted toward her, and what Mrs. Newell couldn't see was the thin white wire that ran out of Evelyn's pocketbook up to the hand she cupped against her ear. Boston was at Detroit.

Between innings, Evelyn took it upon herself to keep everyone supplied with french fries, hamburgers, and hot dogs.

Alf and Michele made for the Grange and Home Arts buildings, where they looked at the cakes and pies and cookies. They squatted down to look in the mason jars of home-canned beets, beans, tomatoes, potatoes, and sauerkraut. They looked at all the paintings, photographs, quilts, and dresses, then went to the Home Show building. They collected brochures on freezers, snowmobiles, woodstoves, and Rototillers.

Everyone recognized Alf's girlfriend and it made him proud to have her hand on his arm as they strolled along. Her new perfume wasn't the usual flowers in bloom. More heady, it caused him to imagine certain passages he'd read in the Bible, passages in the Old Testament that were not usually sermon fodder on Sunday morning. These were passages he'd come across while trying to stay awake in church.

Rachel wanted to see everything. She wanted to be inside the crowds, to move as they moved. She drew Bruno along through the colors and noises and smells of the midway. The carnies were sending out strings of words that looped through the air. She held onto Bruno by the waistband of his jeans. When she was behind him, he could feel her nails against his spine, and when she took the lead, she put one hand on his belt buckle and her other hand rested on the side of her belly where she felt a catch in her ribs from the slight swell of her stomach.

They watched people throw baseballs for canes, basket-

balls for mugs, and hoops for teddy bears. She wanted Bruno
to win her a panda bear, but he'd been down that road
before.

"French fries, Bruno. I want some french fries," Rachel
said.

"You shouldn't be eating that kind of food."

"Stuff it, Bruno. Get me some fries with lots of vinegar."

Bruno bought her the fries and she ate them one at a time
while they watched a skinny kid win a panda bear.

"The kid works here, I know it," Bruno said.

Above their heads was a gondola, and off to the right a
Ferris wheel. They passed the merry-go-round and came to
an opening between tents. Here the midway veered off.
Bruno and Rachel turned down this last leg of the fair. First
came the haunted house and then a variety show with a
bearded woman, a snake-skinned man, and a contortionist.
For two bits you could enter a van with a whale in it, and
then there was a small tent with such fare as a two-headed
calf and a six-legged dog, the thought of which almost made
Rachel sick right there in front of everybody.

At the end of all this was the hootchy-kootchy show. A
crowd had already gathered. On the stage was a stubby little
man with a derby hat and red garters on his sleeves. He
was droning on to the crowd, particularly to a man at the
front of the stage. No women, children, or men with pace-
makers were allowed inside, he said. Three girls walked out
onto the stage behind the barker. Their blue, white, and
black nighties looked dingy in the glare of the light bulbs
at their feet. They wore silver high-heeled sandals with puffs
of cotton at the toes. They looked tired.

A man behind Bruno and Rachel said he'd seen fried eggs
that were bigger than the first girl's tits. Bruno tugged at
Rachel, but she said she wanted to stay and watch. Bruno

saw Alf and his girlfriend walking by and he called over to them. The four of them stood together inside the crowd.

"You look so good, Rachel," Michele said as all around the men joked and laughed at the barker's words.

Rachel smiled.

"What do you think of the fair?" Alf asked, staring up at the stage.

"It's something else, I'd say," Rachel replied. "Bruno, I want to go in and see the show. Take me in."

"You can't go in. They don't allow women."

Bruno looked over at Michele and saw the shock in her eyes. Alf looked surprised, too.

"Then *you* go," Rachel said, "and tell me everything that happens."

"I don't want to go to any damn strip show."

"Alf, you go, too, and then you can tell Michele about it."

Alf stepped back. He wanted to go in, but not with Michele there. He'd always wanted to see the show. He'd heard a lot about them.

"I'll get two tickets," Rachel said. She was gone before anybody could stop her. A few minutes later she was back with the tickets. She presented one to each brother. The men standing around them were watching the two couples, watching Michele and Rachel, as men often watch girls. Bruno and Alf knew they had no choice. This was the last show of the evening and rumored to be the best.

Although neither had ever seen the show before, each thought the other one had, so they pretended that it was no big deal, just a waste of money. For their friends it had been the highlight of the summer. They'd arrive at the fair with their show cows, horses, or sheep, and stay over the three or four days the fair ran. They'd have water fights and sneak beer and try and go out with girls, but they never got too

135

far. The more daring boys, the ones with a few sparse hairs on their lips, would swagger up to the stage and go in while the younger boys watched from the crowds, huddled together in their tee shirts and jeans.

Bruno and Alf had listened intently to the stories afterward about what the girls would do with hot, buttered corn on the cob, and how the girls would snatch the eyeglasses off some unsuspecting man near the stage and do things with them. The younger boys, including Bruno and Alf, would look down and shuffle their feet and say "bullshit," knowing in their hearts that it must've been true because it all sounded too unbelievable to be made up.

Inside, the tent was dark and the bodies were packed tight. The more daring leaned on the stage, their heads in the light that flooded out from the center tent pole. Bruno leaned over to Alf and asked if any of those guys in the front row were wearing glasses, but Alf didn't get the joke.

When the tent was full, the door at the back of the stage opened and the first girl came out, the one in the white nightie. She was carrying a cassette recorder. The men hooted and yelled. She smiled at the crowd and then snapped on the music. She set the recorder on a chair and began to sashay around the stage, holding the hem of her nightie in her fingertips. She danced like a little Shirley Temple. The song ended and she left. Another song started and another girl came out. She immediately took off her nightie and held her tits out, cupping them in her hands. Then she held her hands above her head and did a few bumps and grinds. She waved to the back of the tent. Everyone turned and saw a state trooper standing there with his hands on his hips.

The crowd grew quiet for a moment and then out from behind him stepped the girl in the black nightie. They all laughed, even Bruno and Alf. She was only a few feet away from them.

The girl in the black nightie moved slowly through the crowd, rubbing against as many men as she could. She held onto Alf for an especially long time, running her fingers through his hair and angling her leg between his. The men cheered and slapped him on the back, almost knocking him over.

When she finally made her way to the stage, two men in front lifted her up and she danced with the girl who owned the recorder. The two women danced near the edge of the stage, shaking their tits in the men's faces and letting them reach inside their underpants. Though Bruno fought it, he could feel the warmth in his groin, and his breath come from deep inside his chest.

The girls danced through two songs and then they blew kisses to the men. Before they left, they kissed each other on the mouth, stealing back not a little of everything they'd given to the farm boys and truck drivers and mechanics and small-time merchants. The men booed the girls as they smiled and waved and shook their hind ends one last time.

"Shit," a man yelled, "ain't nothing but a bunch of goddamn woman queers."

The call went up for more, and then after a long pause, a slow drum beat came from the recorder. The light from the tent pole went out and in an instant came back on. Standing at center stage was a black woman, naked to the world. The men were silent as she performed an acrobatic dance that had her snaking and slithering on the stage and then rising bolt upright with her arms sweeping the air.

"Let's get the hell out of here," Alf said, his voice desperate.

The two of them hurriedly passed though the tent flap,

not seeing Bruno Sr. and Larry Newell standing in the shadows. Bruno Sr. was smiling.

Rachel and Michele stood where the brothers had left them. They were sharing a cardboard tub of french fries soaked with vinegar and catsup, Rachel's third of the evening.

Bruno laughed and hugged his wife. He'd never seen her so happy before.

"So?" she said, dancing back and forth on the balls of her feet.

"So. So what?" Bruno said, sliding his hand up the back of her blouse.

Alf fidgeted and Michele concentrated on the fries. Rachel held her arms up and wiggled her hips, then threw back her head and laughed.

"You got it," Bruno said, and held her about the waist.

They looked at Alf and Michele, who were also working up smiles.

"We'd better go," Alf said. "It's getting late."

"It was so good to see you, Rachel," Michele said as the two of them walked away. "I'll stop in to see you soon."

Later, in the truck, Rachel sat close to Bruno, her small body tucked in against his side, his arm around her shoulders. He could feel her hair move as she turned her face up to his ear.

"There's going to be fireworks tonight," she said.

"I know," Bruno said, sliding his hand along her ribs down to her hip and slipping his fingers into the waistband of her shorts.

"I don't mean that," she said. "Alf was getting pretty tight in the jeans."

Bruno laughed and pulled her even tighter against his

side. He couldn't remember a time in his life when he'd been happier.

As the baby grew inside Rachel that autumn, even Bruno Sr. came to care for her more, not because she was his son's wife, but because she was pregnant. His was the same concern he showed to any of his bred heifers. Her belly swelled and her breasts became full and heavy. She comported herself about the farm with almost regal bearing. She walked with her shoulders back and her pelvis thrust forward a bit more each day, her body tentatively seeking its changing center of gravity.

All about her, the grand procession of the year wheeled round and swept toward its end. By Thanksgiving the darkness and cold were inside the barns and sheds and houses. It stayed there throughout the day, hiding in corners, corners where the floor met the wall, and wall met wall, and wall met ceiling.

For a time, late in October, Indian summer set in. Some took this as a moment within which to breathe and rejoice. Rachel threw open the windows and walked in the meadows, picking Indian paintbrush and collecting leaves. Others, including Bruno and the rest of the family, used it as a last opportunity to batten the windows with plastic, nail down loose roofing, and lay bales of straw around the foundation of the house.

It grew cold again, and the men worked late into the night, chopping corn and filling the trench silo. By midnight their breath came in slow, white clouds that drifted in the blue cast of the machinery lights.

Bruno Sr. chopped corn, driving alongside the rows. From

the tractor he controlled the computers that gauged the process, ferreting out any stray metal that might hit the knives. Up to his left he had a spotlight he used to see the chopper and wagon strung out behind him.

Alf ferried wagons back and forth between the trench and the cornfield. He was under pressure from his father to always be ready with an empty wagon. Bruno Sr. pushed him hard. While none of them liked to work so late, it was to their advantage because the frozen ground made it easy to get over wet holes.

Bruno's job was to pack the trench. Hour after hour he drove the D-6 back and forth over the growing hummock of corn. It was slow work and he had to force his mind to stay awake. He'd think of Rachel. Usually this got his horns up, so that he stayed up even later than he should when he finally got back home. One night he fell asleep. The D-6 came out of the trench, crossed the road, broke through the fence, and rolled over a quarter mile of open pasture. He woke up when it jolted down a steep embankment, almost bouncing him off as it dropped out from under him.

Cows were beginning to freshen daily. The new heifer calves were put under Rachel's charge, and the bull calves were shipped for veal.

Rachel grew lonely. There was no time for her and Bruno except late at night. The shortened days forced her to stay inside the tenant house or up at the main house with Evie. Evie was the only one around for her to talk to. One night, Rachel felt as if she were going out of her mind. It seemed to her that she was always alone and that it was always dark.

"Oh, Evie," Rachel said. "He doesn't love me anymore."

"I don't know what you're talking about," Evie said, staring out the window of the darkened room. She could see the lights of the tractors a long way off in the cornfield.

"We don't talk anymore."

"He's all right, what more do you expect from him? Get me a match."

"Evie, it's not like it used to be."

Evie turned toward Rachel, her huge body sweeping gracefully within the small kitchen. "There's stuff you can't have, Rachel, and as far as love goes, you don't know a damn thing you're talking about."

Rachel went back against the chair. She saw in Evie's eyes, if only for a moment, something she hadn't seen before. Rachel saw her now as a woman, a woman who hurt in the same way she did.

"Oh, Evie, I never realized . . ."

"Realized what? You don't know anything."

"I mean, you and Bruno Senior."

"You never realized because there isn't anything to realize." Evie turned away and didn't speak to Rachel again that night.

Rachel went home and made supper and then napped until Bruno got in late that night. When he finally came in, he woke her up. He held out a hand and in his palm were tiny white bones. She looked up at him, still half asleep, her eyes soft in the light. She looked as if she were going to cry.

"Alf found them," Bruno whispered. "He had just hooked up the old man for the last load. He saw them when he bent down. He scuffed the dirt away and there it was. It was along the road, you know. Up in this corner."

Rachel looked at him, all the time her eyes growing darker and beginning to fill with tears. He saw in her face that she didn't know what he was talking about.

"It's a hand. A child's hand. Years ago they used to bury

their dead in the fields. The rest of him is out there some-where."

Rachel stared at her husband.

He dropped the bones into a cup on his bureau and then undressed. He shut off the light and fell into bed beside her. When she heard his breathing level out and felt his body twitch once or twice, she knew he was asleep. Only then did she allow herself to cry, scared to death of the bones he'd brought into the house and feeling foolish that she was. The next day she walked down to where the meadow met the river and threw them in. Bruno noticed them missing, but forgot to ask her about it.

Autumn shut down in a single day just before Christmas when a blizzard pounded its way up the Connecticut River. Bruno could see it coming that morning from the high mowings where he was spreading shit. He saw the blue and gray heads moving over and around the foothills of the Green Mountains. On occasion a bolt of lightning would jag out of the mass, leaving a blank sky when it disappeared. He ran out the load and wound his way down the road. He knew it would be a bad one.

The forerunner of the main front arrived about noon with wind and lightning and sleet. One gust took a cupola off the barn roof and dropped it in the stock pond. Lightning danced and sparked about the feedlot. For a moment the barn flushed with a faint glow. One string of cows rose up and the opposite went down on their knees, blaring out in pain. The glow traveled the water line until it grounded out in the floor, leaving the cows stunned.

The squall lasted for two or three hours and then the body of the storm moved in, dropping twenty-five inches of snow in three days. Wind and cold followed the snow, moving, shaping, and packing it in sinuous and complicated contours. The clothesline was buried, the machinery was buried, and one side of the barn was buried.

On the second morning, Rachel woke Bruno with a scream. The bedroom windows were covered with snow. He held her close to him and stroked her head. Over and over again, she said she was sorry for scaring him.

They dug out, cutting lanes in the snowbanks, pounding into the drifts with the loader, and shoving them aside with the bulldozer. Rachel came out of the house that morning and looked solemnly at how her world had changed. She watched the three men working as a team to open up the yards. The heavy machines they drove pushed within feet of each other at full throttle. Evie was shoveling snow from the walks and porches, cutting out blocks and heaving them aside.

Rachel went back inside and sat by the window. She felt like a child left alone in the house. She was afraid. She took out some old sheet music and looked at it. She turned to a Chopin polonaise. The notes came together in her mind. She didn't make music with them, but she could read them like the words on a page.

She became buoyant. After awhile it took no effort for her to keep herself afloat. The composition reached out to her, moving of its own accord and taking her with it.

Bruno came in after milking and found her still sitting there.

"I fed your calves," he said. "I'm going to hire a boy to do your animals until you're ready again."

Rachel smiled, set aside the music, and started to speak. She opened her mouth, then stopped. She thought a moment before starting again.

"You're a good man, Bruno," she said. "You're a damn good man."

Bruno smiled. At first he had been afraid of what she was

about to say, but he'd seen the panic come across her face and then disappear. He thought to ask her what had been on her mind, but decided not to. "Rachel," he said, "for Christmas, let me buy you a piano."

"No, no," she said. "You can't."

Bruno was taken aback. "Maybe later," he said.

"Yes, maybe later. Maybe later. Come here," she said.

He walked to her and bent to give her a kiss.

"No," she said, "here." She pulled him down to his knees and held his face against her stomach. She held him for a long time and finally fell asleep.

It was a few days before Christmas when Evie came around to see Bruno and Rachel at the tenant house.

"Your father would rather not have Christmas this particular year," she said. "He does want you to have this, though." She handed them a check for a hundred dollars. "Alf will be at the Newells' house, and I guess I'll just cook a small turkey. I know you kids understand."

"Yes, Evie," Bruno said. "It's all right."

"Wait, Evie," Rachel said. She walked into the other room and came back with packages for Alf, Michele, her father-in-law, and Evie. "Could you hand these out, please?"

"I'll be happy to," she said, hugging them both at once.

After Evie left, Bruno folded the check and tossed it in the stove. "The thought's enough."

"Yes, it is," Rachel said.

Bruno never did tell her it wasn't his father's signature, but the same scrawl he'd seen many times on Evie's grocery lists. "So," he said, "should we get a Christmas tree?"

The next morning he went up to his father's house after chores and found his snowshoes in the attic. He threw them in the bucket of the front-end loader and then drove as far up the mountain as he dared. From there he snowshoed back into a stand of blue spruce and chopped one down.

He hauled it back to the house, and he and Rachel decorated it with candles and tinsel.

While Bruno did the milking on Christmas Eve, Rachel cooked a roast. She washed and curled her hair and put on a long, white dressing gown. Under it she wore only a bra. Her breasts had begun to ache from their heaviness.

When Bruno came in, he stamped his boots and shimmied out of his overalls, hanging them on a nail by the door. While they ate and drank wine, he told her the story of the baby Jesus, which, of course, she knew better than he did. She was careful that her questions didn't reveal anything, but drew him out in his telling of the event.

"And that's why," he finally said, "that every Christmas Eve, the animals in the barn are able to speak like people."

This last statement truly amazed her, for she'd never heard such a thing.

"Bull," she said.

Bruno laughed. "All this time you've been leading me along, playing like you don't know anything. Now how's it feel?"

She was embarrassed, but he kissed her and then told her he had a present for her. "Come sit by the tree," he said. When she did, he bent down in front of her, lifted her foot, and rested it on his leg.

"What do you want to do, sell me some shoes?" she said, wiggling her toes.

He put his finger to his lips and told her to shush or she'd break the spell.

From his breast pocket he took a bottle of perfume. He dabbed some on her foot and then, reaching up her leg, he rubbed some inside her thigh. He stretched out his arm and touched the hollow of her neck. She sat back and looked at him.

Then, from his pocket, he took out a bottle of red nail polish. He held her foot in his left hand and with his right he painted with short careful strokes. He held her foot up to his mouth and blew the paint dry. Then he did her other foot.

When he finished doing her toes, he did her fingers. She looked down at what he was doing, but didn't speak. Her hands looked small and fine in his, which were rough and chapped. The polish gleamed in the candlelight.

He held her left hand when he was done. He looked up and saw the water in her eyes. Without looking away, he reached into his other pocket and took out a gold wedding band. Still looking at her, he slipped it on her third finger and then folded her hand inside his. Rachel began to weep.

Bruno held her. "I'm afraid I'm losing you," he said over and over again. He took her to bed and held her until she fell asleep. Only then did he stop fighting his exhaustion, and fell asleep himself.

Around midnight, Rachel woke up. She put a log in the stove and made some tea to settle her stomach. She made a fist and looked at the ring. She rubbed it and felt its smoothness. She opened her hand and placed it on her stomach. She felt ugly and beautiful, then felt sad.

Outside, the path of the moon had come round to the kitchen where she sat. She saw the barn and its black windows. In the milkhouse she saw the glowing red light that indicated the compressors on the bulk tank were working. Rachel pulled on her overcoat and slipped her bare feet into

Bruno's pac boots. She grabbed a flashlight and stepped outside. As the cold air filled her lungs, she coughed, expelling a burst of warm air that floated in front of her face. She made her way to the barn.

The milkhouse was bathed in the glow of the red signal light. The compressors roared like jet engines. Rachel opened the side door a crack and slipped inside. She stood quietly, just a little afraid of the dark. To her left and to her right were rows of stanchions with cows' heads poking through. They coughed and belched and calmly chewed their cuds.

She switched on the flashlight and started toward the calf pens. The door to that part of the barn was half-open, and she stepped in. There before her in the light a man stood staring at her. He was huge, bundled in his overalls and wool coat. She started to scream but held it back with a hand to her mouth. Half a dozen cows hurried to stand, ramming their shoulders into their stanchions, snapping tight the few inches of chain that secured them at the top and bottom.

When she finally got hold of herself, she realized it was Bruno Sr.

"What in hell are you doing here?" he said.

She struggled hard to stop from shaking. She couldn't cry and couldn't speak. She later thought that this was the closest she'd ever come to being scared to death. She stood before him feeling as if she had been driven back into her childhood, a childhood full of fears and whispers and loneliness.

"Bruno told me," she said in a voice so soft the old man could barely hear, "that on Christmas Eve the animals in the barn can talk."

"Never heard such a thing," he said.

Rachel took a deep breath. She felt weak and cold.

147

"Go to bed," he told her and then turned back to the calves that had gathered up to the pen where he stood.

"Good night," she said, and left.

It was bone cold the rest of the winter. Alf and his girlfriend began to have lovers' quarrels in preparation for engagement. Their tiffs were public shows, usually consisting of her trying to civilize his bad table manners and him trying to educate her as a cook. This banter disgusted Bruno Sr., who gave up church during the December blizzard, and it amused the Newells, who by now were considered tedious and pretentious by the rest of the family. Mr. Newell became known as Old Blowhard to Evie, but of course she never called him that in front of anyone but Bruno Sr.

Evie began biweekly trips to the chiropractor in Brattleboro. She stood up one day and declared she'd hurt her back. None of them wanted to reckon with her, and so every second Monday afternoon Bruno Sr. trucked her down the interstate so she could be wrenched and twisted and turned upside-down on a table she was strapped to.

Afterward, she'd insist on stopping for hamburgers, french fries, and a milkshake. Bruno Sr. would sit across from her sipping on a coffee, watching what he imagined to be dollar bills being wolfed down by the huge woman.

Each Monday night while they milked the cows, Bruno Jr. asked his father how it had gone. Bruno Sr. would relate the size of the dent she put in his wallet, and then one night he straightened and smiled at his son.

"I suppose she'll be ready for spring training," he said, and then laughed at his own joke. "Spring training," he muttered again.

Bruno felt a warmth wash over his face and body. He

took this joke they'd shared as a sign of his father's love for him. Inside his chest, he could feel his heart, and for the first time in a long while he was happy to be home.

That night he told Rachel everything that was said. This meant, he told her, they all had a future, and that the worst was over, but she didn't say anything. She only looked his way and let her black eyebrows rise slightly on her forehead.

Two days later, Bruno was back in the doghouse. He and the hired boy had been getting the ensilage every day from the trench. The deeper in they got, the longer it took. Because the corn was mounded so high, seventeen, eighteen feet, it was frozen and hung up in the air.

"By damn, we can't be waiting on you all day to bring in that corn. There's stuff to be doing," Bruno Sr. said, looking at the mound—huge even a half mile off.

"The corn is froze. There's overhang you have to pick around or the whole thing will come down."

Bruno was right. The top layer of corn was higher than the bucket would reach. He'd been picking at it from the edges the last few weeks, trying to get it to drop, without him under it.

"There must be a hundred ton sitting overhead. You want me to blow in there and get crushed? I'm sick of your shit. You hate Rachel, you hate she's pregnant, and you want me dead. I'm just a goddamn hired man to you."

Bruno's words hurt the old man, but he didn't let it show.

"Me and Alf'll get the corn," Bruno Sr. said quietly.

In January there was a thaw. Two tractors moved ponderously down the muddy road to the trench silo. Alf was on the Ford loader and Bruno Sr. was on the Ford 9000, the Gehl forage wagon jolting along behind him. Water and mud squeezed out from under the tires, deep ruts forming behind.

When they got to the silo, Alf immediately began to dress up the trench, piling spillage that had built up and been frozen and was now thawed. Bruno Sr. pulled in behind him, aligning the wagon for easy loading. He then leaned back on the tractor seat, with one heel on top of the clutch and the other on top of the brake. He packed his cheek with tobacco and then crossed his arms. Alf started loading the wagon, dumping buckets of corn over the side.

Bruno Sr.'s mouth gaped and closed with the action of the loader. Days like this made him feel old and young at the same time. The sun shone down on him, relaxing his body, drawing out the aches from what had been a hard winter. He stretched like an old cat that had been sitting in the window all day. He thought of his dead wife and tried to remember which goose it had been. There was a lame cow he wondered about, and there was talk of a change in milk price.

A hydraulic hose blew on the loader. Bruno Sr. felt some wisps of fluid on his cheek. Alf cut the power and shifted to neutral. The two of them grabbed wrenches from the tool box and began to repair it.

Bruno Jr. found them there that evening, crushed under the tons of corn that fell from the top. The tractors were still running.

That night, Bruno Jr. milked the cows by himself.

By March, Rachel was eight months pregnant. Her stomach was huge and it weighed her down. Her breasts were full on her chest and her back hurt. At night Bruno rubbed her legs. He rotated the heel of his hand on the small of her back, to soothe the strain, until he fell asleep beside her, often still moving his hands in his sleep. He was doing all the work himself but she made him strong. Rachel herself was exhausted but couldn't sleep. Some nights she lay awake and spoke to him.

"I don't want to cut my hair," she whispered to him, though by now he was sleeping. "It's heavy and takes time to wash, but I can't cut it. Everybody cuts their hair when they're pregnant."

Bruno's hand stopped moving, resting on the small of her back.

"Bruno," she whispered, but he didn't answer. She sat up in bed. He still had his clothes on, so she undressed him. She took them all off until he lay there naked and white except for a trace of body hair. She moved the rocking chair near the bed and sat down. She watched Bruno and then looked about the room. On the dresser she saw the scissors and for a moment thought she would get them and cut her hair, but then she looked back to Bruno. The thought went as quickly as it had come, but it still unnerved her.

She sat in the rocker and studied her husband. She had her ankles crossed, and her hands rested lightly on her belly. Her navel had started to pop out. She looked at him laying there naked.

After a while, she got down on her knees and started kissing his leg. She licked the scar on his knee and kept kissing her way up his leg until she came to his hip. She put her chin on his pelvis and blew across his flat stomach, but he didn't move. She moved closer and blew again across his body, and then she bit him. She bit him hard, hard enough to leave marks that would last for three days.

Bruno yelled and thrashed his body like a giant fish. His sudden movement knocked Rachel on her rear end. She sat, smiling up at him, leaning back on her hands, her legs crossed. He looked at her, not knowing if she was real or something come to him in his dreams. Her smile widened, and Bruno, still afraid, pushed himself against the wall. He grabbed the sheet and pulled it up around him.

"I want you to make love to me," Rachel said, unfolding her legs.

Bruno stared down at her. He reached out and she went to him. He didn't understand what it was all about, and was surprised by the strength in her body and the measure of her need. It was like their third or fourth time in the dorm room when the sweat fell in drops off her forehead onto his chest.

Bruno felt good the next morning. He looked at his face in the bathroom mirror and smiled. "Man who fuck in morning, live short life," he said out loud and laughed. Rachel was still asleep, her hair thrown straight back, fanning out on the pillow above her head. Bruno dressed and went to the barn. He did the chores, feeling happy with his life, happy with Rachel.

There were several heifers Bruno detected in heat that morning, so he and the hired boy skipped breakfast and stayed in the barn to breed them. Already he was changing the sire program. His father had leaned toward Arlinda and Bootmakers. Bruno was banking on young unproven sires, sires with high predictions. He'd cleaned out the semen tank and refilled it with a greater variety. Some of the semen straws had cost him seventy-five dollars and some had been free to experiment with.

Rachel got out of bed a few hours after Bruno left the

house. She ate toast and tea and then dressed to go out. She wore Bruno's overcoat because it was the only one that would fit her. When she walked out on the front step she could smell the earth as it thawed. She grabbed the doorknob and, feeling dizzy, held onto it. She could see the Bavasi house. In her mind it seemed to pitch and roll for a moment. The side door opened and Evie shuffled out in black rubber boots that came up to her knees. She dragged a broom in one hand and a rug in the other. She hung the rug on the clothesline and began whacking it with the broom. She held the broom like a baseball bat. Rachel felt better. She smiled and set out for her walk.

Once away from the farm the air was not as heavy with the smell of animals and mud and cowshit. She could now smell the pine and hemlock to the north of her. She passed the corn trench, staring into it as she went by. Further along, she began to feel strong again. Her feet and legs didn't ache. She began to forget she was pregnant. She stretched her arms and shook her head, whipping her hair across her face. She passed through another stand of hemlock and then down a hill. To her right and left, meadows, still buried in snow, opened up to her. She could see where a tractor had swung around the one to her right, down near the riverbank and back again to where she stood. She began to follow its track, walking in one of the ruts. All about her, rows and rows of corn stubble popped through the snow, the ends left sharp from the chopper blades that took them down six months before.

This was her favorite meadow to walk in, the lower meadow. The river bordered three sides of it. As she came near the bank she could see huge, gray chunks of ice silently flowing by in the black water. The baby inside moved, kicking her sharply in the ribs. She grabbed her side and held her breath until it settled down. She looked away from the river, which made her dizzy again. She was tired and wanted to rest, but was determined to complete the circuit.

In the distance she heard dogs. They sounded wild and frantic. Bruno had warned her about dogs that roamed with coyotes, but these noises sounded as if there were a hurt animal. She continued on until she reached the gully where the sound came from. Afraid to stand too near the edge, she got down on her knees in the wet snow and crawled forward onto the bluff. Fifteen feet below her, four dogs were tearing away at the body of a dead Holstein calf. Its belly was open and steam rose from the viscera spread out on the ground. The dogs' faces were covered with blood and they snapped and growled at one another. The calf's head was thrown back in her direction and its eyes were open.

Rachel watched, slowly shaking her head, using whatever strength she had left to keep herself from crying. Finally she got up and began the long walk home, knowing what she would do when she got there.

Bruno got back to the house at noontime. He called out Rachel's name but there was no answer. He fixed himself a sandwich and then began to wonder where she was. He picked up the phone and dialed his father's house.

"Evie," he said, "is Rachel up there?"

"She's not here, Bruno. She took the wagon into town. Said she had some errands to run. Said she'd be gone most of the afternoon. Maybe into supper. She said you were to come up here to eat."

Bruno hung up without saying good-bye. It wasn't like Rachel to do such things. Bruno finished his sandwich and then sat down at his desk to do some bookkeeping. There in front of him was an envelope with his name on it. He felt a chill run the length of his body. He knew it was from Rachel. She had never written to him before. He was afraid to open it, but he did.

Dear Bruno,
I love you very much. Sometimes I think I always have, even before I knew you, but how could that be? I will try to come back, but right now I want to be home. I know you do not understand. I will call you.

Love,
Rachel

Bruno slumped back in his chair. He felt like the fool his father had always made him out to be. He thought of the old man as being somewhere in the room, dancing from foot to foot, wagging a finger at him and laughing.

"Shut up," he yelled. "Shut up, goddammit, and die. Die, you old bastard, die."

He slammed his fist down on the desk again and then he sucked in his breath, ballooning his chest with air. He held it as long as he could before letting it out in a long sigh. He made coffee and took it back to the barn to drink.

Rachel sat quietly on the bus heading south to New York City. The signs on Route 91 ticked by as she traveled through Vermont, Massachusetts, and Connecticut. A satchel of clothes was on the seat beside her. She didn't know why she was going, she only knew she wanted to be home.

The bus stopped in Springfield and she called ahead. Her mother met her at the Port Authority. She was waiting there when the bus got in. They clung to each other and cried.

155

Rachel's mother stroked her hair and rubbed her back. She kept saying, "My little girl, my little girl." Rachel and Bruno's baby was squeezed in between them.

The morning after Rachel left, Evie brought doughnuts to the barn for Bruno. He stopped assembling milkers and ate one. Her doughnuts always tasted like rawhide. He turned back to the job he'd been doing.

Evie came up close behind. She reached around and hugged him, enveloping him in her fat arms. "My son," she said. "My son."

Bruno shook her off and turned to her. "What in hell's gotten into you? I'm not your son."

"But your father told me you were my son. He told me right after your mother died."

Bruno looked at her.

"I'm not your son. He was full of shit—and if you believed him, you're full of shit, too."

"I raised you. You were my baby."

"Bullshit," Bruno said. "Go back to the house. You're starting to go crazy, Evie."

Evie stood there.

"Go on, get back to the house."

Evie sighed and toddled back to the house, shaking her head, lolling it back and forth on her neck, confused as to what the truth was. When she got back to the house she began to bake. She baked cookies and a cheesecake and an apple pie and cream puffs. She then sat down and had a little of each while she listened to an early morning call-in show on the radio.

Bruno finished chores and then went in for breakfast. After he ate, he made several phone calls until he located the hired man who used to eat dead calves. He was in Derby Line collecting welfare.

"Everett, this is Bruno Bavasi, Junior."

"Who?"

"Bruno. Bruno Junior," he yelled into the receiver.

"Oh, young Bruno," Everett said.

It was hard for Bruno to understand what Everett was saying because Everett had a harelip. Bruno hadn't heard him talk for eight or nine years and was out of practice.

"Everett, this is Bruno Junior. You working?"

"No," Everett said, "but I got a situation with the state. I heard about the accident."

"Everett, you get down here by tomorrow. I need your help, I'm short on hands."

"I don't know. I've got Grace and the kids. I'm disabled, you know."

"I ain't asking you, I'm telling you. You don't have your ass in that barn for milking tomorrow morning at four-thirty, I'm coming for you and then you will be disabled."

Bruno slammed down the phone. "The goddamn fool."

"He'll be here," Evie yelled from the kitchen, laughing.

The next morning, Everett was parked in front of the house. He had another woman tagging along with him. They were drinking coffee from a jar. Bruno yelled for them to come in.

"I see you made it," Bruno said.

"We sure did. We drove all night. This here's Grace's sister."

The woman dusted off her coat and stepped forward, but Bruno ignored her.

"We left at two o'clock," she said. "I kept the coffee on the seat between my legs so it'd stay hot."

The woman's voice was hoarse and her front teeth were

missing. Bruno stopped and looked at her. She was short and broad across the shoulders. He smiled, and when Everett and the woman saw that, they both laughed.

"Where's the rest of the tribe?" Bruno asked idly. He hadn't slept since Rachel left. He'd been staying up to his father's house, and jumped every time the phone rang.

"I got shed of Grace. If she wants me back she'll have to come crawling on her knees," Everett said, and then he came close to Bruno's face and added, "I think she's been cheating on me. With my brother."

Bruno had all he could do to keep from laughing.

"Everett's got a new woman, Evie," Bruno yelled into the kitchen, whereupon Evie came out.

"Grace get sick of your shit, Everett?" she asked.

"Well, let's just say there's room for you now."

Everett made a move to grab her, but she slapped him in the head with a wet towel.

"Everett," Bruno said, "you go to the barn and clean the stables. This afternoon Evie'll move my stuff up here and you can move into the tenant house."

Everett nodded and started to leave, but Bruno stopped him.

"You go near one goddamn calf, dead or alive, and you'll wish you hadn't." Bruno waved his hand and Everett left.

A month went by and still there was no word from Rachel. He had a phone installed in the barn just in case she might call.

Grace moved back in with Everett. The two oldest boys were old enough now to shovel shit, so Bruno put them to work. Bruno paid them twenty-five dollars a week. He made out the check for all three, Everett and his two oldest boys, and gave it to Grace to manage.

One night Michele came by to visit. When Bruno heard

Evie greet her, he hid in another room where he could listen.

"Ives told me Rachel left Bruno," Michele said.

Evie didn't say anything. She only fiddled with the knob on the radio trying to get the ball game.

"Poor Bruno," Michele said. "I know just how he feels, losing Alf the way I did."

Evie turned up the volume, and Michele's voice had to compete with the static.

"Where is he, Evie? I'd like him to come to church this week. I feel it will do him good. I know it has sustained me. I'd like to take him to a movie. He needs something to take his mind off things. In one fell swoop, he lost his family and then Rachel."

Evie turned the volume down and looked at Michele.

"There just ain't no justice, is there, honey?" she said, and then turned the volume back up. She found a Bruins game and sat there listening as if she understood until Michele left. Then she shut off the radio, turned out the lights, and went to bed. Bruno had fallen asleep on the divan, the phone on the floor next to him.

The last half of April he began to dream that Rachel had called. He woke up in the morning happy for the first few moments, then sadness and tiredness would set in again. He remembered having long conversations with her, but he couldn't recall anything they talked about. He took to asking Evie at breakfast if she'd heard the phone ring, but of course she hadn't.

"You can get on the ground in a few days, son," she told him. "Once you get to plowing, you'll feel better."

Bruno didn't say anything. He finished his breakfast and went out to the barn. Just as he was about to walk in the door, he heard a scream that went through him like a cold knife. He ran out behind the barn to the tenant house and there he saw Everett's younger boys watching two barn cats go at it. The boys had tied their tails together and then thrown them over the clothesline.

Bruno cut the line. When the cats hit the ground they broke free of each other. The boys ran for the house, where all that time Everett had been standing on the front step drinking his coffee.

"If I didn't half need you," Bruno said, "I'd kill you, you son of a bitch."

Everett turned, but Grace slammed the door on him before he could get inside.

"Get to the barn, you old puke," Bruno said.

Everett set down his cup and went back to the barn, not realizing what all the fuss was about. Bruno picked up the cup and knocked on the door. Grace let him in. When the kids saw him, they scattered into every corner. Some crawled under the beds. One little girl got in and pulled the covers over her head.

"Got any coffee, Grace?" Bruno said.

Grace handed him a mug without saying a word. She poured herself a cup and sat down across from him. Neither of them spoke. One by one the kids poked their heads out and stared at him, but other than that no one moved. Bruno sat and drank coffee until the pot was empty. Finally, without a word, he stood and turned to leave. Grace stopped him at the door.

"Your Rachel," she said, "I hope I can meet her sometime."

Bruno didn't say a word, he just left.

Later that day he sent Evie over with a check for a hundred dollars so Grace could buy the kids some new shoes. He had Evie load them all into the station wagon and take them

160

to town. From her grocery money, Evie added a little bit extra so they could buy new socks and underwear.

Bruno tried to make his peace with Everett, but in the end felt cheated because Everett had long since forgotten the altercation.

"Get the implements greased up, then," Bruno said, "if that's all you care to talk about it."

That night the phone-call dream seemed more real than ever before. The next morning he remembered everything. He remembered talking about the baby. It was a boy and she was going to come back the very next day. She said the boy looked like him, and that she'd named him Samuel.

When he woke up at four-thirty to milk the cows, he felt as if something had come in the night and cast a spell on him. He felt charmed as he stepped out into the twilight and walked to the barn.

He went through the day saying "Samuel" over and over to himself. He rechecked the plow that Everett had worked on and then he walked the cornfield to see if the wet holes had dried sufficiently to be plowed. In the distance he saw a tiny figure, which at first he took to be a woodchuck. For a moment, he made the figure out to be Rachel. As he got closer, he saw it was Everett's little girl. They didn't speak, but she followed him about the fields the rest of the day.

By nightfall, he was exhausted. He ate the supper Evie put in front of him and then had her draw a bath for him. He moved a radio into the bathroom and turned on the game. The Sox were at Fenway.

Bruno sat back in the tub and looked down at himself. His skin was stark and pale in the fluorescent light of the bathroom. His legs were slightly bent as they stretched out before him. Bent because he didn't quite fit in the tub and

161

bent because it hurt him to straighten them out flat. The red scar on his left knee looked like a salamander poking its head out of the water. Between his legs there was a thatch of black hair and under the water he was shrunken from the heat of the bath. Just above the hair, he could see where the teeth marks had been after Rachel bit him the night before she left. He imagined them to still be there.

Evie sat in the kitchen listening to the game and reading from the newspapers she and Grace had brought home from the grocery store. She was reading about a woman who was held as a sex slave by a tribe of love-crazed Amazons. This was Carl Yastrzemski's last season. Outside it began to rain.

The next morning, Bruno was on the tractor before the sun was up. Everett and Grace and the boys were doing the milking. Grace was good with the cows. She understood their cycles. She could sense their changes long before the men could. She could diagnose the onset of mastitis or ketosis before there was any sign of it. She was a good woman to have around cows, Bruno thought, driving onto the corn ground.

Even Everett changed when he got around animals. He was a different kind of man. He was gentle and spoke in whispers no one could understand because of his harelip. He was gentler with the milk cows than with his own kids.

A band of red stretched out between the skyline and the shaggy tops of trees set still and black against the horizon. Above that, the clouds were starting to break up, clouds the color of woodsmoke, with white seams between them.

Bruno looked up and felt small as he witnessed the world begin to turn around for another day. He downshifted, dropped the plows, and let off the clutch. The tractor surged forward. Bruno looked back over his shoulder and watched the coulter blades slice through the ground. He watched the plowshares sink down sixteen inches and roll the earth neatly off the moldboards. He watched the unbroken furrow furl out behind him. The birds came in and walked stiff-legged through the fresh-turned ground.

At the end of the field, Bruno raised the plow and turned back toward the rising sun. Inside the tree line, its light burst from a prism of water on a dead maple. For a moment it sparkled and gleamed, but as Bruno approached it disappeared in the steel gray sky.

Bruno stared at the spot where the light had come from, trying to hold it in his mind as long as possible. Then he stopped the tractor and stood on the seat. He looked all around, trying to find it again someplace else, but it wasn't there.

Bruno was on the tractor that entire day. He plowed the lower meadow, stopping only to eat the lunch Grace brought down to him.

"I won't be in to milk," he told her. "You and Everett watch out for those two cows with bad quarters, and we're still dumping the milk off that Holmes cow."

Grace nodded. She was the one who'd alerted Bruno to these animals in the first place. "Bruno, you need rest."

Bruno looked at her. It was the first time Grace had said anything to him about his own well-being. He looked at her now as she stared off across the meadow to where the land stopped at the river.

"My father used to work for your grandfather. He used to bring me down here at night after chores and we'd fish for horned pout. We had a kerosene lantern we'd fire up to draw them in. If they got you, it hurt."

Bruno was surprised at this. He didn't know that Grace had grown up on the farm. He'd never heard her spoken of. Her knowledge of the land made him feel a little bit of

163

a stranger to it. He began to think back on all who had come and gone, and began to feel less sure of his own grasp. He looked down at his hands. They were big and raw and the skin was peeling from the calluses on his palms.

"One got him once right in the back. I pulled it in hard and handed him the pole. The line swung around him and it got him on the back. The spot swelled into a big red knot. Didn't go away for days."

Bruno stood up and dusted off the seat of his pants.

"You find Everett and begin the milking at four sharp. I'll try and get up to help."

Grace packed what was left over, picked up the lunch basket, and started to leave. Then she stopped, set the basket down, opened it, and took out a thermos of coffee and two doughnuts wrapped in wax paper.

"They're for later," she said, handing them to him. "My father always liked to have a thermos of coffee on the tractor with him."

Bruno watched her trod up the dirt road, then he got back on the tractor. He wrapped the thermos inside his coat and put it under the seat. He pulled back onto the meadow, lined his tire up in the dead furrow, and then dropped the plows and accelerated the power at the same time. The tractor hunkered down and then surged forward.

It was near dark when he finished, and the dew had begun to settle in. The air had cooled and the shadows were now so long that they ran into each other, covering the land. Bruno swung across the newly plowed ground and began up the dirt road to the barn. While driving, he pulled his jacket from under the seat. He unwrapped the thermos and put it on the floor between his feet. Then he put his jacket on. It was stained with oil and grease and smelled like the barn. On one arm was a big stain, a blood stain from late winter when he'd had to pull a calf from its mother, a calf too big for her to squeeze out on her own. Bruno zipped up the jacket and turned the collar up against the night air.

When he got to the corn pit, he pulled the tractor over, put it in neutral, and climbed down. He walked over to the spot where his father and Alf had died.

"I just wanted to tell you," he said softly, "that the lower meadow is all plowed." Bruno stood and listened for a moment, then smiled. "By the way," he added, "it's the first time it's ever been done in one day."

Bruno turned and walked back to the idling tractor. By that time his own words were coming back to him, making him feel small and ashamed. He climbed back on the tractor and slowly drove back up the road to the barn, the lights of which he could see far off in the night. For the first time since Rachel had left, he was in no hurry to get there.

The Greyhound pulled into Keene late that afternoon. Rachel was the last one off the bus. She was carrying her son on her hip, and the driver helped her down the steps. She waited for everybody to get their things from the luggage compartments on the sides before she stepped up. The driver stacked her things neatly on the sidewalk. She had decided against bringing all of the baby's stuff, just enough for a few days' stay, since even the bare minimum took up quite a bit of space.

Rachel looked up and down the street until she spotted the station wagon in front of Lindy's Diner. She smiled when she thought of Evie perched on a stool, eating doughnuts and drinking coffee while she waited. Rachel crossed the street with a slow measured limp to balance off the weight of the baby. Evie was inside, sitting in a booth that faced the street. She was smoking a cigarette and looking across at the bus depot. She had watched Rachel cross the street, but now that Rachel was inside she still kept looking out the window.

Rachel went to the booth and sat down. Evie didn't say anything.

"Evie, it's me," Rachel said, but Evie still didn't speak. "Evie, did you tell him I was coming?"

Rachel put her feet up on the seat and held the baby in her lap. Across the street, her things were stacked on the sidewalk where the bus driver had piled them. That was what Evie seemed to be looking at.

"You're angry," Rachel said, "but I'm not going to apologize for what I did."

Evie put her cigarette up to her lips and drew hard on it. She held the smoke deep in her lungs, then blew it out. When she breathed again, she kept her mouth clamped shut and kept staring out the window.

It began to rain, a spring shower that came up fast and hard. Evie watched the rain hammer on the streets and cars and sidewalks. A waitress came to the table and asked Rachel if she'd like to order anything. Rachel asked for tea and dry toast. The baby watched all of this. He didn't move his head, only his eyes. It was time for him to nurse again.

"Are you hungry?" she whispered to the baby. "Of course you are. It's time for your supper."

When the waitress came back with Rachel's tea and toast, she asked Evie if she wanted more coffee. She called her by name, but Evie only sighed and kept looking out the window, watching the rain fall. She could see people huddled under the awnings over the shop windows, and another group under the marquee of the Colonial Theatre.

Rachel sipped at her tea and was staring out the window

when the baby began to cry. Rachel unbuttoned her blouse and then cradled the baby in her right arm. She held her breast with the other hand and drew on it two or three times to relieve the pressure. When she felt it come, she held the baby up to it. He took it in his mouth immediately, making sucking noises as he drank. He'd been good about nursing right from the start. The nurses at the hospital had tried to discourage her from nursing because it meant they had to bring him to her more regularly than if he was on a formula. She was glad she'd resisted them.

Rachel reached across her front and pulled her blouse closed as best as she could. She settled back against the red vinyl seat and looked out the window again. The diner was quiet, and the waitresses stood together in front of the glass doors to the pie shelves. One leaned forward, her elbows on the counter, and the other stood with one arm across her stomach and her other arm bent at the elbow, her hand up to her chin.

The men at the counter had stopped eating. They were looking back over their shoulders, their faces blank. The cook stood in the doorway to the kitchen, a towel in one hand and a spatula in the other. Outside the rain had slackened, but still no one had moved back onto the street.

Rachel felt tired. She hadn't slept since she'd made her decision to come north. She dozed against the cushioned seat, forgetting where she was. She'd open her eyes and see the rain and then she would close them again. She began to imagine that she was back with Bruno and that everything was all right. They were alone and living in the slate-roofed tenant house. They were in bed together and beside the bed there was a crib and the baby was in it, asleep.

She dreamed that Bruno was lying in the bed with his body aligned with hers. He was pressed against her, his chest to her back. One of his arms came over her side and he held her breast in his hand while his other arm stretched out on the pillow under her head. She could feel his face tucked into the hollow left between her neck and his arm. In her dream, she was awake and Bruno was asleep. She felt small lying there against him. She could hear it raining outside the tenant house. It was close to morning, closer than she had realized. A false dawn cast its light against the maples outside the window of their bedroom, the bedroom where she and Bruno lay together again as if nothing had ever come between them. She watched the light lose some of its radiance as the true dawn approached. She pushed her body against his and felt him tighten his hold on her and she wasn't afraid anymore.

Rachel let herself wake up long enough so that she could switch the baby to her other breast. The people in the diner quietly began to move again. Rachel settled back into the booth again. She looked over at Evie, who was now looking at her. The old woman's face was drawn and tired. Her eyes were wet, her hands folded in front of her.

"Evie?" Rachel said quietly.

"What, honey?" Evie said, tears starting to come at the corners of her eyes.

Rachel didn't say anything. She sat nursing the baby and looking across the table at Evie.

"All your things were caught in the rain," Evie said.

"They were, weren't they," Rachel said, looking across the street.

"We'd better get them in before they're ruined," Evie said.

Rachel held the baby up to her shoulder and patted him on the back. Then she set him down on the seat beside her and buttoned her blouse.

"He's milk drunk, isn't he, honey," Evie said looking at the baby.

"He gets that way," Rachel said.

"His father always did, too," Evie said.

"Does he know I'm here?"

"No. He'd already left for the barn when you called and then he went right out on the plows."

Evie stopped smiling and pinched her lips together. She looked back out the window again. The waitresses began to make more noise now as they worked the counter. They poked at the men and told the cook to get his ass in gear. At first the men tried to listen to Evie and Rachel, but the waitresses snapped at them to mind their own business.

"I was going to send you away," Evie said, still looking out the window.

"But you didn't," Rachel said. "You didn't, so it's all right."

In the barn that night, Grace and Everett milked the cows. They moved about silently, wasting little effort. In the milkhouse, the vacuum pump developed enough suction to milk a dozen cows at once. Periodically, fans kicked on to vent the hot air generated by the animals' bodies and the motors. The bare light bulbs were flecked with whitewash and fly droppings. Each was surrounded by a glowing haze of light that reached its brightest moment a few inches out and then quickly dulled. They created pools of yellow on the ceiling and in the air, pools that melted into one another, pools that Grace and Everett walked through silently, looking as if they were moving from one place to another, their bodies growing and shrinking, becoming lighter and darker.

During the milking, a cow was beginning her labor in

the back barn where every day now cows were freshening. Hers was a big calf. The rest of the animals quieted down as the mother heaved and panted and groaned. She was a heifer that Bruno's father had bred back in September. The cows he'd bred last fall were now coming in. For the next five months all the calves born would be from heifers and cows the old man had bred before he died.

Everett and Grace took turns checking on the heifer. It was her first calf, and there was a chance it was too big for her to deliver. The old man had a tendency to breed with big bulls no matter the age or size of the dam. Neither said anything, though. They knew it wasn't time to help. They continued with the milking. The two cows with the bad quarters came in together. Everett started to hook up the milking units to all four quarters but Grace poked him in the ribs and shook her head.

Finally they were down to the last few cows. Grace took off her apron and started for the back barn. Everett followed her. Along the way she picked up two lengths of baling twine that were laying on a window sill. The heifer was standing when they got to her. One of the calf's legs was already sticking out of her. Grace pushed her hand in along the leg and found the other one, still inside, bent at the hoof in such a way that it was lodged inside the opening. She straightened the leg and drew it out in her hand. She then tied a piece of twine to each leg so she and Everett could both pull while the mother pushed.

At first they didn't make much progress, but then the mother began to heave with more determination. The other cows stood still. They patterned their breathing with hers. They stretched their necks and sighed. The contractions began to take control of the mother's body. The calf started coming, first the knees and then the nose and then the eyes, and then it came like a diver. Everett reached over and took both pieces of twine, one in each hand. Grace ducked in under the calf. It came faster, weighing more every second. For a moment she had it in her arms and then she went down under its weight and it was on top of her. Everett pulled it off and immediately spread its legs. It was a heifer. It would be kept and raised.

The Boon

My father was a drinking man. He always drank pints—pints of Hiram Walker, pints of vodka—until February 11, when he got his hands on a fifth. He hiked into the woods and drank the whole thing. Somewhere in the night, all by himself, he went from being passed out to being dead.

I tracked him down the next day. You could see where he'd circled the tree before he sat down on a root. He was slumped against the trunk, his cheek on the bark as if he were leaning against his mother's leg. Rain streaked his face and dripped off his nose. His hands and his cheeks were the only thing that struck me as being a little different. Otherwise he looked like he belonged in those woods. He looked like he'd come home.

I picked him up and packed him out to the road, his body draped in my arms, a good fifty pounds lighter than when he was in his prime. I laid him down on the seat next to me, tucking his knees against his chest and slinging the seat belt over his body. I drove him to town.

He was buried the next week. They set him down in the hole and then cuffed the dirt over him. The funeral was nice but nothing special. The way he would've wanted.

A half dozen of his old cronies from the war years showed up. At the grave they rocked back and forth on their feet. They clasped their hands in front of them, and behind them, and then gave up, one by one, and thrust them into their pockets. Each one might've been thinking that it could've been him.

I say the war years because it was during the war that they teamed up. They were all at the University. One had bad eyes, another bad knees, and a third couldn't hear too well. My father had high blood pressure.

They were in a fraternal organization. Now they're doctors, lawyers, accountants, and engineers. Professional men. They loved to hunt.

Hap stood nearest. "Hap" is short for happy, though his real name was Harold. He was my father's best friend. Hap and my father grew up together. They went to the same high school, the same high school I went to. After they graduated, they hopped a freight and headed west.

They helped build Boulder Dam. They slept in the Painted Desert and, in San Francisco, crashed a Harley that belonged to the guy next door. He was a policeman. Hap was in the sidecar, my father was in the saddle. They drove it up the front step, along the veranda, and through a window.

The dark side of their trip west was when they took on a couple of railroad bulls in Kansas City. They were making their way back east for school. Both had decided on civil engineering. As the story goes, they beat the shit out of them and then hid out for a week in the hobo jungles around the yards. The dicks got tough. Every night, gangs of them would descend on the jungles with billy clubs as big as baseball bats. They'd break bones and crack skulls in their rage over what Hap and my father had done. One night they squeezed into their culvert just before the attack. From where they hid they could see the big rangy agents go two-on-one getting a hobo down and then putting the boots to him.

When they told me the story, Hap, fat and red-faced, worked up a lather as he strained for words not in his engineer's lexicon to describe the sight of lips half torn off, noses like rose bursts on the face, and eyes swollen shut. He did better on the angle of broken bones and displaced joints.

My father sat back, uncomfortable, preoccupied. For him it hurt that such uncalculated things could happen. His words, cool and sure, sliced through Hap's dramatics. "It's unfortunate what happened to those bums, but they should've known better."

Things finally cooled off after a bum turned up dead, looking like hamburger. According to Hap, when the bulls found him riding the carriage under an inbound freight, they dangled railroad spikes on wires between the cars. The spikes bounded off the ties and snapped into his body until the train slowed and stopped.

"He had no business being there," my father said, ashamed of his role in the affair and, at the same time, outraged by the shame.

It didn't bother me, one way or the other. Sitting there listening to the story, I only wished they'd been a little slower on the draw and felt the clubs lick their own shins and maybe taken one aside the head. I didn't want either of them hurt, just a little scarred, maybe an ugly stitch over the temple or a bit of a limp, something I could see, some mark I could fix on. But there wasn't any. The bums were fools and those two weren't, so they came home and went to school and learned how to build dams and roads and bridges and sewage-treatment plants.

My father was the first of them to bite the dust. They must've been relieved in a way, thinking that he'd broken ground for them. He'd been the drinker. He was the one who always made last call. He was the one who always cajoled or shamed them into having just one more, and of course they'd always comply for the sake of a bond welded years ago.

He was a likable man—brilliant as far as that goes. Anyone who met him, liked him. Perhaps people sensed that he was consuming himself, caught up as he was with drink. In seeing that, people first would feel sorry for him, but ultimately overwhelming relief, because he had served to unburden them. He was no threat to them, only to himself.

After the service I handed the minister a twenty, for which he dug down especially deep into his soul and gave me my money's worth in a gaze and a handshake. For a second he thought of saying something in an attempt to pluck my soul from the gates of hell, but then thought otherwise, sucked in his lips, and shook his head as if all things were beyond human understanding. I looked into his sad, cloudy eyes and smiled. I nodded my head up and down, broke off the handshake, turned and walked up the hill.

Vic, the lawyer, called after me. We had a few things to talk over.

"Not now, Vic," I said. I was tired and needed to sit.

"I'll come by tonight," he said. "The boys want to take you out. We can talk then."

"Sure, Vic," I said, "you come by tonight."

Sitting in my father's chair, I watched the low sunlight coming through the double-hung windows cast a veneer of reds and oranges over the room. It was those things that were the memories of my mother, enshrined in many small ways and places about the room—her books, her doilies, her hand-painted glass eggs, and her teakwood boxes that sat on the shelves.

I thought that I couldn't remember the last time any of this had been moved. Her memory was in the room, resting on things. It was like tarnish on copper or the water marks on wallpaper where the ice backed up, channeled into the roof and down through the walls. Her memory was evident but indiscernible. It had no edges.

I looked at the most immediate things my father left me: an ashtray full of cigarette butts, a water tumbler next to the chair in front of the television set, half a pack of Camels, a six-inch saw-tooth folding knife used for cutting banana stalks off trees, and a cameo he gave his mother and she gave back to mine.

I sat in the room like a stranger. I felt like a visitor, a hitchhiker picked up on the highway and driven to someone's house for the night or worse than that. The sun went down.

As much as I wanted to be, I wasn't a part of that house. I ate and slept there, but never lived there. This was the house my mother and father built. The one they raised me in. It was a relief, I told myself, to have that grave capped off and square over his belly, a relief because I spent most of my life either bringing him indignity or hiding out. I loved to hide out. I'd hide out in the cellar or attic. When I got a little bigger, I'd hide out in run-down houses and on the back roads. Now I hide out in the woods, a long haul from anywhere.

The lights of an automobile banked through the picture windows and reflected off the mirrors and glass. I went to the door and let Vic in.

"Say, Trooper, how you holding up?" he asked.

"I'm okay," I said. "No problems."

"I know it's a little soon, but I'm the executor of your father's estate."

"I'll make coffee," I said.

He began to cover the kitchen table with papers. "I hate to have to do this to you, son, but I have to be back in

177

Concord tomorrow morning, so I'd like to go over these papers with you and then the rest of the boys want to meet us at the roadhouse. Just like the old days."

Vic spoke as if I were my father. I was never a part of the old days.

We drank coffee while Vic laid things out for me. The house was mine, as was our lodge in the Northeast Kingdom of Vermont, and there was even some money, I didn't know how much.

When you look at all this as the fruits of a man who worked his butt off for forty years, it's not that impressive. But then again, life's cheap if its worth is based on what it leaves behind. A man marries a woman, produces a son, and then has to die.

"As I see it . . ." Vic said.

But I stopped him. I held up a hand.

"Sell this house, Vic. Sell it as soon as possible. Sell everything in it, except a few things I can get in the pickup. Can you handle that?"

"Sure I can, if that's what you want. I can take care of it. What's your thinking?"

"I just want out from under it. I'll go north and live in the lodge. We can bank the money, can't we?"

"Yeah," he said, "sure we can. If you don't want much, you can probably get by the rest of your life on the interest. It'll pay the taxes up north and keep you in groceries and gas."

"Sell 'er out, then."

My decisiveness impressed him. He liked decisions, good or bad. "All right, let's go meet the boys."

They were all there at the roadhouse. They leaned up against the bar, their leather elbow patches wet from spilled

178

beer. They clapped me on the back and looked me in the eye. They had just a little fear in theirs, or at least that's what I tried to see.

I'd been in the roadhouse before, the bar we sat in that night. I was there with a hitchhiker I'd picked up down the highway. When she got in the truck, she showed me a pickle fork she carried for protection. I took her up to the roadhouse, where we spent most of the night. She acted a little crazy, a little vacant.

When the police came for her, the only thing I could say was I didn't know she was a fourteen-year-old runaway from Concord. She looked all of seventeen. She and I had even talked about running away, getting married, and having kids.

The next night my father sat me down for a father-son talk.

"Did you pick her up?" he asked.

"Yes, sir," I said, pleased with an easy question for a change.

"Did you know her?"

"No, sir," I said.

"Was she a stranger?"

"I said I didn't know her," I told him.

"You trusted her?"

"She seemed okay."

"You trust strangers?"

"No, sir."

"You just said she was a stranger and you said you trusted her. You trusted a stranger. You have to think. These are facts. You ignore the facts and you're in trouble. Analyze the situation, son. It's not just you who suffers the constant indignities you bring on this house."

"Yes, sir," I said.

He couldn't help it, I told myself, it was just his way. He was a civil engineer.

Each one insisted on buying my first drink. There was me and Hap and Vic and Lewis and Billy Guyette. Every one a success in his own right.

I knew Vic was feeling good at the thought of having me up north. He didn't much care for me. He had a daughter about my age. One Sunday afternoon we got caught playing stinky-finger out in the woods when our families were on a picnic. She was a beauty with long, curly black hair and a Roman nose. A few years ago she ran off to Alaska with a welder.

Vic thought I'd corrupted her. He thought I took her virginity, but God knows she probably lost it on the crossbar of a ten-speed, or took it herself in the bathtub when she was eight. She was spitfire. Vic set me up with a beer and a peppermint schnapps.

As the night wore on, it saddened me to watch these old men trying to carry out a ritual, a testament to the one who'd gone first. They moved and drank like lame, ancient dogs, not handling their booze too well, and not thinking on their grief at all.

I'd rather see this, though, than have one of them think he knew what they should be doing because he'd read it in a book. I was heartened to see them muddle through. I admired them for it.

They told the same old stories. Each one took turns finishing after another had started. The stories ran together. They argued over whether it was April or May, or Waco or Tucson. They tried to remember whether the girl had had red hair or black, and which one of them she'd wanted the most.

Thankfully, exhaustion finally overtook them. They were drained and fatigued, but none wanted to be the first to leave. Sensing they needed a sign from me, I stretched and yawned and said I was tired and, if they didn't mind, I'd like to go home to bed. This, they all agreed, was a good idea.

Hap stopped me on the way out. He said Vic had told him of my plans, and he thought they were fine. "I'll be up," he said, "and we'll go hunting like we did before."

"You come ahead," I told him.

"I'll call."

"No phone up there."

"Oh, well. I'll just come ahead," he said. "Two or three days into the season."

"You do that, Hap. You come on ahead."

Hap had gone to meetings with my father once or twice, but these got in the way of friendship so my father talked him into going to the bars instead. Hap stopped pushing and things relaxed for a while. Then when my mother died a few years back, it all went to hell. Hap stopped coming around and our families didn't get together so much. It's understandable.

Hap had that drunken friendliness about him, though he wasn't a drunk. I liked him and still do.

The house was sold within two weeks. Vic crowed about how he'd pulled a few strings and done me some favors. He used the words "expedited" and "liquidated." He told me I had a tidy sum in the bank and that I could count on a solid income. He said that I couldn't go whoring around, though, and laughed.

I told him I didn't do that anymore. I was too old.

"Too old?" he wailed, but then he backed off as his eyes rolled up in his head and he saw me and his daughter in the bushes with our trousers down around our ankles.

I had intended to drive straight through the next day, since it was only three hours. But when I got on the interstate, things seemed to be happening too fast. People were roaring past me. I took the first exit I came to and topped off the tank. Instead of going back up the ramp, I took a parallel route, weaving my way north, in and out of small towns up the valley.

I felt better traveling at thirty-five, taking in the sights, branching off onto any side road that pointed north.

The spring thaw was setting in. Brooks were opening up and flowing freely, swollen with run-off from the hillsides. Bent grasses were showing in the high meadows. The road seemed to bleed water. The tires of the truck sucked it up and sprayed it into the wheel wells.

The other people on the roads drove old cars and trucks and didn't pay me much mind. No one knew me. I stopped at a diner just outside of Rutland for lunch. I was the only one in the place except for the woman who was both cook and waitress. I asked for a menu, but it struck me I'd seen hundreds like it and they all were the same. I handed it back to her and ordered sausage and eggs and fried potatoes and corn muffins, if she had them.

She had a friendly, comfortable look about her. I thought it would be nice to be her friend, maybe even to sleep with her. I imagined unzipping her dress and sliding it off her shoulders, then unsnapping her bra and pushing down her panties so she could step out of them. I imagined running my fingers along the red lines where the elastic had marked her skin.

She brought me my food. While I ate, she stood at the

other end of the counter flipping through the pages of a magazine. She drummed her fingers against the top of a napkin dispenser, shifting her weight from one leg to the other and looking out the curved windows, first to the south and then to the north.

She poured me more coffee and asked if I wanted anything else. Just the check, I said. She pulled the pencil from behind her ear and tallied my bill, set it to my right, and then went back to her magazine.

The bill was for three dollars and change. I laid down a five and a one, then I hid one of my mother's hand-painted glass eggs beside my coffee cup and left.

It was dusk when I reached the lodge. That first night sleeping by the fire, rolled up in blankets, I dreamt about Vic's daughter. She turned into the waitress in Rutland and we were eating breakfast together. It was the only dream I remember having that summer.

Work at the lodge went along smoothly. It was mostly a matter of winterization. I insulated the interior and finished the walls. I skirted and insulated around the foundation so the water could be left on when it got cold.

The work took me over. It was a good summer, there on the edge of mature timber, miles up the dirt road from the highway. I'd go four or five days without seeing anyone.

Every other day or so I'd discard an item of clothing, first my tee shirt and then my jeans, until I got down to gym shorts. Finally I gave up the shorts and went about my daily routine in a jock strap or bare-assed.

It was a beautiful spot. The shrubs and seedlings formed islands and peninsulas in the forest until, further in, the tree crowns shaded the ground. I wandered in and out of the light, going no place in particular. I took to wearing a pistol and a baseball cap.

Later that summer, I struck up a relationship with a girl in Burlington. She was in summer school at the university, a teacher doing course work. She reminded me of Vic's daughter by the way she walked.

One evening I took her back to the lodge. She had a big basket with her and said it was a surprise. She liked the lodge, she said, she liked to touch the wood. I asked her about her surprise. From her basket she took out candles and wine and food.

After being in the woods for a month and chasing her from one bar to the next for a week, I told her I wasn't exactly interested in eating food.

The next morning she watched as I pulled on my work-shoes, strapped on my gun, and grabbed my baseball cap.

"What the hell?" She laughed and slipped on her panties and tennis shoes.

I gave her the grand tour of the lodge and its grounds and then we hiked into the forest.

She told me she had to leave the next day, and in a way I felt relieved, though I still think about her in Connecticut or Massachusetts or wherever she is assigning her students an essay on their summer vacation.

The night Hap arrived, I was elbow deep in a fresh kill. I was working on cutting away the tenderloin for supper. He got out of his jeep, yawned, and stretched his neck like a big, ungainly bird. He had a bottle-ass from too many years of sitting at a desk. His feet were flat and splayed out as if he were walking in butter.

He called to me, but I acted like I didn't hear him. I kept the knife in tight, close to the bone, cutting at the meat in short, smooth strokes. He came up and clapped me on the back. I still didn't acknowledge him.

"Forget to tag that one?" he said. Then he laughed, as if he were in on some joke.

I stopped what I was doing and looked him up and down. He also had a pistol strapped to his gut and what looked like a brand new Remington 1100 with vented ribs slung over his shoulders.

"You look good, son," he said.

"I'm doing all right, got my clothes back on," I said.

"Last time I was up here," he said, scanning the site, "it was me and your old man and Vic. We played five-card stud all night long and got drunk. I don't think any of us even got a shot at a deer."

"I remember him telling me," I said. "He almost wrecked the truck on the way home. He had to lay over in some town."

"It looks like I got here at the right time," Hap said, eyeing the tenderloins.

We went inside the lodge. From the kitchen window we could see evening grosbeak and goldfinch pecking at the seed I'd spread on the ground.

"I brought you some nectarines," he said. "That's the fruit this month, you know. Me and the wife joined a fruit-of-the-month club out of Medford, Oregon. Gifts right out of the orchard, guaranteed."

After supper, Hap and I smoked cigars he'd brought with him. The splits I'd thrown in the fire popped and snapped. Hap pulled brandy from his duffel bag and we had a drink.

"So," he said, "you getting much?"

"Nothing, Hap," I told him. "Been dry all summer."

"How's 'bout the college in Burlington?"

"Nothing, Hap, not a thing."

Hap rolled his cigar between his thumb and his forefinger. The diamond on his little finger glinted in the firelight. I wished he hadn't come.

"I'll never forget the time," he said, "when me and your old man were in Mexico. Just down from Corpus Christi they got a place called Boys Town. The girls come right up and sit on your lap. They take your hand and stick it up their dress or down their blouse. They all carry health cards, but that don't matter. We got the clap anyhow." Hap roared, as if getting the clap in the Mexican whorehouse was the funniest thing in the world.

"You know what you do," he said, "you carry a pint with you so you can dip your finger in it. You slip that finger inside her and if she's got any sores, she'll scream." Hap laughed again.

"Hap," I said, "we'd better get to bed if we're to go out in the morning."

"Yes," he said, "of course."

We both stood up and he grabbed me in a hug, clamping his arms around my shoulders. "I'm glad we could do this," he said. "I'm so glad."

I didn't say anything. I just turned and left, feeling that the time I'd lived since February had just evaporated. I felt it leave my life, and then I was in those woods again, following footprints in the snow.

That night I made that walk a hundred times until, just before dawn, I fell asleep for an hour or two. When I woke up I decided that I had to get rid of Hap as soon as possible or everything would end up going down the tubes. I was determined to get him a kill as fast as I could.

That morning we started without breakfast. I directed Hap along a ridge that rose above a copse of willow and alders. The thicket provided thermal cover for the deer at night, and was latticed with trails that shot up the ridge. From where Hap was, he'd be able to sight in on anything I kicked out.

I moved quickly and cautiously. I didn't want to get a deer myself; I just wanted to send one Hap's way. It was rough going. Eight or ten saplings seemed to spring from each root, branching out to connect with the growth next to it. There were a lot of signs. Five years earlier I'd taken a deer in this very place.

When I was a hundred yards from the edge, Hap fired. He fired into a stand of beech in front of me. To my left, I could see him huffing down the ridge, his body thrown back to keep from toppling down the hill. He held his gun across his stomach.

I got to the boy first. He was flat out on a platform he'd rigged between two branches about chest high off the ground. He was dressed in a full deer hide, with the legs hanging down the side. Blood was coming from a hole in his forehead, right at the hairline. It had already formed a pool that his cheek lay in. The headdress of deer antlers was folded back against his body.

I touched the boy's back and could feel through the hide where the rifled slug had ticked down his spinal column, smashing vertebrae as if they were china plates standing on edge, fronts to backs. His ass end gaped open where the slug had left his body. On the ground lay a single shot, twelve-gauge Harrington and Richardson.

I figured the boy to be about fourteen.

Hap sat on the ground, his back against a beech tree. His face was white and shiny with perspiration. His lips were stretched so tight across his teeth they'd almost disappeared.

For a long time we didn't say anything. We looked at the

dead body as if it were something we'd come across in the woods, something that both belonged and made sense, made sense in the way the alphabet does or a run of consecutive numbers. Then again, it made sense in another way, the way a five-legged dog or Siamese twins do.

"The kid had no right being there," Hap said.

"I don't suppose he did. At least not dressed in that fashion."

There was another long silence.

"You're going to stay right here," I said, "while I hike out and get the sheriff."

Hap didn't say anything, but I knew what he was thinking. I gave him time to work up his guts. I scuffed my boots. I emptied the shells from my gun and tucked them in my shirt. Just when I thought he wasn't going to say anything, he spoke with all the strength left in him.

"Dammit," he said, "there are other options."

I smiled. "About the only other option I can see, Happy, is you can take off one of those hundred-dollar hunting shoes and your thermo-insulated sock. Then you can tuck that gun barrel up under your chin and slip your big toe in that trigger guard."

He looked at me strangely, caught up by the notion, mulling it over as if it were a decision he could make. I returned his look and didn't smile. I held him that way until he buried his chin in his chest and began to sob.

As I think back to that time, I hate myself for using that dead boy the way I did. None of this was any concern of his.

In This Life

I.

I HAVE A BLACK-AND-WHITE SNAPSHOT of my brother Harley and his best friend Dunfee. Around the scalloped edges, the paper is yellow and worn. This is the only photograph of Harley that exists from after the time of his accident.

Dunfee sits in a rocker. His legs are crossed. Poking up from between them is a Winchester. He is wearing a bandoleer of ammunition slung across his chest. Harley stands next to him. He wears a Colt on his hip. His shirt is open. His chest is a hairy V spreading out to his shoulders and neck. Across his stomach is a sawed-off shotgun. It hangs from a strap that goes around his neck. His arms are crossed. They are huge. One elbow rests on the stock and the other on the barrel. Whoever took the picture cut his head off.

In the book there is another snapshot, this one of the inside of a Buick. The photographer must've been laying on the hood. He took the picture through the windshield. There's a girl in the front seat who's combing her hair in the rearview mirror. A boy is sitting next to her. He has his face buried in her neck. The boy is Dunfee and she is the Contas girl. Someone told me Harley was in the back seat, sleeping off a drunk.

There are baby pictures in the book, too. There's one of Harley on his back, his feet in the air. You can't tell if he's a boy or a girl.

In my mind, the only stupid thing my brother ever did

189

was smash a road flare with a brick. When it exploded, the sulphur burned off half his face. He turned to me at the very moment and I watched it happen. It sparkled like a thousand tiny Christmas lights and then they all came together. He ran to the house, his head a great light, while I stood with my neck drawn into my spine as if all my vertebrae were fused solid into one small, sweeping column.

My mother changed the bandages every day for a month. I can still see her in the morning light, wrapping his head so he could go to school, the old bandages stained red and yellow in a pile at her feet like tangled streamers.

"It's coming nicely," she'd say to him, looking over his shoulder at me, standing in the kitchen doorway, staring at his back. "Don't be afraid," she'd say to him, with her eyes on me.

She kept his back to me all that month, saving whatever he looked like for herself and the doctor they went to once a week. I'll never know what she saw and how she felt as she bandaged what was left of her oldest son's face, once in the morning and once at night, beginning and ending her day the same way.

For both, it had to have been a grave act of will. When he trembled, she cooed to him as if he were a baby, and toward the end of the month, she built him up, said things meant to give him courage.

At night I'd look over at him and see the white bandages with black holes left for his eyes, ears, nose, and mouth. I dreamt night after night that his face was the moon. In those dreams I'd take his head under my arm and soar as high as I could, but always swoop back to earth because it was too heavy to keep aloft.

After a while, the threat of infection was gone. The blisters dried, the dead skin was all cut away and the blood-red splotch diffused, spreading out through his body until it was gone. She unwrapped his head for the last time. Instead of a mirror, he asked for me.

"I want Robert," he said. My mother called, and I came from the other room where I'd been standing with my cheek against the wall.

"Your brother wants to see you."

He was on a stool by the kitchen sink. His shoulders were rounded and his head was cocked back. I padded across the room barefoot, staring at the floor as I went. I stopped in front of the stool where he sat and looked up at him. He turned his head my way and then slowly lined his eyes up with mine. He stared down at me that way until I wet my pants.

"Get to the bathroom," my mother yelled, but I couldn't move. The wetness stained the front of my pants and, when they could absorb no more, trickled down my leg and onto the floor.

"Get," my brother said, and I did.

I stayed on the toilet until I'd counted all the tiles on the wall in front of me. I counted out a row and a column and multiplied, and then I counted them one by one to see if it really worked.

When I washed my hands, I looked up at the new medicine cabinet and understood for the first time why it didn't have a mirror. Over the last month my father had moved about the house like a ghost, carrying all the mirrors out under his arm—the one in the hallway, the one on the inside of my mother's closet door, and the one over the dresser. For a while he cupped a small one in his left hand and shaved with his right until he finally gave up and grew a beard that my mother trimmed once a week. Where they went, I don't know. I think he hid them somewhere and that faces are stored inside, but I know that's not true.

Some nights, after the bandages were finally taken off, I'd wake up for no reason and force myself to look at him. He slept soundlessly, flat on his back with his eyes open. The moon would show on his face and chest. These were the only times I allowed myself to look his way.

I hid a note under his pillow telling him he'd go crazy sleeping in the moonlight, but took it back before he found it.

During the day my brother wore a cap with the bill skewed low over that half of his face. He wore sunglasses and kept his collar turned up. He guarded his face, using an elaborate series of gestures and postures.

One night I looked over and he was gone. The window was open.

I went to it and looked out, but I couldn't see him. I went back to bed and lay there, watching the curtains drift in the night air. Finally he came back.

"Where have you been?" I asked him.

"In the corn."

"What's in the corn?" I said, but he didn't answer for a long time. We could've reached out and touched each other's arm or leg or chest, but we never did. We just lay there.

"Listening to it grow," he said. He repeated it once more and didn't say anything else.

For the next few nights I fought to stay awake. I wanted to follow him. I'd close my eyes for only a moment, though, and he'd be gone, or sometimes it'd already be morning and I'd be surprised how fast the night had slipped away.

And then I did it. I watched as he climbed out the window. He held his shoes by their laces, clenched in his teeth. I watched him hike one leg over the sill and then the other. He perched there, carrying himself on his hands, and then was gone. I went over to the window and looked out, but he wasn't there. I climbed higher into the opening, craning my neck, scanning the black shadows that lay between the lawn and the woods. I still couldn't find him. Then, I looked down. He was standing right below me, looking up, his face inches from mine.

"Do you want to come?" he said.

I didn't move. I tried to see his mouth but I couldn't. His eyes were more like an animal's, the way they seemed to come from out of nowhere. He held up a hand and I grabbed it. My feet hit the ground first and then I rolled. When I came up, grass cuttings were stuck to my back and chest. I followed him around the house, out the driveway, and down the road. The trees above our heads formed webs of shadow at our feet. So much moon came through that there was still color in places. Lines were sharp and the very edge of everything glowed in its light. The night seemed to run all the way round the world and come back to meet us. We were running down the seam where the two ends met.

We came to the cornfield. The corn was new and rolled out in front of us in leisurely rows that tucked into the tree line at the other end.

"Now, listen," my brother said, squatting down. "It sounds like cereal when you pour milk on it."

I couldn't hear anything, but I told him I did because it didn't really matter.

We sat in the corn many nights after that. Harley smoked cigarettes and I threw stones. Later we'd return to the house, our bodies greasy with sweat and covered with mosquito bites. We'd sleep late, getting up in time for lunch.

Toward the end of July, we started looking in people's

windows. That's how we first got hooked up with Farina.
He had a plot of land down by the river where he parked
his trailer for half the year. The other half he spent in
Florida. A lot of people went to Florida in the winter. I
wasn't sure about Florida, myself.

We were in Farina's garden. Harley stood among the
sunflowers and I sat on a pumpkin. The inside of the trailer
was bathed in the blue light of the television. He wore boxer
shorts and a white tee shirt that had straps for shoulders.
We were watching the late movie that came from a station
in Albany. Jimmy Cagney was bouncing around like a ban-
tam rooster.

Farina got up to go to the refrigerator and then he yelled
for us to come in. I was for taking to the woods, but Harley
started for the trailer. Farina pointed to the sofa and told
us to sit.

I'd never been inside a trailer before. Everything was
attached to the wall. We were sitting close to him. Harley
wouldn't look at the television. He kept staring at Farina,
leaning toward him and moving his head a little bit at a
time.

"Quit that," Farina said, without looking at either one of
us. Harley turned away and looked at the television.

Farina was huge. His head was like a giant bullet. He
didn't have a neck and his glasses looked as if they'd grown
into his face. He sat in a reclining chair that had a bedspread
draped over it. He gripped the arms of his chair and looked
over his stomach at the set. I liked the trailer. It was something you could take into orbit if you ever needed to.

"You boys fish?"

Neither of us said anything. We watched the late show.
I thought for a second about the fact that neither of us had

any clothes on and then made a decision not to think about it.

"Catfish?" he said, but we still sat. The reception wasn't all that good. It took concentration to sort out the people, except Jimmy Cagney. He was duking it out with someone. He seemed to push his punches into the other guy's head.

"Bullhead, horned pout?"

"Horned pout," Harley said.

"Good, now we're getting somewhere. How about eels? You ever catch eels?"

"Not on purpose."

"How about if I hired you two nighthawks to catch some? I love to eat them, but I don't care too much for catching them. I got boat and tackle."

"Harley," I said, "we aren't allowed on the river."

"Shut up," he said.

It's hard to hold onto that first week of nights we spent on the river. We crawled out the window at midnight and were back in bed by three or four. Our world was in the lantern light that pooled on the water and cast huge shadows on the rock wall at our backs. The shadows were ours and when we moved in the swirl of water where the brook flowed into the river, mine would disappear inside his. Then the boat would move and I'd come back out, twenty feet up the wall. I liked it when that happened.

After a time, Harley would tell me to pull us in so he could check the trotline. Hand over hand we'd work, Harley taking in the catch and baiting the hooks while I pulled us to shore.

Farina's boat was a flat-bottomed dory with sides that curved up to my waist. We let it drift off a point of land where the brook water mixed with river. Outside of our light we could hear the big fish break where the river was deep and didn't go in circles like it did here, but pushed on to the ocean, bearing its tonnage of earth and what comes from it.

Night birds hunted the shallows, using the moonlight to find what they were looking for. Muskrat and beaver came down to the water to fish. I imagined great schools of young eels coming up the river to live out their lives before they returned to the sea to spawn and die. I imagined them to be quick and handy like pickerel.

Harley threw the garbage fish in one bucket and the keepers in another. We took time during the night to chop the garbage fish, mostly carp, into bait. The rest we took home and dropped into the springhouse. Whenever we caught a turtle, my brother painted his name on its shell with oil paint. He'd leave it in the bottom of the boat until it dried and then he'd throw it back in. He told me there were turtles down there as big as the boat. He thought about getting some baby ducks so we could catch one that big, but he never did. Usually we didn't talk much.

At the end of the first week we caught our first eel. It took the line as deep as it could. Harley pulled and pulled. He knew it was something different. The line wasn't heavy, but it was hard going. The action was unlike any other fish. The line quivered and sawed the water. First came the head. Its mouth was open, a hole wider than the body. Its eyes rolled and looked straight at me.

When Harley got the head in, he put his foot on it and began pulling in the rest of the body. It was thin in his hands and then, once it was in the boat, puffed up.

Harley grabbed it by the head and ripped out the hook, but then he lost his grip and it was thrashing around. I thought about bailing out, but I wondered if maybe this was some master plan and there were hundreds of them waiting down there, waiting for this one to scare us out of the boat. I wanted to be home. I wanted my mother to have locked us up inside the house.

Harley finally got hold of it and held it up in the light. It was steel gray and marbled with spots of different sizes. Its smooth, slick body twisted and snapped, whipping the air between us. Harley dropped it in a five-gallon bucket and threw a tarp over it. The eel banged against the sides, making the bucket bounce and skitter.

When we hauled the line in for the last time, it was almost morning. By then we'd caught four more. Harley carried the eel bucket and I carried eight horned pout strung through their gills on a branch. We'd never gotten home that late before. My mother would see us getting in. I was tired, more tired than I could ever remember being. I walked along behind Harley, the fish tails slapping me in the leg with every step. The bucket he carried was heavy. Whenever he broke stride or switched hands, it knocked against his knee and sloshed water down his pant legs. I made a game of stepping in the puddles left behind him. It would be time to eat breakfast when we got home, but I was more interested in sleep.

Harley went directly to the springhouse. Inside, an iron grate covered a stone vault. In the spring, the water boiled up out of the grate and flowed down the hillside, but in August it was three or four feet below the ground, black and quiet. Harley dumped his bucket over the grate. The water flushed in through the latticed bars, while the eels twisted across the grid work. Harley poked their heads through with a stick and their bodies slithered in after. The water below splashed and churned and then became quiet again, except for the trickle of ground water seeping in and dripping down the stone sides. I dropped the horned pout in the eel bucket and went to the house.

My mother was at the stove cooking French toast.

"I thought we'd have something special. I haven't cooked breakfast for you in quite a while."

I sat down at the table and watched her. She dipped bread into the egg and milk and then flopped it into the frying pan. It sizzled for a second and then began frying.

"I'm told you two are in the eel business," my mother said, turning over the piece of bread with a spatula.

I didn't know what to say. Through the screen door I could see the springhouse. The door was off its hinge, but you couldn't see inside. My mother brought a plate of bacon and French toast over to me. I looked at her and could see she'd been crying. Her face was older than I remembered. She kept blinking her eyes.

"Well," she said, "I should like to see them."

I pushed back my chair. I didn't want her to see them. I wanted to be in bed, wrapped up in the sheets. I went to the door and held it open for her. She smiled and nodded her head as she passed by. Her legs were stiff and she hunched forward as she walked. I called to Harley when we got to the springhouse. We stood on the path and waited for him to come out. When he finally did, he was naked and water was running off his skin. The morning light caught in the round water beads that skimmed his white body. He held up an eel in his right hand, his arm crooked toward his head. He smiled and his eyes were black holes in his face.

"That's nice," I heard my mother say in a voice I'd never heard.

She turned and left us there, but I couldn't look away.

I'd never really seen my brother before, and I knew that if I moved, he'd be gone.

II.

The third week in April, the yellow perch run in Chippewa Bay. They come to spawn, as they've done since long before there were names for any of this.

There was a young man used to live here who went off to war. They made him a scout because he knew how to move in the woods. He was captured by the Confederates at Shiloh. They trussed him up and sent him down to Andersonville, where he lived off rainwater and lizards. After the war he made his way home to the bay.

His father killed a turkey and the neighbors came by with beans and succotash, salt potatoes, pork rinds, pies and bread, cider and ale. The neighbors set up sawhorses with long planks across the top. People ate and danced to fiddle music. The men clapped him on the back and the women kept his plate full.

The children held hands and snaked their way in and out of the crowd. The boy at the front of the line planted his heel and wheeled them around. The last little girl was lifted off her feet and sent tumbling across the lawn, curled up in a tight little ball, her skirts above her head.

The young man sat back and took everything in. He never thought he'd see the bay again with its hundreds of tiny islands and clear blue water. Like so many young men, he died a few days later because his intestines had shrunk up and the muscle was gone.

Harley and Poncho's daughter began fishing before morning. Poncho told them about the bay and how his wife, Aggie, had loved it. He helped them load the truck. They brought deck chairs, two poles apiece, and a bucket of minnows. Harley rigged an air pump to a car battery so the minnows wouldn't belly up. It chilled the water and pumped air in the bucket for the bait to breathe.

Harley felt like a rich man sitting next to Elizabeth. The morning darkness seemed warm and generous. They were the only ones there on the edge of the bay.

They were both tucked inside blankets, watching bobbers that floated ninety feet out. The water lapped at the dock. The last of the night birds and the first of the morning birds were just now crossing each other's paths.

Elizabeth loved Harley. He never spoke unless something was on his mind. She thought he'd make a good social worker, and liked the idea of him helping people solve their problems. When they got back home, he'd stay with her and Poncho. He could go to college at Keene State and still help her father with the business.

She looked at his face in the cast of purple light that was just now coming over her right shoulder. He didn't move his head. The skin on his neck was tight. His chin was drawn and one side of his face looked like it would crack.

She told him once that if she had a magic wand she would tap his forehead and make the burn scars go away. Without looking at her, he told her that if he had a magic wand, he'd repair tractors for farmers because they'd keep their mouths shut. They'd keep calling you back, but they wouldn't allow themselves to believe in it or tell anyone else.

When he told her that, she knew it would be safe to love him, but not to talk about his face. Then she decided that she wanted to marry him.

Harley told Elizabeth about a young man who died of constipation. She didn't laugh, though. Her period was three weeks late and she didn't want to think about death. Harley didn't laugh either, but he never laughed much anyway.

An old man and a boy came down to the dock. They set out their gear and waited for the fish to bite. The old man opened his thermos and it was empty.

"Grabbed the wrong one," he said to the boy.

Harley heard the old man, so he went over and offered him a cup of coffee from a new thermos he and Elizabeth had bought down the turnpike at a Dunkin' Donuts. Harley liked their coffee, and Poncho always stopped there in the morning before work. He offered the boy a doughnut, but instead of taking it he kept looking at Harley's face.

Harley wanted to push him into the bay, but then he thought of Elizabeth and he smiled. "I'll just leave a couple here, and if you change your mind you'll have them."

Harley went back to his chair and wrapped himself up. The darkness was breaking to their right, but the islands across the bay were still black shadows that humped out of the water. The closer morning came, the cooler the air felt.

Harley let his head go back. He could feel the skin of his neck stretching out to the cool air. He imagined that he had trouble breathing, but didn't. He felt Elizabeth's hand come inside his blanket and find his leg. For a time this seemed the only spot on his body he could feel. He forgot about not being able to breathe, and looked up for what was left of the moon. It was a sickle in the sky, and only a few stars were left to disappear. He decided that he'd begin to like the morning and maybe sometime he would like the day, too.

"Harley, I think we have a bite."

Harley sat up and looked out. All four bobbers had sunk out of sight and the lines were swimming back and forth. Harley grabbed the rod with the most pull and began reeling in. It was a young walleye. He thought for a second about keeping it, but let it go since the season for walleye wouldn't open for another three weeks. The second line held a small yellow perch. He twisted the hook out of its jaw and threw it back, mouth first, to open its gills.

He turned to look at Elizabeth. She was holding a line in each hand. She had two fine perch, keepers. She handed one to Harley to take off the hook while she did the other. He held it behind the gills and twisted the hook. A stream of white sperm ran down his wrist and onto his pants. He looked up at her. Smiling, she reached out a fist and slowly opened her fingers. In the palm of her hand was a mass of pink eggs. Harley felt his neck flush with blood. Elizabeth laughed out loud, loud enough for the old man and the boy to look their way and wonder what was so funny.

Before Elizabeth was developed, before she had breasts and hips and hair that settled about her shoulders, Poncho brought her onto the job with him. Sometimes she would sit under a tree and watch the heat rise on the new asphalt. In August she braided her hair and brought Kool-Aid to sell for a dollar a cup, all the men bought some because her mother was dying and each one of them knew it.

Poncho bought her a string of real pearls. She wore them

around her neck as she marched from man to man doling out the drinks. When work started up again, she twirled around and around in the shadow of his bulldozer. Poncho would yell down to her—"Oh my gal, she's so mean, puts my shoes in the washing machine."

Later on, she was old enough to stay home alone and nobody saw her that much. Poncho's wife, Aggie, was dead of a brain tumor. Down at the Legion he told the men about the trips the family took to Hanover every week. He told them about the holes they drilled in her skull and the headaches she'd suffered until she said she couldn't suffer any more. Then she'd tear about the house, screaming and crying.

"If her head ever blew," he said, "it'd be like the time foolish Rodney changed the wheel on his tractor. Remember? That split rim blew and spread him all over hell and back."

Poncho's chin jerked into his chest as he started to laugh and then remembered it was Aggie he was talking about. He pushed back his chair and set his elbows on his knees. He stared down at the floor through the diamond he formed with his fingers.

"I'm not complaining," he said to no one in particular. "I'm not complaining."

Poncho finally crawled out from under his hospital bills and went into business for himself. He couldn't read or write so he hired my brother Harley to work for him. Poncho liked Harley. He liked to look at him and ask him questions about the burns on his face, but only when they were alone.

Harley kept the books and took care of the contracts. They did a lot of work for the company, but now they were their own bosses. The company liked it better that way, too.

Every Friday I met them down there at the Legion and listened to stories. Poncho usually had the better ones, and

203

the best ones of all were about him. One story turned into another. The name of a person or a town or a job started up someone else. By evening just the names were enough to tell the whole story. Someone would say, "that Thursday morning last January" or "the rock cut job," and everyone would laugh or shake their heads and say, "Oh, Christ."

Me and Harley sat at one end of the table. It was good to see him, and I hadn't seen him much since he left home. He was strong and smart, and was going to night school to learn how to be a social worker. No one seemed to mind his face. When he came around, people didn't notice him because he kept quiet most of the time. He saw his best friend, Dunfee, once a year when they went hunting, but mostly he kept to himself.

We'd talk about the health of our parents. I told him they wanted to see him go back to school full-time and finish his degree. Then we'd talk about money or the price of diesel fuel or how the weather really has been different since we landed on the moon. Usually, though, we just listened to the others. I was happy just to be with him.

The Garofalo brothers were usually there, too. They were newlyweds. Billy married the mother and Bobby married the daughter. They all lived in a small house with only one bedroom. The four of them liked to chat late into the night. They slept in shifts so that two of them were awake to carry on the conversation at all times.

Poncho was the center of everything though. He wore army shirts with the sleeves ripped off at the shoulders. Aggie's name was on his bicep inside a heart. He had it done for five dollars at the Eastern States Exposition in Massachusetts. Something like that today would cost fifty.

"The hospital set me up with the chaplain," he said. "He

was a nice fellow. I let him help me out as much as I could, but there was just so much I could do for him."

The Garofalo brothers nodded their heads. Their wives had taken pots of beans and pies over to Poncho's house when Aggie died. They told the brothers that they could see beautiful dresses hanging on every door. Elizabeth wasn't home. She was back in school.

"How's the girl, Poncho?" Billy Garofalo said.

Poncho thought about it. Since Aggie died he thought over every question before he answered it. Some people stopped asking him questions because they didn't want to wait around for the answer.

"Billy, she's fine. She's real fine. I couldn't have made it without her. She's had some hard years to live through," Poncho said, then he stopped to think some more.

Harley watched him, which was part of his job. Poncho got drunk on Friday nights and Harley would have to drive him home and leave him in the truck. Then he'd get in his own truck and drive off to his house in the woods. I've never seen Harley's house. I don't know anyone who has, except maybe Dunfee.

This Friday in late October, Poncho and Harley were celebrating. A big job had come in well under budget and Poncho had made a lot of money. He made enough to put in the bank and also buy a new truck, though he didn't really need one. Harley told him there were tax advantages, and Poncho wanted one with four-wheel drive.

They were drinking at the bar. Harley was happy, too, having played a big part in arranging for fill from a farmer's gravel bank at less than a third of the going rate.

The other men came in. Bobby Garofalo had a cast on his arm. He'd fallen off a roof that morning and broken his arm. It wasn't the arm he nailed with, so he was back at work in no time. Poncho kidded him about what a sneaky way this was to get a few hours off.

"The boy just wasn't watching what he was doing," Billy said. "If I said it once, I said it a thousand times, 'safety first.' I showed him time and again how to twist in the air and sink the claw of that Estwing in the sheathing. Why, I've hung twenty feet in the air from my hammer."

When Billy got wound up like that, spit flew from his mouth. I tried to imagine him dangling in the air by one arm, but couldn't picture it.

"Well, when his arm's healed up, you give him a good spanking," Poncho said.

"I would, but he's generally a good boy."

Everyone laughed, even Bobby.

"Now, boys," Poncho said, "me and Harley have a little wager going on here."

Poncho emptied his glass and ordered a round for everyone at the bar. The Garofalo brothers took their beer and thanked him. Other men moved closer, taking the beer as an invitation.

"We are wondering how long it will take a vehicle to seize up once its vital fluids have been drained off."

Harley didn't know what Poncho was talking about. He put his beer down and pushed it away. When Poncho started talking this way, he knew enough to stop because he'd have to drive later.

"We were wondering," Poncho said, "how long it would take the engine to seize up once the oil and/or the water had been drained out. We've got certain ideas about it and we were wondering what yours were."

Billy and Bobby looked at each other. More than once Poncho had taken them down the rosy path with one of his schemes. Billy put both hands on the bar and looked up at Poncho.

"If we were to commit ourselves to a set time that was, let's say, different from yours, how would we arrive at the truth, Mr. Poncho?"

"Well," Poncho said, "Harley here started the whole thing. He suggested that we each kick in a hundred dollars. Fifty for him and fifty on the bet. If we could get enough bets, he'd be willing to start up his truck and drop the heat plug. Then we could put the timer on it."

Harley didn't like the idea of setting up the engine in his truck, but he trusted Poncho enough to let him keep going. Since it was payday, the Garofalo brothers didn't have any trouble getting four other guys to kick in. The deal struck, they climbed in their trucks and left for Poncho's house. Dozens of other men followed. Harley drove Poncho's truck for him. Poncho told him not to worry since he was giving him his old truck as a bonus. This made Harley feel better about the bet, and he decided to put up some money, too. Poncho told him he couldn't bet, because his interest was already being taken care of. Instead, Harley had to buy back as many time slots as he could, and when they won, Poncho would use the money for the down payment on his new four-wheel drive. They arrived and the trucks pulled in one after the other, word having spread throughout the Legion and over CB's.

Harley met Elizabeth the night the engine seized up. He was sitting on the porch watching the men standing around a fifty-gallon drum that had a fire burning inside. Fitch, a welder, was telling a story about cutting into a steel barrel with his torch and having it blow up from fumes that were still inside. Fitch had sinus problems from inhaling gases when he was younger. He was a dangerous man on a job. He mostly got hired to do work other men were afraid to do. People at work kept an eye out for him, thinking they might be able to see him die.

Poncho held the book on the wagers. As more men showed up, Fitch and a few others complained that Harley was making more than the truck was worth. Poncho agreed to let everyone who bet split their times. This meant Harley, too, but he didn't say anything about it. It made the men feel better that way.

Elizabeth came out on the porch and sat down next to Harley. He didn't know she was there until she touched his arm.

"You bring him home on Friday nights," she said. "I always cook extra food but you never stop in."

Harley watched as others showed up. They all wanted to bet. Poncho gave them another split. Times were being divided into seconds and then Harley stopped listening. He couldn't hear them anymore.

"When you leave him in the truck," she said, "he's hard to get into the house."

Harley felt like he'd wronged her. And though he wanted to think she was being unfair, he couldn't.

"I'm sorry," he said, wanting her to go back inside.

"Where do you go?"

"I go home to bed."

"Have you eaten supper yet?" she said. "Come inside."

Harley followed her inside the house. He'd never been inside before. He sat at the table and she put a plate of macaroni and cheese in front of him. Harley looked around the room. The closet under the stairs was open. Dresses hung on the doors and shoes were piled on the floor.

"Those were my mother's. Some of them fit me."

Harley nodded his head. The dresses were beautiful.

"I watch from the window," she said. "I watch you get out of our truck and then walk over to yours. In the mornings I see you from my window upstairs. It's dark, though, and I can't see your face."

"It's not much to look at," Harley said.

He stopped eating and set his fork down. He looked up at her. She stood near his chair. She smiled at him and told him there was dessert if he wanted it.

"That would be fine," he said. "I'd like that."

Poncho came in through the back door.

"Oh, baby, what a story," he said. "It looks like you and me, mister, we each have a new truck and a lot of pissed-off compadres."

Poncho dished out some macaroni and cheese for himself. He sat down across from Harley. His face was red from too much drink. He took a wad of hundred-dollar bills from his shirt pocket and set it down on the table.

"You won," he said.

Harley and Elizabeth looked at the money. Harley picked it up and put it in his pocket. Poncho didn't say anything. He held his plate close to his mouth and worked the fork with his other hand. He didn't stop until he was done.

"I see you finally got your hooks into him," he said to Elizabeth. "Now don't you let him go."

She didn't speak. She turned away, went back to the stove, and started cleaning up. Poncho cleared his throat as if to speak but got a beer instead. When he passed by the closet he hung the dresses inside and closed the door. Then he went outside and sat in a chair on the porch.

Harley took out the wad of bills. He pulled out a hundred and took it over to Elizabeth.

"This is some of Poncho's money," he said. "He told me he wants you to buy some more dresses that fit."

"No he didn't, but I'll take it for groceries if you'll come again. It would mean a lot to him."

Harley reached out and handed her the bill. She took it and they smiled at each other. Harley walked out to the porch and handed Poncho the money. He held back two hundred dollars to spend on the boys down at the Legion.

"Where you going?" Poncho asked.

"Home," Harley said.

"It's just like you, you son of a bitch, to leave me before I'm done with you," Poncho said smiling. "You stay here tonight. You haven't got any truck, remember. At least not till tomorrow."

"I guess you're right, Poncho."

That weekend Harley closed up his camp and moved into Poncho's house. They loaded his belongings in Poncho's new four-wheel drive. When they passed the Legion, Poncho recognized a lot of the vehicles out front. He turned around and parked in front where everyone could see his new truck. Harley bought all the drinks that afternoon. Poncho let the boys get him drunk, which softened up the hard feelings of everyone except Fitch. He stood next to Harley with his back turned. He spoke about Poncho and Harley loud enough so Harley could hear. Billy Garofalo told him to shut up, but he kept on talking. Harley went over to Poncho and began steering him to the door.

"Bushels of clams next week," Poncho yelled. "Bushels of clams at my house."

Harley drove the truck. When they turned onto the highway, Poncho sat up and lit a smoke. He stared ahead.

"You can take them, but you can't shame them," he said. "It wouldn't be right. You let it go. If the day comes when you love a girl like I did, there won't be room for it in any part of you."

Poncho had Harley pull over beside the road. He then got out, unzipped his trousers, and pissed in the bushes. When he was done, he rummaged behind the seat until he found Harley's bottle. He climbed into the cab and settled down. By the time they got home, he was asleep.

Elizabeth was standing on the porch. She wore one of the dresses that hung on the closet door the night the engine seized up. Harley got out of the truck and stood with his elbows on the hood and his hands folded. They stood that way looking at each other for a long time, as if in a picture that was taken in this life and would be forever.

Chippewa Bay was cold that second morning. They were a long way from home but didn't seem to mind. They took the Old Towne out onto the bay. They canoed to a far island and fished where the sun would come up first. Too many people were fishing off the docks. The canoe was deep in the water, loaded with food and clothes and fishing gear. They wore coats and gloves. The temperature had dropped suddenly, as it often does in April. Harley thought it might even snow.

Elizabeth was in the bow and Harley fished from the stern. The perch were fat with eggs and sperm. They floated in the water on the bottom of the boat, white and pink and yellow. Harley tried to keep it cleaned out but gave up. By noon the sun was high and they'd already caught another fifty.

Harley took his shirt off. The sun felt good on his back and neck and shoulders. When Elizabeth turned to look at him, he looked away. She hadn't seen him in such light before.

"It's okay, Harley," she said, and then wished she hadn't.

211

He put on his tee shirt and pulled his cap low. She turned away and decided to leave him alone. She looked out into the bay.

"I love you," she said. "That's all."

Harley didn't want this to happen. He wished for another strike on his line and finally it came, so they could talk about this fish as if it were different from the others.

At two o'clock they paddled back to shore. Harley steered them to the far end of the dock so he wouldn't scare the fish away from the others. They loaded their gear into the truck and together they hoisted the canoe onto the ladder racks. They drove back to the hotel.

Elizabeth watched Harley fillet the fish. He handled the knife cleanly, cutting away the meat in sharp, even strokes. Eggs and sperm and guts covered his hands and wrists. He kept wiping them on his trousers to keep them as dry as he could. When he finished, he cranked them through the scaler, peeling off the skin.

Elizabeth wrapped them in tin foil while Harley threw the heads and bones in the dumpster. They took the fillets to the chef and gave them to him. This made almost two hundred fish fillets in two days they'd turned his way.

"You know," he said, "you'd be surprised how little fresh fish I really get."

"We can't do much with them except give 'em away," Harley said.

"Hey, I've been meaning to ask you, you get burned in the war? I bet you were a cook. Good buddy of mine got scalded just like you. I been burned. Occupational hazard."

Harley nodded his head. Elizabeth wanted to say something, but decided not to.

"Now when you two come down to dinner tonight, you

tell Lenny that I have something special for you and I'll send out a couple of nice steaks."

"That'll be good," Harley said. "We appreciate it."

Back in the room Harley watched television while Elizabeth took a shower. He'd never seen so many channels before, and wondered what good they were. He used the remote control to flip from one to another until he finally fell asleep.

When he woke up, Elizabeth was on top of him. She had his shirt unbuttoned and she was running her fingers over the skin on his neck and face. Cool water was dripping from her hair onto the places her fingers touched.

"The light," he said.

She got up to shut it off, then pulled the shades. She undid his trousers and then got back on top. Water kept running down on his face, her fingers gripping his shoulders.

Then they rolled on their sides and lay quiet. Harley looked at her. He thought that if he died just then it would be all right, and then wondered if it was because he was afraid to go back outside or if it was because he didn't need to ever go outside again. They slept and didn't wake up until the next morning, when it was time to pack up and leave.

They crossed the bridge into Canada and drove east. Just outside of Montreal, Elizabeth told Harley she'd missed her period.

"So what does that mean?" he asked.

"I could be pregnant," she told him.

Harley thought about handling the hundred perch, the eggs and sperm on their hands, their clothes, and sometimes even in their hair.

They spent the night in Montreal. Harley wouldn't go out of the room and Elizabeth didn't mind. She sat at the window and looked down on the city. After Harley had fallen asleep, she got in bed next to him and curled up against his back. She wanted to tell him that she thought she knew she was pregnant, but she wanted to be sure.

From there they pushed on through Granby and Sherbrooke. They took Route 112 to Maine, where it turns into Route 27. They made the Kennebago River by evening and slept off the road in the truck.

In the morning they set out in the Old Towne to where the Kennebago falls away into the Rangeley. The river was high, and there was still snow in the mountains. Ice could be found in the backwaters and beaded on the roots of trees where the river undercut the bank. It sparkled in the morning sun, and the clear air cut through their mittens. Years ago the river was choked with logs and Frenchmen in caulksoled shoes. The rumble of dynamite could be heard up and down its length.

Harley watched Elizabeth from where he sat in the stern. She kneeled in the bow, her paddle dipping in and pulling water. It was hard to see her move in the heavy sweater she wore. He wanted to see her ponytail hang down between her bare shoulders. He wanted to see her back shine in the sunlight as he followed her down the river. Behind them, their fish lines played out a hundred feet. Harley had bobbers set back five feet on the lines so they would troll a little deeper. They used worms and grubs and a lure that Poncho said was magic. The last time he'd used it was on the Kennebago twenty years earlier. The fish struck all day long. Harley didn't rush to set hooks. He gave them time to set themselves. He threw back most of the catch except for six browns that were each over twelve inches long. These he cleaned as Elizabeth paddled, heaving the guts onto the bank when she swung near enough. These he kept in the creel wrapped in wet grass.

By noon the sun was high enough to come in through the spruce and pine that lined the river. They took the east fork into Kennebago Lake, came up on the north side, and made camp. Harley stretched a tarp over a rope he tied between two trees. He dug a fire pit and then stowed away their gear.

Elizabeth took out a bar of soap and went down to the lake to bathe. She took off her clothes and went in up to her waist. The water was cold. Before long she couldn't feel her legs. Harley sat on a rock and watched her.

"Come in," she said.

"No, that's quite all right," he told her.

"I'm not going to sleep with a man who stinks."

"Then you can sleep under the stars," he said, laughing at his own joke.

She splashed water on him, but he didn't move. He smiled as she worked the bar of soap into a lather. She rubbed it up her arms and across her chest. She did her neck and stomach. Harley laughed when she reached under the water and washed herself. He told her not to pee in the lake, but she didn't hear him. She dove under and came up on a run to the shore. Harley met her with a towel. He wrapped her in it and began rubbing her body. The fine white hairs on her arms stood up and her nipples were hard. Harley lifted her in his arms like a child and carried her onto the rocks that were warm from the sun. He sat down with her on his lap and they both looked out at the line of trees on the other side of the lake. Harley reached into his pocket and fished out a cigarette. In the same pocket he found a stick match. He snapped it off his front teeth and lit his smoke. He

215

looked down at Elizabeth. She was asleep. He held onto her for a while longer and then laid her down on his coat.

Harley went back to the camp and started a fire. He cut up onions, potatoes, and carrots, and stuffed them inside the fish. He sprinkled them with salt and pepper and wrapped them in tin foil. He worked each package down into the fire. He checked on Elizabeth and then took his twelve-gauge and went back into the woods.

He hiked back a quarter mile following a stream until he finally came out where a logging road crossed it. Clear water ran over logs that had been laid side by side to form a corduroy road. Tight ruts ran from each side of the bridge, off into the woods.

Harley turned west and walked slowly down the center. After another quarter mile, the road broke out onto a marsh. Spikes of jack pine and cedar rose up among the cattail and reeds. Harley could see ducks splashing in the shallows, shaking their black plumage. He threw a stone behind them and as they flew up across his path, flapping out their wings, stretching for elevation, he shot two of them.

He split their necks with the point of his knife and then carried them back down the road by their feet, letting them bleed out as he went. It was getting dark. He reached the corduroy road that crossed the stream and struck out through the woods. The leg of his trousers was wet with blood.

The stream began to drop sharply toward the lake. Harley pulled himself up the banking and stepped out of the woods into the campsite. Elizabeth was sitting by the fire. She was dressed and wrapped in a blanket. She looked up at him. Harley held up the ducks and smiled.

"Don't ever leave me again without telling me," she said.

Harley went over to her. He could see that she'd been

crying. He wished he hadn't gone off the way he did. He could feel his neck stiffen and his arms grew weak.

"I woke up and you were gone," she said. "Then I heard the shot and I knew you were all right, but then I thought something awful had happened."

She began to cry again. Harley went to her and held her. She punched his chest once and then again, harder.

"Don't ever do that," she said.

He pulled her tighter into him until she stopped.

"Roast duck," he said.

"Yes, I know. They'll be good."

Elizabeth took a smoke from Harley, something she rarely did. He went to the duffel bag and took out a bottle of Canadian Club. He poured some in a tin cup and gave it to her. She sighed and settled back. Harley thought he might like to talk, but decided to wait until they were on the lake and she felt better.

Harley poked at the fish that were wrapped in the bottom of the fire. They needed to cook a bit longer. He held the ducks by their feet over the campfire. The pinfeathers hissed and crackled, singed away by the flames. The skin began to show on each one. Taking one bird at a time he cut across their guts. He reached in with his palm and loosened the entrails at the top of the cavity. He flipped each bird onto its back and cracked the backbones by snapping the tails back. He cut around the vent and removed the guts. With the flat of the hatchet he broke down the breastbones and then, with his knife, cut free the breasts, a large upper fillet and a small lower one.

He made a spit with two forked branches and an oak split. When the meat began to heat up, the grease dripped into the fire, hissing and snapping. Harley looked over at

Elizabeth. She had finished her first drink and had poured more in the cup. She handed him the bottle.

"Give me your pants," she said.

"What for?"

"I want to rinse them out. They're covered with blood."

Harley stood up and stripped off his trousers. His long underwear was stained where the blood had soaked through to the leg and onto his lap.

"Those you can burn," she said.

He followed her down to the lake. The sun was almost gone. He watched her hands work the fabric and the blood rinse out into the lake. It turned black in the last of the clear water as the long shadows came from the west. She slapped the trousers against a rock and told him to hang them by the fire.

First they ate the fish. The white meat was tender and fell cleanly from the bones. They drank Canadian Club, and Harley told her stories about when he was a boy. The first one left her quiet. It was about leaving home. He wanted her to laugh so he started in on another one and made up a whole new ending for it. He told her about the time her father contracted to dig a cellar hole for a man from the city who only wanted to pay just so much. Poncho dug down six foot and left it. By the time they framed it, everything cost more because it was so high in the air. Elizabeth didn't understand why that was so funny, but she laughed anyway.

Harley felt good. He took the duck breasts off the spit and gave her one. They were hot but tasted good. Both were hungry and they ate everything they'd cooked. They filled their cups with whiskey and sat back. The moon was climbing out of the east and crossing the lake. Harley threw wood on the fire so he could see. He started telling her another story, one about Dunfee, but she stopped him and told him she knew she was pregnant. He thought about what she said. He didn't know what else to do but put his arm around her and hold her.

"That's good," he said after a while, and they didn't speak again that night.

The next morning was the coldest of the trip. Billows like steam came off the lake and rose into the sky. The blankets were stiff with a fine coat of frost. Elizabeth was tucked inside against his ribs. Harley pulled himself out and jumped around. He pulled on mittens and another pair of socks. The fire was smoldering. The bottle of Canadian Club was next to it. His head hurt until he swallowed a mouthful of whiskey. He felt the heat in his throat and stomach; it was the shortest hangover he'd ever had.

Harley got down on his knees, piled tinder on the embers, and blew into them. They smoked and finally caught. He banked the fire with sticks and limbs and then a log. Then Elizabeth was by his side, standing as close to the fire as she could get. Harley made coffee while she pulled the duffel bag near the campfire. She put on her clothes and then pulled on a pair of Harley's wool pants and one of his flannel shirts. She put on her down jacket and zipped it up. Harley put on a double layer, too, and then they drank coffee.

After their first cup, Harley made pancakes and fried bacon. They ate near the fire, folding the strips of bacon into the pancakes. The whole world was white as the mist off the lake drifted in around them. They couldn't see beyond the camp.

By ten o'clock the lake was still white. The sun hadn't come out and it looked like snow. They decided it was best to get back on the river and try to make the eight miles to Haines Landing between Rangeley and Mooselookmeguntic lakes.

They broke camp, packing everything in two bundles. These they stowed in the bottom of the canoe.

Elizabeth got in first. She had trouble moving in all her clothes, and it took time for her to reach the bow. Once she was settled, Harley got in and pushed off. They paddled hard across the flat water. At times Harley couldn't see her, though she was only eighteen feet away.

When they reached the fork in the river, they swung away from shore to cross into the current. Harley looked behind. He saw first the land and then the trees disappear from sight. He turned and saw Elizabeth's back, but he could see no farther. He began to worry that they were going in circles. The water was flat but he knew the currents were strange. He thought they might get turned around, go back onto the lake, and get lost.

The canoe banged against something in the water, jolting to the right and left. Harley fell forward to keep himself from going over the side. His face hit the thwart in front of him. He split his lip and bit into his tongue. His nose was broken. He pushed himself up and looked for Elizabeth, but she was gone. He stood up in the boat and searched the water. There was nothing. No sound, no widening circles of water, no rising air.

He sat down in the boat. His whole face felt like it was on fire. He wondered for a moment if she'd been there to begin with. Maybe she was still on shore, or maybe she'd never even come on the trip. He rubbed his eyes with his fingers and held them there. He pushed in and saw the red glare expand and contract. He pushed the heels of his hands into his eyes and saw the red as if it were the glow from a cave. He beat his eyes trying to hold the great flashes of light, as if they held the answer to his question.

He started diving. His clothes and shoes dragged him to

the bottom where he wanted to be. He reached out in the dark but couldn't even see his own hand. The currents pulled him one way and then another. He didn't know which way was up. He fought to get air and then went back down again and again, and after a while he stopped. He climbed into the canoe and began to look for the shore.

He built a fire when he reached land, and dried out next to it. It began to snow. He pulled the canoe near to the fire and tipped it over for shelter. The gunwale sheltered the flames from the snow. He swung the butt end of a log into the fire and then fell into a half-sleep, waking only to slide the burnt end along to keep the fire going.

He dreamt that he found Elizabeth and floated to the bottom with her. They lay there wrapped in each other's arms as lovers would, and then he had to go because he didn't have the strength to save them both. She held him tight and then pushed him away, knowing what she had to do and knowing that he wouldn't leave her otherwise. Later on, the dream became to him the way it really happened.

He slept on the bank of the Kennebago while the late spring snow came down, muffling the forest and piling up around the canoe, holding in the warmth. He slept for two days until finally he made his way to Haines Landing, where he told his story. Inside he was different after that. We all were, but none of us knew how.

III.

In the season between fall and winter, Harley and Dunfee hunt deer. They go back in the woods where they have a

221

shack. There they drink beer, talk dirty, and shoot deer if any happen to wander by the front porch. They are both reputable hunters, their skill respected by all who know them.

This year was no exception. Dunfee had taken up with the Contas girl and now was trying to get shed of her so he could leave. Harley waited in the truck, his face knotted with burn scars. He had tried his hand at social work, but didn't like it. People wouldn't let him do his job. They wanted to talk about him and his life, or else they wouldn't open up to him at all. When that happened, he'd talk about the weather or the ball scores.

Harley owned his truck. The frame was twisted. The truck didn't track down the road in the direction it pointed, and was always headed for the ditch. The frame bent up between the box and the cab. This made the headlights bank down toward the road at night and everything you put in the back rolled out. It happened to Dunfee. He and Harley were in Brattleboro trying to drink their way through town. By two in the morning they were still in the same bar, so they decided to give up. Harley drove and Dunfee stretched out in the back. He wanted to look up at the sky as it rushed out behind him. When Harley hit the gas pedal in front of the Howard Johnson's, Dunfee slid for the road. He finally dropped out on the bridge that spans the river. He lay there between Vermont and New Hampshire, the stars above him caught in the green steel girders arching over his head.

Harley didn't know he'd lost Dunfee until he got home and looked in the bed of the pickup. He was too tired to go back and find him, but he did take the time to cut out a tailgate from a sheet of plywood, so it wouldn't happen again.

*

It was morning, but the sun had not come up on the Contases' property yet. From where Harley sat, he could see the girl's father beating a goat over the head with a stick. It seemed to Harley like the kind of work one wanted to get an early start on. The goat would shake his head and then the old man would smack it right between the horns. Three children were watching from the front porch, where they sat in old bucket seats. They were quiet, and Harley wondered if the old man was trying to teach them something.

A limb stuck out in front of Harley, sticking up from the front of his truck. When he drove up the road, he'd run over it and it had wedged underneath. It looked like an old woman's hand reaching out with the palm down.

Dunfee was inside the house, where he'd spent most of the summer. He was packing his belongings in a paper sack. The Contas girl was looking out the window at her father hitting the goat. She thought he was starting to look tired. He was taking a breather between hits. Each time he'd bring the stick down as if he was chopping wood, only a little slower than the time before. She lay down on the bed and asked Dunfee when he'd be back.

"Harley's waiting in the truck," he said.

"Harley doesn't have a face," she said.

"And you don't have any brains."

The Contas girl laughed. She rolled onto her back and stuck one leg straight in the air. Her ankle was caked with laundry soap. Underneath, poison ivy blisters were starting to dry. The rest of the leg was pretty, though. Dunfee looked at it. He saw how it went all the way to her ass. He knew Harley was waiting in the truck. Dunfee touched her. He knew he didn't plan on coming back here again, but probably would.

Harley and Dunfee had gone to school with the Contas girl. The three of them had become friends because they all lived on the same way to school. They were older now and better friends, mostly because no one else stayed around. Twice the Contas girl had gone off for a year at a time. She went off to have babies. Harley and Dunfee didn't think much about it, figuring it was her own business. Other people spoke about it, though. Dunfee got in a fight once because of something said about her by one of the other boys. He didn't talk to her for a long time after that.

Harley didn't fight much. Most people left him alone because they didn't know what he would do. But he was always there for Dunfee. He backed him up so no one would take a sucker punch. Harley was a big boy. His face was always secret.

When Dunfee fought, he went into a rage. He'd come flying through the air, all black shoes and hairy red knuckles that were just scabbing over from the last fight. He didn't fight anymore, though. He didn't have to because now people knew enough to mind their own business.

The sun finally came up on the Contases' property. It got hot inside the truck. Harley got out to stretch his legs. He was happy to be unemployed. He pulled up his collar and rested his elbows on the hood. He had enough money to get him through the winter. His house wasn't much, but it was paid for. He'd lived in a tepee once, and that wasn't so bad.

Mostly he was happy that it was hunting season. He liked to be alone in the woods with Dunfee. When they were boys, they took more than their share. They stayed out of school the whole season. For a fee they began shooting deer for other people to tag. They never collected the money, though, so everyone thought Harley and Dunfee were giving them a break. People bragged about how much they paid because they thought everyone else was paying. They told their friends that Harley and Dunfee were expensive, but well worth the price.

One year they shot deer for the patients on the third floor at the county farm. They carried the old men and women down the stairs to their deer and gave them the stub off their license. Most of the old people didn't have teeth or stomachs left, so the venison went to the prisoners across the road.

Harley and Dunfee talked about becoming guides, something neither had ever tried. But they didn't pursue it since they didn't like the idea of showing the woods to outsiders.

Harley went away to school and Dunfee worked only when he had to make ends meet. The last few years, though, they did as little as they needed to. They got by.

The old man was slowing down. The goat seemed to be enjoying it. Harley tried to pull the limb out from under his truck. It wouldn't come. He got down on his knees to see where it was caught. There was a patch of antifreeze on the ground. It was still dripping from the core. He couldn't figure out how the limb had punctured it.

Beside the road there was a plastic gallon jug. The kids were watching him. He cut the top off with his hunting knife and set it under the radiator. Antifreeze was expensive.

Harley looked at his watch and then took it off. He put it in the glove box and slapped the door shut. He thought about asking the old man if he wanted him to take over for a while, give him a break. Harley went over and offered him a smoke. The old man took it. Harley had one, too.

"Don't have a spare pack on you, do you?"

Harley shook his head.

The old man was looking at the goat. He was sizing it up as if he had more work to do before he'd be finished. "I'm so tired," he said, "it seems like I've been tired all my life."

Harley pulled up his collar. He held his hand up to his face the way someone would for a moment, but he left it there. He finished his smoke, and wanted to say something to the old man. But he didn't know what. He went over to where the kids were sitting on the porch. Their heads were together. He expected them to start singing Christmas carols or maybe an old Supremes tune. There was an extra bucket seat out of a Ford Mustang. Harley sat down and lit another cigarette. The old man started back in on the goat. This time he used a four-foot piece of inch-and-a-half black plastic water pipe.

"How come he's doing that?" Harley asked the kid sitting closest to him.

"He got his shoe wet yesterday. It made him mad."

Harley butted out his cigarette and lit another one. He struck the match off the bottom of his front teeth. The kids watched him do it.

Inside the house, Dunfee and the Contas girl made love. They did it in a friendly sort of way. Dunfee had to be careful. He let her tell him what to do, because she often had pains inside her. It had to be done just right or he'd hurt her. When he made a mistake, her eyes would roll back in her head, and she'd lie there as if she'd been stabbed. Sometimes she'd make him stop altogether.

The first time, Dunfee was drunk. It was late at night and neither of them had intended for it to happen. He and the Contas girl had driven over to the college to see Harley, but they couldn't find him. They were on the athletic field, lying in a pile of foam rubber that the pole vaulters used to land in. The Contas girl had started to bleed. Dunfee balled up his tee shirt and gave it to her. She clutched it between her legs and closed her eyes. She didn't cry. She only lay there in the moonlight, the smell of mowed grass all around them.

Dunfee prayed it would stop, and finally it did. He swore to himself he would marry her, go to church and give up his drink, but he never did any of these things. It took him a while to forget his broken promises, but he managed to do so.

Every time the old man hit the goat, the sound echoed from the end of the pipe. The goat cocked his head to listen. The old man missed and fell over. The pipe skittered off the goat's right horn and down the side of its face. The old man stood up and held his back.

"There goes his back again," said one of the kids.

The old man walked into the house, holding his back up as if he were trying to carry a bag of groceries behind him. Harley went to the truck and got a six-pack off the front seat. He went inside, too. He'd never been in the Contases' house before.

He stopped inside the front door. There was an aquarium on a stand against the wall. A brown trout took up most of the room in the tank. It looked white in the light that came

227

up from behind it. Air bubbles rose up under its chin and spread out around its head to the surface. Harley wanted to reach in and stroke its back, but he knew he shouldn't. He pulled back a set of drapes and went into the living room. He could see the backs of the kids' heads. They were sitting on the sofa watching television, a console set with the front smashed in. Wire mesh was tacked over the opening. Snakes were inside, lying quietly among the wires, tubes, and broken glass.

A plastic box sat on top of the set. Inside were white mice. Some were running on a treadmill, while others wormed their way in and out of tunnels. The kids didn't say anything. They stared at the snakes that weren't moving.

"How come you guys aren't in school?" Harley said.

The kids still didn't speak, so he let it go. He figured it was none of his business. He went into the kitchen, where the old man was sitting at the table. He was surrounded by chain-saw parts. He was eating a sandwich and having a glass of water. Harley saw three different kinds of casings. He wondered if the old man was trying to come up with one saw from these assorted parts, a sort of hybrid.

The old man finished his sandwich and his water before he took a beer. He drank it down without stopping and then opened another to sip on. Harley had a fresh one himself. From the other room, they could hear the Contas girl telling Dunfee what to do.

The old man told the kids to turn on the radio, and they got a news station. There was a lot of snow in Montana, a lot more than usual. A man in Texas wanted to raise the *Titanic*, maybe move it to San Antonio. It sounded to Harley like a good idea.

The old man clapped his hands to the sides of his head. "You don't have any NyQuil on you, do you?"

Harley didn't say anything. He drank his beer and fiddled with a carburetor. He tried to concentrate, but it didn't make any sense to him. He'd had cases like the old man when he was doing his counseling. They didn't say much, even when they spoke. He usually sent them home. He figured they had enough problems.

"So what do you do for a living, Mr. Contas?" Harley asked.

"Move pianos. Work's been slow."

The old man finished his second sandwich. He bummed another smoke off Harley, who left the pack on the table. He set it on an Oregon bar. The roller head was burned out, purple and black from overheating.

The kids took the box of mice off the console set and put a twelve-inch portable on top. They rigged the rabbit ears with tin foil and then plugged it in. A spark whipped out from the wall and the kids laughed. The one who was holding the cord grabbed his hand. He laughed, too.

It was quiet in the other room. Dunfee and the Contas girl lay on the bed. The air was damp and warm. Her eyes were closed. She held a finger to her lips. She held it there a long time. Dunfee felt foolish. He always felt foolish after he finished making love. He felt a little piece had been given up of its own will. It had gone away and become something else. The girl got up after a while and walked around the room as if she were trying out her legs. She walked slowly, one step after another, remembering as she went.

She stood by the window. "Harley's still here, you know."

Dunfee sat up. He wondered why she didn't get pregnant, but then stopped thinking about it. He put his feet on the floor and his elbows on his knees.

*

Harley was on the other side of the drape that separated the Contas girl's room from the kitchen.

From where he sat, he could hear her say, "I can feel you seeping out of me."

He looked at the old man. He didn't seem to hear. Harley wasn't sure if he had heard it himself. He set the carburetor down and looked at his hands. He drank another beer. He made himself hear again the words he thought she'd said.

After a time Dunfee and the Contas girl came out. She wore a dress that looked like a man's shirt. Harley caught himself wondering what color underpants she had on. She gave him a hug. He could feel her warmth coming through the dress. Dunfee nodded at him.

"There's a storm coming down the river," she said. "It should be here any minute."

Dunfee made a stack of sandwiches and handed them out to the kids. The Contas girl took one and so did the old man. They sat eating their sandwiches and drinking beer. It was warm in the house. Harley looked at her. He tried to remember when she had been ugly, but he couldn't. He tried to remember anything that was ugly, but couldn't do that either. The kids sat on the couch, watching the little portable television.

"I hear work's been slow," Harley said to her.

"Keiper wants him to chop rowan but he won't."

Harley nodded at her, but didn't say anything. He picked up a muffler.

"You don't have any Stop Leak, do you?" he said to the old man. "I popped a hole in my radiator."

"Use an egg white," the old man said. "Pour it in there. When it gets hot, she'll swell up and plug the hole. I ran from here to Springfield with a baby grand on. Went through a half dozen large, but I made it. He slumped back in his chair when he finished talking. He picked up his beer can with both hands and finished it off.

"You got any eggs then?"

"No. They're bad for the heart."

Dunfee was sitting on the kitchen counter. Harley looked up at him. Dunfee was watching the girl. Harley pulled his collar up tight to his cheek. The girl was looking out the window. She held her legs together. Her hands were folded on her lap. Dunfee jumped off the counter and grabbed the last beer. "So how's life?" he shouted.

Harley smiled. Before he could speak, the girl said, "It doesn't hurt so much anymore," and then everyone was quiet. No one moved. She looked out the window.

"Whole days go by and I don't even think about it. I don't think about him or you or nothing," she said.

She stood up and looked at the kids. She took stock of them. She pointed at each as if she were counting the hairs on their heads. The back of her dress had a red stain on it. It was an old stain, dry and almost black.

She sat back down and the power went off. It surged back once or twice and then was gone. The lights, the refrigerator, the television, and the aquarium, everything was gone. Harley didn't mind. He sat up and stretched. The darkness was everywhere in the room, except for some light that came in through the windows over the sink, but it wasn't much.

He began to think about going to the woods with Dunfee. They were headed for the woods, that he knew.

Harley looked at the old man. His head was thrown back and his mouth was open to the ceiling. His bony chest barely moved inside his shirt.

Dunfee went to the Contas girl and told her not to cry. She told him she wasn't going to. They stood apart, looking at each other. The kids came into the kitchen and looked at everyone. They drained the empty beer cans into one and passed it among them. Harley could hear the old man sucking air into his lungs. He sent one of the kids out to his truck to get another six-pack. Dunfee and the Contas girl went back into her room.

The one who went for the beer came back and gave it to Harley. They all sat down together like a family and watched him open a can and begin to drink it. Harley let go of his collar, went around the table making up names for each one, and then he toasted them. He gave a little speech for each name.

The kids smiled. The one he named Roy got up from the table and went to the drawer next to the stove. He took out a box of Ohio Red Tips and passed them out. The kids stood up around the table and began lighting them, snapping them off their front teeth and throwing them in beer cans.

Harley sat back and watched. He felt the tiredness that lovers feel after a fight. He thought about how good it was to be in the Contas girl's house, watching the tiny flares come from the kids' mouths, one after another.

How to Bury a Dog

THREE NIGHTS AGO I had to bury a dog. I've buried five dogs in my lifetime. Three of them I had to shoot. After you shoot your first dog, you become known as someone who will shoot a dog if the dog needs to be shot. There was another dog, my own, that got into a porcupine. Everyone expected me to shoot it, but I didn't. I took the quills out with pliers. As I was doing it she gashed my arm with her teeth, but I knew she didn't mean to.

Burying a dog isn't like burying a cow or horse or skunk or woodchuck or even a cat. Once, when I was a kid growing up on the farm, I was supposed to bury a cow, but instead me and two of the hired men pushed it into the Connecticut River and then spent the rest of the day drinking beer and fishing for carp.

Carp are an ugly fish and none of us would eat one, but my uncle used to take them to the city, where he sold them to some Negroes he knew. He'd bring us back the money, but I knew he always kept some of it for himself.

When we got back to the barn for chores, I told the hired men to keep their mouths shut because they weren't too bright and my grandfather would see liar written all over their faces. So when he asked me if we buried the cow, I looked him in the eye and said, "What in hell do you think we did with it, float it down the river like a tugboat?"

"You probably did," he said, "knowing you."

A week after that we were in the milkhouse washing

milkers when a car with Connecticut license plates drove in. A man with a suit got out and asked for my grandfather, so I took the fellow over to the house.

"Are you Sam Chickering?" he said.

My grandfather just nodded his head, not being one to offer any information unless it was necessary.

"You lose a cow about a week ago during the storm that came down the river?"

"Why?" my grandfather said.

About this time I knew what was about to be said, but was more fascinated than frightened. I stood fixed on the spot, intrigued by how all this was unfolding in front of me.

"We traced the ear tag to you through the State House in Concord," the man said, as he dropped an ear tag on the table. "We fished her out of a sluice gate at the hydro plant in Hartford. That cow is going to cost you some big money, I'm afraid, Mr. Chickering."

"Ain't my cow," my grandfather said.

"But it's recorded at the State House that you own this identification."

"The cow belonged to him," my grandfather said and pointed a finger at me. "And he wants it back."

The old man got up and went to his files and pulled the cow's registration. Sure as hell, the registration showed my name and was dated the day before the cow died.

"See there," my grandfather said and pointed to the name and date of ownership transfer.

"But the cow's dead, sir," the man in the suit said.

"Dead!"

"Yes, as near we can tell, it died from drowning."

"The boy paid eighteen hundred dollars for that cow and now it's dead?"

"I'm afraid so, and it has caused the state of Connecticut far more expense than it's worth."

"You keep it, then."

"But we don't want it."

"What's the boy to do with a dead cow?"

"What's the state of Connecticut want with one?"

"Bury it, by Jesus!" my grandfather yelled, his face red and swollen. "The boy's lawyer is Tot Belk in Keene, New Hampshire. Go talk to him about what in hell you do with a dead cow. We have to eat supper."

It was worth losing two of my show cows for that night in the kitchen. Each time I bury a dog I think about it, and I think about how burying a dog is different from burying a cow. You wouldn't think a cow could float that far, would you?

The last dog I buried was three nights ago. I hadn't planned on doing it, but then again the most notice I ever received before was a day or so.

One time in the dead of winter we got snowed out so we went to the bar. The neighbor woman called and said she'd already called six other bars looking for me. Her dog had been killed and she needed it buried. I told her we'd be right down.

All of us were fairly drunk when we got to her trailer. The dog was across the road, rolled up in the snowbank like a big rum ball. I asked her how she expected us to bury the dog when the ground was frozen. She said she didn't know about that, but she wanted it done before the kids got home from school. *Please,* she said.

We threw the dog in the back of my pickup and started driving. Before long we were back at the bar trying to figure out what to do with the dead dog, a black Lab, in the back of my truck.

"Did you ever notice," my friend Herb said, "how people who live in trailers have big dogs and people with money buy little dogs?"

"Bullshit, Herb," my friend Web said. "My sister lives in a trailer and she has a little terrier."

The bartender, Alice, came over and told us that she thought Herb was right, but that she also knew Web's sister and that she did in fact have a little terrier.

Just as things were starting to heat up between Herb and Web, in walks a man who was in the fire department and always wore a beeper.

"Who's got the dead dog in the back of the pickup?" he asked, like it was a big joke.

"I do," I said.

"What're you planning to do with it?" he asked.

"That's what we're trying to figure out."

"I read in the *Reader's Digest* that in Siberia they burn bonfires all night to soften the permafrost," he said.

"*That's* what we'll do." Herb slammed his fist down on the bar. "We'll go up to Eagar Hill and burn one of those big slash piles. Then tomorrow morning we'll bury the dog before work."

By the time we got up to Eagar Hill we were really drunk. The man from the fire department had come along as the expert, this being his idea.

We drenched the pile of slash with five gallons of gasoline and, from a good distance back, threw a flare into it. The whole mess exploded, shooting a ball of fire as big as a foreign car into the air. Then the brush settled down to a nice healthy burn.

We stood as near to the fire as we could, drinking beer. Caught this way between a lake storm and the bonfire was tiring. Before long I couldn't even keep the beer in, and had to take a leak on the average of two to every bottle I drank. We promised to meet back there before work. It was time to go home.

The next morning I was late picking up Herb and Web, so we had to go straight to work. We didn't even have time for coffee. We had foundations to pour and tent in. By the time we arrived on the job, two concrete trucks were already waiting.

At eleven o'clock, the last bucket swung into the hole. I motioned the line down and Web, who was on the street, relayed the message to the crane. I pulled the lever to open the gate. The big Lab dropped from the bucket like a boulder into a pond. Concrete splashed the whole crew. The man on the vibrator laid it on the dog and we all watched him sink under. Nobody said anything.

The dog I buried three nights ago was different.

Terry and Melanie are neighbors of ours. We've known them for quite a while. Melanie teaches with my wife and on occasion I've worked on jobs with Terry, who's a steel-worker. Melanie's pregnant.

Terry jobs out a lot. He doesn't mind working all over the country. Myself, I like to stay close to home.

I got home three nights ago and my wife was on a royal tear.

"What's wrong now?" I asked.

"That damn Terry. Melanie was doing the phone bill and found two calls to Bermuda."

"And so?"

"He slept with a woman when he was down there last summer on a job."

"He called her from his home phone?" I said.

"What difference does that make?"

"Well, it doesn't seem very smart." My wife didn't reply because I think she was disappointed that I saw him as stupid instead of a cheat. We looked at each other for a moment, then she walked to the kitchen. When I do things like that, I'd rather she hit me in the head. It's easier to deal with. But I knew she'd get over it.

Finally I got her to laughing, but you know there's always something you lose that I suppose you can never get back. After supper I left for Terry's.

The yard was dark when I got there. Terry's truck wasn't in the driveway, but I decided to go in anyway. Slipped inside the front door was a note. I figured Terry had left it for Melanie, so being nosy I unfolded it as I walked inside.

Melanie was sitting at the table.

The note said:

> *I have hit a dog in front of your house. The neighbors told me it was yours. There was nothing I could do. It ran out in front of me. I know how you feel. We lost our dog in September. We had her for ten years. I can't tell you how sorry I am. He is just a little north of here beside the road.*

"What's that?" Melanie asked. I handed her the note.

She read it quietly and then wiped out the dishes on the table, then threw a cup for good measure.

"Shit," she cried, "that's the topper to the worst week of my life."

"Where's Terry?"

"Down at the damn union hall."

We stood facing each other until I became uncomfortable. "So how's the little one?" I said, reaching out to pat her stomach. At first she pulled back but then gave me a half smile and told me the little one was fine.

"Does Terry have a shovel?" I asked quietly.

"In the shed."

"You sit here and have some tea and I'll go take care of the dog."

"No, I'll come, too."

We found the dog a hundred yards up the road on the left-hand side. Skid marks showed that the driver had crossed lanes to avoid the dog. They pointed to where it lay crumpled in the ditch.

Dogs are pretty tough, I have to say. They rarely show blood and guts when they get hit, unless of course they're run over by a trailer truck.

This one was an Australian sheepdog that weighed about fifty pounds. He was already pretty stiff. I set him on the tailgate and then we drove slowly back to the house.

"Where do you want him, Melanie?"

"Put him on the edge of the lawn. Are you sure you can dig a hole? The ground looks pretty hard."

"No problem." I almost told her about the time we tried to bury the dog on Eagar Hill. I wanted to tell her it was just a dog, but I thought Terry should do that.

We got to the edge of the lawn and I started to dig a hole. I figured two-foot by three-foot would be sufficient. I set the sod to one side of the hole and the dirt to the other.

"Do you have a flashlight or lantern?" I asked.

"I'll get one," Melanie said.

While she was gone, I stood between the hole and the dog and smoked a cigarette. It was a clear, crisp night with a lot of stars, but the hole was black. Without a light I wouldn't be able to keep it square.

She came back with a stack of newspapers and some matches.

"Maybe these will throw some light," she said.

We lit a crumpled wad next to the hole. It showed the top to be nice and square, but the sides tapered in at the bottom. I dug quickly in the dying light. We lit another wad and I dug some more.

After a bit I couldn't see the bottom from the shadows, so I took to throwing the burning paper into the hole to get my bearing. I continued like that until the hole seemed deep enough.

"That should do it," I said, but she just stood there clutching the sweater draped over her shoulders. I laid the dog in the hole as easy as I could, but its head stuck out. Without thinking, I stepped on the dog's head and forced it down into the hole. Melanie let out a gasp.

"Should you be out here in the cold like this?" I asked.

"I'm all right," she said resentfully.

I shoveled the dirt into the hole and then laid the sod back in neat squares. By summer they wouldn't even notice the place.

"When's Terry getting home?" I said, but again she didn't reply. I followed her back to the house. She gave me a beer and made like she was yawning, so I left.

When my wife got home last night, I asked her how Terry and Melanie were doing.

"Like two lovebirds," she said.

"Did they get a new dog yet?"

"Who the hell cares?" she said, and then laughed.

About the Author

Robert Olmstead was born in New Hampshire in 1954. His work has appeared in *Black Warrior Review* and *Granta*. He is currently writer in residence at Dickinson College, in Carlisle, Pennsylvania, and is a graduate of the creative writing program at Syracuse University. He has worked as a contractor, teacher, and farmer. *River Dogs* is his first published collection of stories.

About the Author

Robert Ottenhoff was born in New Hampshire in 1948 and was educated at Hillsdale College, ... the University of ... where he received a ... degree in ... literature. ... and is a professor. He currently lives and ... Maryland with ... He has served as a ... teacher, and ... this is his first published collection of stories.

VINTAGE
CONTEMPORARIES

"Today's novels for the readers of today."

—VANITY FAIR

"Real literature—originals and important reprints—in attractive, inexpensive paperbacks."

—THE LOS ANGELES TIMES

"Prestigious."

—THE CHICAGO TRIBUNE

"A very fine collection."

—THE CHRISTIAN SCIENCE MONITOR

"Adventurous and worthy."

—SATURDAY REVIEW

"If you want to know what's on the cutting edge of American fiction, then these are the books you should be reading."

—UNITED PRESS INTERNATIONAL

On sale at bookstores everywhere, but if otherwise unavailable, may be ordered from us. You can use this coupon, or phone (800) 638-6460.

Please send me the Vintage Contemporaries books I have checked on the reverse. I am enclosing $_____ (add $1.00 per copy to cover postage and handling). Send check or money order—no cash or COD please. Prices are subject to change without notice.

NAME_____

ADDRESS_____

CITY _____ STATE_____ ZIP_____

Send coupons to:

RANDOM HOUSE, INC., 400 Hahn Road, Westminster, MD 21157

ATTN: ORDER ENTRY DEPARTMENT

Allow at least 4 weeks for delivery.

VINTAGE
CONTEMPORARIES

___ LOVE ALWAYS by Ann Beattie	$5.95	74418-7
___ FIRST LOVE AND OTHER SORROWS by Harold Brodkey	$5.95	72970-6
___ THE DEBUT by Anita Brookner	$5.95	72856-4
___ CATHEDRAL by Raymond Carver	$4.95	71281-1
___ DANCING BEAR by James Crumley	$5.95	72576-X
___ ONE TO COUNT CADENCE by James Crumley	$5.95	73559-5
___ THE WRONG CASE by James Crumley	$5.95	73558-7
___ THE LAST ELECTION by Pete Davies	$6.95	74702-X
___ DAYS BETWEEN STATIONS by Steve Erickson	$6.95	74685-6
___ A FAN'S NOTES by Frederick Exley	$5.95	72915-3
___ A PIECE OF MY HEART by Richard Ford	$5.95	72914-5
___ THE SPORTSWRITER by Richard Ford	$6.95	74325-3
___ THE ULTIMATE GOOD LUCK by Richard Ford	$5.95	75089-6
___ FAT CITY by Leonard Gardner	$5.95	74316-4
___ WITHIN NORMAL LIMITS by Todd Grimson	$5.95	74617-1
___ AIRSHIPS by Barry Hannah	$5.95	72913-7
___ DANCING IN THE DARK by Janet Hobhouse	$5.95	72588-3
___ NOVEMBER by Janet Hobhouse	$6.95	74665-1
___ FISKADORO by Denis Johnson	$5.95	74367-9
___ ASA, AS I KNEW HIM by Susanna Kaysen	$4.95	74985-5
___ A HANDBOOK FOR VISITORS FROM OUTER SPACE by Kathryn Kramer	$5.95	72989-7
___ THE CHOSEN PLACE, THE TIMELESS PEOPLE by Paule Marshall	$6.95	72633-2
___ FAR TORTUGA by Peter Matthiessen	$6.95	72478-X
___ SUTTREE by Cormac McCarthy	$6.95	74145-5
___ THE BUSHWHACKED PIANO by Thomas McGuane	$5.95	72642-1
___ NOBODY'S ANGEL by Thomas McGuane	$6.95	74738-0
___ SOMETHING TO BE DESIRED by Thomas McGuane	$4.95	73156-5
___ BRIGHT LIGHTS, BIG CITY by Jay McInerney	$5.95	72641-3
___ RANSOM by Jay McInerney	$5.95	74118-8
___ RIVER DOGS by Robert Olmstead	$6.95	74684-8
___ NORWOOD by Charles Portis	$5.95	72931-5
___ MOHAWK by Richard Russo	$6.95	74409-8
___ CARNIVAL FOR THE GODS by Gladys Swan	$6.95	74330-X
___ THE CAR THIEF by Theodore Weesner	$6.95	74097-1
___ TAKING CARE by Joy Williams	$5.95	72912-9